*The Widow's K*

# ACCOLADES FOR THE SECOND WIFE

Amazon 2016 Kindle Book Awards WINNER

The McGrath House Independent Book Awards 2016 WINNER

Maggie Award for Excellence FINALIST

B.R.A.G. Medallion HONOREE

"This book goes to dark places but the healing interactions between all the people who love Alisha are achingly tender and the heart of the story." ~NPR

"Paul places the violence in direct contrast to Alisha's Indian family, who have taken David deeply into their hearts, and who serve as his strength while he copes with her disappearance." ~Sonali Dev, *Award Winning Author*

"The Second Wife is one of those rare novels that will lurk in the back of your mind for weeks. With stunning precision, Kishan Paul throws the reader into a world of clandestine organizations and brutal politics. The gripping characters wrench your heart and make you cringe with fear. A rollercoaster of suspense and emotion not to be missed." ~Aubrey Wynne, *Bestselling and Award Winning Author*

"I cannot think of another book I've read this year that moved me, made me gasp or still make me full of emotions days after reading it. So thank you Kishan Paul, this book was my favorite and will be one I will re-read often to feel the feels and emotions again." ~Guilty Pleasures Book Review

# THE Widow's KEEPER

## Book 2 of The Second Wife Series

## Kishan Paul

Kishan Paul Publishing

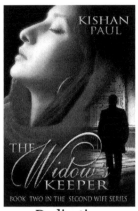

The Widow's Keeper: Book 2 of The Second Wife Series

Copyright © 2017 by Kishan Paul

ISBN: 978-0-9985294-1-7

Edited by Tera Cuskaden Norris and The Editing Hall

Cover by Original Syn

Formatting by Anessa Books

# DEDICATION

*To the wounded souls: Your pain is not always visible but it is very real. I hope you find joys along the way to ease the ache.*

# ACKNOWLEDGMENTS

The Widow's Keeper has been by far the hardest book I have ever written. As difficult as it was, I could not have done it without the help of so many.

First and foremost, I am thankful to God and HIS many blessings.

To my amazing husband and kids: Never underestimate the power of family, and thank you for being the strong force within me. (And yes, those were awful Star Wars references.) But seriously, I love you and thank God every day for gifting you to me. I could not do what I love if it wasn't for you.

To my fans: The Second Wife was turned down over sixty times by agents and publishers before I finally decided to publish it myself. I was told it was too dark. Too hard to sell. Thank you for seeing the beauty in the darkness that is Ally and Dave's story. Thank you for loving them as much as I did. I am humbled daily by your encouragement, your messages, and comments on social media, and your love for the stories and characters that fill my brain. It still shocks me that you buy my books, write reviews, and tell your friends about my stories. Thank you! You are the reason I continue to write.

To my fabulous pundits: One of the best parts about being a writer is meeting people with crazy cool jobs and having an excuse to ask them about what they do. There were so many components to this story where I had to do just that, and it was fascinating. To Craig S. Swafford LCDR SEAL, USN (Ret.) for teaching me about guns/weapons, surveillance, and on how a soldier might think. To Holly Fox, former Special Agent with the Federal Bureau of Investigation and former Hidalgo County Assistant Criminal District Attorney, for educating me on proper surveillance and protocol, and what is realistic and what's not. To Bindhu Oommen for letting me text you with different medical scenarios and not being freaked out by my how do you kill people questions.

To Nicole Ulery, my ever-patient author's assistant: Thank you for pushing me and reminding me on a regular basis just how much time had passed since I published The Second Wife. Your frequent reminders made me glue my butt to the chair and write this story. You have taken a heavy weight off my shoulders, and by doing so, I am able to focus on what I love most—writing. Thank you for all that you do and for being you.

To my editors: Tera Cuskaden Norris and Chris Hall. You have been a part of The Second Wife journey since Book 1. What would I do without you two? Thank you for calling me on the parts of the story that made no sense, on pushing me to go deeper, on challenging me. By doing so, you have made me a better storyteller and writer. Also thank you for being patient with my comma abuse. I am not even going to lie and tell you I will get better.

To my beta readers: For your critical eye and your honesty: Renee R, April Stone, Kristen Sanchez, and Jennifer Daniels. You were the first to lay eyes on this story and it wasn't pretty. Thank you for pointing out the plot holes and making it more authentic.

To Kish's Collective: I swear you folks are awesome. Thank you for being the monkeys in my circus. I am humbled every day by your words and encouragement. Thank you for believing in me. Love you guys!!

# PROLOGUE

TWO YEARS AND TEN MONTHS POST-SAYEED

*R*azaa ran a hand through his thick, black hair and knocked on the hotel room door. He scanned the hall of the five-star building as questions flooded his brain. What if he had the wrong address? Or for that matter, what if he had the right one and the man turned him away? He answered each question the same: Those were risks he had no choice but to take.

Over two and a half years ago, the life he considered blessed vanished. His father was murdered, and he and his fourteen brothers were ripped apart, scattered across the globe. Forced to live with strangers and take on new identities, he had no contact with the rest. But if their situation had turned out even half as bad as his, he could only imagine the brutality they endured. Marks of his one year with his foster family were forever imprinted not only on his body but seared into his mind.

A few yards down, a door slammed shut, making the nervous young man jump. He sucked in a breath and knocked a second time. If he could survive the past two and a half years, he could survive the next few minutes. Somehow, he managed to escape his hell only to enter another. He traveled the world as a migrant worker searching for the familiar faces of his family. Food and money were scarce and the beatings plentiful. The memories of pain flooded him, making his eyes prickle and burn with emotion. He blinked to cool the heat and kept his gaze fixed on the hardwood surface in front of him.

When the deadbolt slid, his heart tried to leap out of his throat. Razaa swallowed it down and rolled his shoulders back. Very soon, he'd come face to face with his only hope.

A man well over six feet tall opened the door, naked, except for a towel wrapped around his waist. His deep black curls hung to his light brown shoulder. Drops from the damp hair spilled onto his muscular, bare chest.

"Can I help you?" His words were spoken with an English accent.

Razaa's hopes fell, as did his face. "I am sorry, I must be at the wrong place," he stammered and walked away.

"*Aap kaon hain*?" The question made him stop in his tracks. He asked the same question as before, but this time in Urdu. The sound of it sent a jolt of calm through Razaa's anxious soul. It felt like home. He turned to face the stranger. "I have lost my family, and I need your help finding them."

The man leaned against the doorjamb, his arms crossed. A smile tugged at his mouth. "And why would I help you?"

He fisted his hands to hide the way they shook and said the words he'd practiced. "Because I am Razaa Irfani. Your brother was my father."

The man's smile dropped but he didn't move.

The young boy crossed his arms, matching his uncle's stance, trying hard to be the man his father raised. Inside however, fear squeezed his throat, making it difficult to breathe much less speak. He didn't know if he was doing the right thing by showing up at the man's hotel room, but he was desperate. This wasn't just about saving himself, it was about saving his family.

As if reading his mind, the man nodded and pushed away from the wall. "Come in, Razaa Irfani."

He gulped down his excitement and followed. Razaa learned long ago to never get his hopes up. Like the sun, they were fleeting.

The hotel room was enormous. A sofa bigger than the cots he'd slept on most of his life sat in the middle of the space, along with two matching armchairs. At the far corner was an open door. Razaa caught a glimpse of a woman asleep on the bed inside.

"Excuse me for a moment while I change," the man said before entering the dark backroom and shutting the door behind him, leaving Razaa alone.

He stayed glued to the floor until his uncle returned a few minutes later. Thankfully, he now wore pants and a shirt. The man sat on the chair and rested his bare feet on the coffee table in front of him. "We both know my brother did not have a son your age, and I don't have a lot of time for this nonsense. So tell me quickly what you want and be off."

"I may not be his blood, but he will always be my father." Razaa stuffed his fists in his pant pockets and cleared his throat. "Sayeed *Babba* adopted me and fourteen other boys from an orphanage in Islamabad a few years before he died. He loved us as his own." The man rested his elbows on his chair and pressed his chin on the tips of his fingers. "I am aware of the boys my brother adopted. I am also aware they died two and a half years ago with him."

"Nay, *Chacha*. We did not die." Razaa noticed the way the man's brows lifted as soon as he called him uncle. He ignored it and continued, "We were separated, given new names, and sent to live with different strangers." His face warmed with emotion. "I have searched for the others, but I don't know where they are. If their lives are as hard as mine, I must find them."

"And what makes you think I'd believe you, much less help you?"

Emotion filled Razaa's eyes. "When my brothers and I would fight, Babba would tell us about you two and your lives together in Karachi. He told us you never fought with him but that you admired him. He wanted us to be like you and him." The young boy's throat tightened. He cleared it and forced out the words. "And we were. We may have been adopted, but we were as close as brothers could be. Chacha, I need your help finding my family."

"Don't call me that," the man snapped.

The tone startled Razaa, but he tried not to show it.

"Call me Shariff." He waved at the sofa. "And sit down."

He slid on to the edge of the couch, keeping his focus on the man.

"So tell me, Razaa, if you and all your brothers are alive, what happened to your Sayeed Babba? Did the As-Sirat not kill him?"

Heat prickled at the back of his neck. Memories of that day, and of his father's bullet ridden body, tortured him. "He is dead but not by the As-Sirat."

Shariff sat motionless for a long while, making Razaa wonder if he should repeat what he said.

"If the As-Sirat did not kill him, then who?"

Razaa cleared his throat. "His wife."

Shariff laughed. "My brother was killed by his wife?"

The disbelieving smirk on his face made the young man shift in his seat. "Yes, Cha...Shariff."

"What was her name?"

Muscles in his body tightened at the prospect of uttering the name of the woman he'd tried to block from his mind since the murder. "Sara."

Shariff's brows. "Sayeed Irfani was murdered by his second wife?"

# CHAPTER ONE

## INTERVENTION

*A*lly gripped the phone to her ear and paced the bathroom. The automated voice on the other end thanked her for her call and promised to return it as soon as possible. Considering she'd heard the same message every day for the past four months, she knew the number and the man's words by heart. She tucked a loose strand of hair behind her ear and sucked in a breath as the message beeped.

"Good morning. This is Alisha Dimarchi. Wife of David Dimarchi. Calling. Again. I'm following up on the status of the investigation around my husband's death." As usual, her voice cracked at the last few words. She cleared it and continued. "I've left several messages and would appreciate a response, please, to let me know I'm contacting the right person."

She'd recited the same words more times than she could count; sometimes they were spoken politely, other times they were filled with emotion she couldn't hide. There was no doubt the agency had her contact information, but she provided it again before the message beeped a second time and the line disconnected.

Ally slid the phone to the counter and willed it to ring as she paced the room. Although in the message she called it an investigation, it didn't appear anyone else viewed it the same way. The police had already closed the case, citing no evidence of foul play in the crash that killed him. No one seemed bothered with trying to understand why her husband had slammed on his brakes and parked his car in the middle of the road in the first place.

The only witness, a shadowy figure in a dark hoodie, had vanished. A nearby store's video showed the person running down the sidewalk seconds after the incident. No other footage of the individual or incident existed.

It was a person no one seemed interested in finding because, as far as the detectives were concerned, her husband voluntarily stopped his car and as a result was rear-ended. And for most people, their logic would have been enough. But most people didn't know David. And most people hadn't been kidnapped and taken to another country. Most people hadn't been tortured and raped for two years. Most people hadn't clawed their way out of hell only to lose the man they loved three years to the day after they'd escaped.

Ally smoothed out the white card in her fist and returned it to the spot under the box of Q-tips in David's drawer. She'd found it there days after the crash. Her fingers brushed against the container. He usually hogged most of the countertop and took longer getting ready than she did. A smile tugged at her lips. Funny how the things she once found annoying she now ached for.

A knock at the bathroom door brought her out of her thoughts.

"Ally *Bayti*, breakfast is ready." Her father's gentle voice echoed through the thin wood separating her from them. Instead of calming her, her muscles tightened.

Privacy was a luxury she no longer enjoyed. Her parents moved in the day she lost David and hadn't left her side since—no matter how many times she'd asked, begged, or ordered them to do so. They worried she'd hurt herself and scrutinized every move she made and every word she uttered. She knew this because their voices floated through the thin walls of her apartment. Even the fan in her bathroom, the one place in the house where she could hide from them, did little to block them out.

"Coming!" She looked up at the image in the mirror and shook her head. Pappa's blood pressure would double if she went out looking the way she did. Ally opened her drawer and retrieved her makeup bag and a hair tie. After smoothing out the top of her hair, she bunched her thick curls into her fist and twisted the band tight around the ponytail. She took out her beige tube of concealer and spread it over the black circles etched under her eyes.

Once the areas under her eyes and the dark hollows beneath her cheekbones were the same shade of brown as the rest of her face, she put away her makeup. Ally stared at the bathroom door, willing herself to leave. Instead of moving toward it, her legs propelled her backwards into the master closet. She turned on the light and shut the door behind her. Tight muscles relaxed the minute the faint scent of cedar and musk filled her lungs. It was the only space that still smelled like him.

She took her time changing, and once she finished, picked up the worn leather backpack in the corner and headed to the large suitcase leaning against the far end of the room. Ally lowered to her knees, unzipping the luggage enough to get her hand through. When her fingers brushed against smooth plastic, she grabbed one of the packets and pulled it out, quickly sealing the suitcase shut and returning it to its spot. Ally tucked the bag into her brown leather backpack and headed to the kitchen. It was time to face the family.

As soon as she walked in, she wished she'd stayed in the closet. Instead of two sets, four pairs of eyes stared back at her. Her big brother, Nik *Bhai*, her sister, Reya, and her parents were all seated around the table. Considering it was the middle of the week and her siblings both worked, their visit had a purpose. Her. She slid into one of the two seats still vacant and stared at the cup of chai in front of her.

Her father cleared his throat. "Alisha, I called the family together because we need to talk with you."

He averted his gaze when their eyes locked. She watched him adjust his glasses and shift in his seat. Her mother grabbed Ally's hand and gave it a squeeze.

"A woman from the Counter Terrorism Department contacted me last night. She said you've been calling them daily, sometimes two times, asking about David's car accident."

She leaned forward on her elbows, her pulse rising. "What did she say?"

Silence weighed heavy in the room. Pappa scratched the top of his almost-bald head and cleared his throat. Her brother's chair creaked when he leaned back. Bhai resembled his father minus thirty years and, unlike Pappa, had a thick head of black hair. He raised his brows at the patriarch, encouraging him to continue.

"Well?" Ally's face heated as the two men silently communicated with each other. After all the messages she'd left, they'd finally called back, but not to speak with her. She pulled her hand out of her mom's grasp and locked gazes with the only person who would look back, her baby sister. "Rey, can you please tell me what she said?"

Rey opened her mouth but Alisha's father answered. "She said you are harassing them. To tell you there is no investigation and to stop calling."

"Harassing them?" She leaned back in her chair and crossed her arms. "Trying to get answers about my husband's death bothers them?" Ally kept her voice low as she scanned their faces. "Is that what you told David when he searched for me?"

Reya reached across and tried to grab her hand. "It's not the same situation, Di. We didn't know if you were alive or dead. There is no question Dave is dead. We all saw him in the coffin."

Ally pulled her hand away and curled her fingers into her palm. "I know my husband is dead," she whispered.

Not a single person in the room met her gaze. "Every night I go to bed dreading the morning because once I wake up I will have to remember *my David is dead*." Although her words were spoken softly, it felt like she screamed them. Four months later, uttering the statement had the same impact as someone ripping her lungs and heart out of her body.

"We wouldn't know what you think because you won't tell us." The hurt in Reya's tone stung.

Ally shook her head. "I don't tell you because you don't understand. You can't understand." She had to get away from them. Away from their looks of pity, their disappointment, and their judgment. She rose to her feet and snatched the backpack from the floor.

Her brother grabbed her wrist when she walked past. "Let it go, Ally. The police and everyone else believe there was nothing suspicious about the accident."

She glared at him. "Two people can look at the same situation and see two different things. You are allowed to perceive his accident one way, and I am allowed to perceive it another."

Nik cut her a look. "Your way is wrong. Your story is created by grief and a need to somehow keep him alive."

The corner of Ally's mouth curved up. "Wow, Bhai, you should give up pediatrics and go into psychiatry."

He rolled his eyes but didn't respond.

She twisted her hand out of his grasp and pointed at herself. "What I believe?" Ally took a step backward from him. "Is the truth. There is no way he would have just stopped his car in the middle of the road. Something made him stop. And no, I don't think it was a cat or a dog or that he was so sleepy that he decided to park his car and take a nap in the middle of the road."

She walked out of the kitchen and grabbed her sneakers from the coat closet. Her eyes burned with emotion. Ally blinked it away and sat on the sofa as she worked on untying the knots in her laces.

*I'm alone.* The realization crept into her consciousness the moment she had lost him. And with every passing day, the darkness grew heavier. No matter how many people suffocated her with their presence, the isolation persevered. Sometimes, in her lowest moments, she found herself wishing she could go back in time. Back to when she was locked away in Sayeed's compound being tortured.

The sofa shifted when her sister slid onto the cushion next to her. Ally's fingers shook, making it hard to undo the knotted lace of her shoe.

Rey grabbed the sneaker out of her hand. "Di, some shitty things have happened to you. You've had to survive them all and then lose Dave." Her sister's voice cracked. "That would put me over the edge, too." Reya placed the unknotted shoe back in Ally's lap.

"You think I've gone over the edge?" she whispered. Her sister's words didn't surprise her. They had just never been uttered out loud before. It was also the reason why Ally had stopped talking to them about her suspicions.

Bhai positioned himself on the coffee table in front of her. "We think you need more help than you're getting."

She pulled the shoe onto her foot and then worked on unknotting the other one. "You've already increased my meds, and I'm in counseling twice a week. How much more help are you wanting me to get?"

He cleared his throat. "The woman from the agency told Pappa about an intensive trauma treatment center for people who've gone through things like you have."

She paused mid-lace. "And what exactly have I gone through?"

Bhai averted his gaze and shifted in his seat. "The rape and kidnapping."

Ally nodded and returned to working on her shoes so she could get away from them.

"We *all* believe you need to go there."

The emotion in her mother's voice made her look over at the woman standing in the hall. Her face glistened, wet with tears, and Pappa stood beside her, holding her hand. "Every night you wake up screaming, and then we're finding you asleep in your closet. It's not normal."

She rose. "Please tell me what exactly is the normal way a woman should mourn the loss of her husband?"

Mummy's gaze locked with hers, but her father answered. "By grieving and letting your family comfort you. Creating untrue stories about things are not going to help you heal. You have to let him go."

Ally clenched her fists as she looked at every person in the room. "Is this what the people at the center told you to say to me when you staged this intervention?"

The room fell silent as each person looked away.

Rey hugged her and rested her chin on Ally's shoulder. "Di, we all love you very much, and no matter who told us to say what, this is the truth. No one person should have to survive the shit you've had to endure. There's nothing wrong with getting help."

She sucked in a breath and didn't bother arguing. Help was exactly the reason she'd called the agency. Ally shook her head and headed for the table by the door where she and David kept their keys.

"I've researched this place," Rey said from behind her.

The keys were missing. She opened the drawer and found it empty. "Did they tell you to hide my keys, too?"

Her sister ignored her question and continued to sell the institute. "It's an eight-week intensive program run by the U.S. government in Germany for soldiers struggling with post-traumatic stress. They don't normally allow civilians in." Rey cleared her throat. "But since your situation is a little different, they are offering you a spot."

"It sounds like a great opportunity, but I'm not going." Screw the keys. Ally turned and headed for the door.

"Let her go. She needs some time." Her brother's words rang true; she needed time. Time to figure out what to do because there was no way in hell she was leaving her home.

As soon as she exited the apartment complex and her feet hit the sidewalk, Ally started to run. *My David is dead.* The words continued to echo in her head, growing louder with each step. She made her way down several blocks of sidewalk, and when she turned into the park, she broke into a sprint. She was almost home.

# CHAPTER TWO

## FIGHTING DEMONS

FIVE MONTHS POST-RESCUE

*D*ave stopped short at the entrance of the park. He leaned forward, planted his palms on his thighs, and tried to catch his breath. Adrenaline surged through him as his heart pumped an erratic beat. The three blocks he'd sprinted clearly had something to do with his current physical state, but just a small bit. The real reason for his panic sat on a park bench a few yards away, alone, with her back to him.

Terror had taken residence in his throat for the past forty-five minutes. Now seeing her with his own eyes, it eased a little, and he was finally able to swallow it down. He wiped the perspiration off his forehead with the edge of his sweat-soaked tee all while keeping his gaze fixed on her. No way in hell was he letting Ally out of his sight again.

A thousand questions raced through his head, but the most important ones were now answered. She was alive. Safe.

Waking up at six in the morning to an empty bed and apartment had scared the living shit out of him. Not only had she disappeared, she hadn't answered any of his calls, and no one knew her location. Once upon a time, it wouldn't have been a big deal, but everything changed with her kidnapping and the years of torture she endured at the hands of bastard Sayeed.

In the five months since her rescue and return home, this was the first time Ally had gone anywhere alone. While he searched the apartment for her, images of finding her blood and shoe in a parking lot almost three years ago flooded him, suffocating him. *This couldn't be happening. Not again.*

It took him a moment to shake off the panic, and when he did, his brain started working. He searched his bathroom drawer for the card his buddy in the CIA gave him. Eddie had said if anything suspicious arose to call the number, and the person on the other end would help. Thank God, he was right. The woman who answered took down his information, and then after what seemed like a decade, called him back, told him his wife was in Fairmount Park, even specified which entrance he should take and which bench. As soon as he hung up, he threw on some clothes and ran.

The three blocks to get to Ally felt like three hundred. The urgency to be near her fueled him, pushing his legs to pump faster, harder. Ally out there alone in the world terrified him. Not only because of his own crazy issues about losing her again but also because of the shit Sayeed did to her. Hell, it took her months before she could close the bathroom door all the way, and now she'd wandered out of the apartment into the city alone?

Once he steadied his breathing and his hands weren't shaking anymore, he walked as casually as possible in her direction. Almost three years of hell faded as he approached. She sat cross-legged on the bench, dressed in jogging clothes and sneakers with her thick, black hair pulled back in a tight ponytail. Her brown skin glowed against the backdrop of the green and red autumn foliage. Aside from the death grip she had on the poor bag of pistachios in her lap, she appeared relaxed and at ease.

His chest tightened. Her MO. The calm, carefree look she let the outside world see. Sometimes she covered it so well, she even fooled him. But the white knuckles always gave her away.

Once upon a time, Ally used to come to this park and run along the river. She said it centered her, gave her a high. The small seed of hope he kept shoving down began to sprout again. Maybe the outdoors would help center her again. Granted, she'd never be the same, but he ached for her to smile the way she used to. The kind of smile where not only the edges of those full, sexy lips lifted, but the corners of her big brown eyes did, too.

When Ally reached into the bag and pulled out a shelled pistachio, her gaze locked with his. The immediate flash of fear on her face when she noticed him didn't sting as much as it used to. She slammed her lids shut and sucked in a breath, releasing it slowly. Once she exhaled, she nodded and stared out at the river. "I should have left you a note."

He cleared his throat and grinned. "That would have been nice. Or maybe answered one of my calls."

Although she kept her gaze on the water, her perfectly arched black brows rose. "You called?"

He shrugged. "Not too many times. Only about seven or so."

She pulled the phone from her backpack, and then cringed at whatever she saw on its screen. "Sorry, I didn't hear it. You're mad, aren't you?"

He shook his head. "No. Not yet, anyway. But the thought you might be dead or almost dead did wander into my mind a couple hundred times, which is why I really need to touch and feel you right now."

She got up and wrapped her arms around him. From the way she held on tight, he wasn't the only one relieved. Dave rested his chin on her head and held her close. Feeling her skin against his, knowing her heart beat so close to his, *this* was what centered him.

"It was very inconsiderate of me after everything you've gone through." Her words were mumbled, probably because of how tight he crushed her to him. Not that it mattered; he had no plans of loosening his grip.

"What happened?" He kept his voice low and calm, void of the worries consuming him.

She shrugged but didn't answer.

He rolled his eyes. "After the multiple almost-heart attacks I had in the past half hour, you've gotta give me something here."

Her head bobbed under his chin. "I couldn't sleep, so I went to the kitchen and heard your cell phone beep. I didn't mean to read the message, but the screen kept flashing on the counter."

He frowned. He didn't remember seeing any new messages. "I don't care if you read my..."

"It was from her."

Dave winced at the way Ally said *her*. He held her tighter, fighting the urge to pull out his cell and scroll through his messages.

Blond and blue-eyed, Kate had been his saving grace when he'd lost Ally, and he'd relied on her companionship a lot to help him through. But he always felt guilty. Guilty he didn't love her the way she loved him. Guilty he was in some way cheating on the only woman he'd ever loved by being with her, even though he had no reason to believe Ally was even alive back then. Regardless, the fact she'd texted and Ally saw it wasn't a good sign.

He cleared his throat and dreaded the answer to the question he needed to ask. "What did it say?"

She shifted her weight and shrugged. "She missed you and still loved you."

*Fuck*. Dave slammed his eyes shut. "Ally. There's nothing there."

"I know." She pulled away and sat down on the bench. "You'd never do something like that."

Although her response should have relieved the tension building in his neck, the way she said it had the opposite effect. Dave slid in beside her and grabbed her hand, unsure of what she'd say next.

Ally stared out into the river in front of them. "Have you seen her since we've gotten back?"

He scanned her face for signs of anger or jealousy but saw none. "We work at the same hospital. It's hard not to run into each other."

"How does she feel about...everything?"

He shifted in his seat. "I don't really ask."

"But you know she still loves you."

The words stabbed at his conscience. "I can't make someone feel or not feel something. Those are not conversations we have."

She pulled her hand out of his grasp. "But you do have conversations with her."

He shrugged. "Very little. What are you trying to say?"

Ally's chocolate brown eyes locked with his. "Do you ever wonder if you picked the wrong person or thought about what life would have been like if I hadn't come back?"

He shook his head. "Never."

She hugged her knees to her chest, rested the heels of her sneakers on the edge of the bench, and stared at the pond. "I do."

Dave opened his mouth to respond but then shut it.

"All the time," she whispered.

Although none of what she said surprised him, hearing the

words cut.

"And after reading the text, I started thinking about all the challenges I brought back with me, and how your life would have been easier if you'd been with her instead."

He let out a breath and shook his head. This wasn't the first time she'd talked about how hard she'd made his life, and it seemed like nothing he said or did could convince her otherwise.

"Maybe I was supposed to be with Farah and the boys, and you were supposed to have a life with Kate. Maybe somehow I messed things up by coming home."

Dave put his arm around her shoulders and rested his cheek against hers. "You know what I call that?"

She shook her head.

"Bullshit."

He paused and stared out at the clear blue of the river, letting his response sink in before explaining. "I had a life with Kate, and I spent it thinking about you. Getting you back was the best thing to ever happen to me. I don't ever want to relive those years without you. Yes, things have been challenging for us, but it's still much better having you here with me than not having you at all. And as far as messing with the forces of nature or whatever you're thinking, that's a load of crap. What if here was where you were supposed to be?"

"I'm not an easy person to live with." She scanned the waters as if looking for an answer.

Dave grinned. "Good thing I am." He nudged her head onto his shoulder and rested his cheek on her hair. "I don't know how many times, ways, and in how many different languages I need to tell you this is where I want to be, but I'll do it. Until the day I die."

"I want you to be happy."

"I am," he lied. Well, it wasn't a complete lie. Having her home made him happier than he'd been since she disappeared. But the way she stared out and got lost in her thoughts, tuning him and the rest of the world out, the way she would jerk away from him as if he'd hit her... It all stung, and no amount of reading or couples' therapy could ease the feeling that he could no longer make her happy. "More than you'll ever know. But I'm still not understanding why you're here."

She shrugged. "I'm tired of being scared of my own shadow."

He ran his fingers up her arm, and although she stiffened, she didn't pull away. He smiled. *Progress.* "So you thought walking three blocks to the park at six o'clock in the morning was the way to go?"

The sound of her laugh made his chest swell. "I didn't say it was a rational thought but it worked."

He inhaled the sweet vanilla of her perfume. "Why didn't you wake me up? You know I'd have come with you."

She pulled his hand off her arm and into her lap, weaving her fingers through his. "You can't fight all my demons for me. I needed to know I could do it on my own. And I did."

"You don't have to push this hard, you know. It's only been five months."

"I know." Ally nuzzled her forehead against his neck. This was something new she'd started doing, and he loved it when she did. "But I needed to know."

"And how'd it go?"

"Scary as hell. I jumped at every noise. I kept wanting to turn around and come home but I didn't."

He pulled her hand to his lips and kissed her knuckles. "It wouldn't have been so bad if you had."

She shrugged. "It would have been for me. So I pushed through it and made myself sit on the bench. But you know what the suckiest part was?"

"What?"

"Realizing I was going to have to do it all over to get home." Ally looked up at him and smiled. "But now I don't have to worry about it anymore because you swooped in to save the day."

Dave kissed the tip of her nose and grinned. "The next time you decide to fight your demons, leave me a note or something. Okay?"

Her face fell. "I keep disappointing you."

He savored the fact she hadn't pulled away. "Baby, as long as you're alive and safe, nothing you do will disappoint me."

# CHAPTER THREE

## THE VISITOR

*A*lly slowed to a brisk walk as soon as she entered the cemetery. She wiped the sweat from her forehead on the sleeve of her shirt. While she weaved through the hundred-year-old gothic tombstones littering the grounds, her pulse eased to a calmer rate. A smile tugged at her lips. Once upon a time, she and David wandered around the property, reading the names engraved into the stones and making up crazy stories about the people buried below.

Now, the worn monuments and mausoleums no longer called to her. What drew her was a simple plot in the far end of the property with a view of the Schuylkill River. It had no tombstone yet, just a marble plaque listing the name and date of the occupant. And she didn't need to create a heroic story for the person lying beneath the slab of freshly plotted grass—she'd seen and lived it with him.

A few hundred yards before her destination, movement to her right caught her attention. A man stood by the entrance to one of the larger mausoleums. In jeans and a black tee, his muscular arms were crossed against his chest. As usual, he kept his black hair cut short and his dark aviators made it impossible to read him. She stumbled at the sight.

Her pulse, which moments ago had slowed from her run, quickened. He must have heard about her calls. As if reading her mind, Eddie nodded. She watched him scan the area. He tipped his head in the direction of the building behind him and disappeared inside.

Ally stayed rooted to her spot and looked over her shoulder. Aside from the squirrels searching for their breakfast and the birds chirping from nearby trees, the place sat empty, as it always did at seven in the morning. The only thing different was the excitement surging through her.

She'd spent the past few months leaving messages at the agency, hoping he'd get them. But why had he come? She bit her lip. What if he'd shown up to tell her he agreed with her family that she was crazy?

Ally shook her head. It didn't matter. David wouldn't have found her without Eddie's help, and hopefully he was here now with the answers she sought. The thought propelled her forward.

Unfortunately, she also knew Eddie. He was stingy with information, rarely sharing his knowledge unless necessary. Which made his sudden appearance even more intriguing. He had something to share, and she intended to hear his thoughts, even if she didn't like them.

At the entrance, she stopped and eyed the thick, rusted lock dangling from the handle. The door sat slightly ajar, open enough for a person to slide in yet still be hidden from the world. Her stomach tightened. Eddie had gone to some trouble to set up this meeting. She craned her head to look inside but saw nothing other than a gray wall. Ally sucked in a breath and squeezed through the cracked opening.

Rays of early morning sun poured in from small slits on the ceiling of the otherwise dark room. A thick rectangular slab of concrete sat prominently in the middle of the space. Large cobwebs covered the white bust of a man situated atop the slab. Most likely, the same man whose corpse slept beneath it.

"How are you holding up?" Eddie stood beside the bust, facing her and the entrance.

Ally grabbed hold of the door. Her face heated. "According to my family and some woman in your department, I've gone crazy."

He grinned. "Well, as of two days ago, I believe you've called us three hundred twenty-seven times." One of his brows lifted, rising over the frame of his shades. "That's a lot of messages."

Her hopes lowered substantially. "So you're here to tell me

you agree with them? That I'm crazy?"

He shrugged. "It's not PC to call people crazy anymore. And no, it's not the only reason why I'm here. I'm here to tell you to go to the hospital in Germany, like they're recommending. Consider it a quiet getaway. A time to heal."

Heat burned her face. Ally stepped closer. "When Sayeed killed your family, is that what you did? Get away and give yourself time to heal?"

Eddie straightened and rubbed the back of his neck. "It's a little weird to be having this conversation with a dead body in the middle of the room, isn't it?"

He knew something. Her gut screamed it. The fact he wouldn't share his knowledge made the anger of the past few months swell. Ally continued her slow approach. "You kill people for a living, I think you can handle a coffin with some bones in it." Her whispered voice shook with emotion. "And that's not what's making you uncomfortable. What's making you uncomfortable is I'm mad, and you don't know what to do with me."

With every step forward she took, Eddie took one back, fueling her contempt even more. "He did *everything* you and the agency told him to do. Everything." She jabbed her finger at his face. "You said leave Farah and the boys behind and never contact them. Every time I even mentioned their names or wondered out loud about what it would be like to see them again, David quoted your words at me. He would say, 'the agency's taking care of them,' and reminded me they could never know I was alive for their own safety. After doing everything you asked of him, what was the end result?"

A muscle on the side of his jaw flexed.

An angry tear slipped down her cheek. "Someone killed him."

"All the reports indicate the death was an accident," he said.

She nodded and swiped the moisture away with the back of her hand. "They also say Sara Irfani died in an explosion in Pakistan over three years ago."

Eddie opened his mouth and shut it. Good. She wasn't finished.

"And you came all the way here to the cemetery and broke into a mausoleum to tell me what the reports say? Oh, and to tell me I'm crazy and need to go into the hospital. Why go to so much trouble when you could have picked up a phone and called, or emailed, or written a letter even? " She grit her teeth, hating the pain she heard in her own voice. "Have I gone through the most agonizing loss of my life? Yes. Am I the grieving widow who's obsessively called the CIA over three hundred times? Yes. But after all these years of doing exactly what you said, don't I deserve to know?"

"And twenty-seven."

Ally shook her head, not understanding what he meant.

"Three hundred and twenty-seven calls, as of two days ago."

She rolled her eyes and continued. "I may be all those, but I'm not stupid."

He let out a sigh and rested the back of his head against the concrete wall. "You're right, I should have called you back. And I'm sorry. About everything. You didn't deserve any of this."

Ally looked over at the cobwebs blanketing the statue beside her. His words caught her off guard. She expected smart-ass comments, not an apology.

"I really liked him. I wouldn't have helped him if I didn't."

"Liar." A spider crawled across the marble statue's nose, making its way to its forehead. "We both know you were itching for a chance to go after Sayeed. David gave you the opportunity. You're saying whatever you need to get me to shut up and do what you want me to do."

"Yes, I want you on the plane, but I'm telling you the truth. David was a good man. A much better man than most of us will ever be. I didn't have to take him with me to Pakistan, and I definitely wouldn't have spent two weeks locked up in a building with him if I didn't like the guy."

She sucked in a breath and let it out slowly. "My husband liked you, too. He considered you one of the good guys. An asshole but a good guy."

Eddie chuckled and pulled off his shades. "How are you holding up?"

A deep purple welt darkened the bottom of his right eye. Instead of asking about it, she answered his question in Eddie style. "How do you think I'm doing?"

"Pretty pissed off."

Ally stared at the stained glass window on the top of the room. "I thought nothing could be more traumatic than my life with

Sayeed. I was wrong. Losing David has been the hardest pain I've ever endured." She cleared her throat and pushed away the tear that threatened to escape. "You still haven't answered my question. Why are you here?"

Eddie nodded. "To talk to you about the hospital in Germany."

*Of course.* A sad smile tugged at her lips. She was tired. Tired of people thinking they knew what was best for her. Tired of no one listening. Tired of pretending she was okay. She leaned her back against the wall and slid to the ground. Ally hugged her knees to her chest, rested her forehead on the tops of her arms, and closed her eyes. "I'm not going."

"It's not up for debate."

She laughed. "Okay, then drugging me and taking me away has worked in the past."

"Right now, I have to say it's not a bad idea."

Ally waved toward the door. "Go home, Eddie. No more jokes. No more lies. I can't do this anymore."

The room fell silent. She listened to his jeans stretch as he moved around the room. He mumbled under his breath for a while before finally sitting down beside her. "Okay fine. Look, there's a problem."

"Does the problem have anything to do with David's accident?" she asked.

"Maybe."

Her head snapped up, and she stared over at him. "I'm listening."

Eddie's legs were bent. His arms hung over his knees, his fingers clasped together as he stared at the mausoleum entrance. "All I can say is there's a situation, and we need to get you in a safe place as a precautionary measure."

Every muscle in her body froze, focused on Eddie's words. "What kind of situation?"

He scowled. "The kind I can't discuss."

"There's a situation *possibly* connected to my husband's death. A situation dangerous enough that you want me to leave, but you won't tell me anything further."

He nodded. "Yup."

She rested her chin on her forearms and shook her head. "I'm not going."

Eddie's whispered string of obscenities filled the room. She ignored them all. After he finished, he cleared his throat. "Please?"

From the pained sound of it falling from his lips, there was no doubt he rarely used the word. Ally looked over at him. His face was bright red, especially the spot between his brows. She kept her voice calm. "Tell me the truth, Eddie. None of this 'because I said so' or 'because I know better' crap."

He was silent for a few beats before answering. "One person's already dead and two others are missing. Not counting the possibility that this could also be connected to your husband's accident."

Her heart thudded harder and harder against her chest. "Who?"

He scowled and stared at the entrance.

She sucked in a breath. "Farah?"

Something flashed across his face as soon as she mentioned his sister's name and disappeared a second later. Ally climbed to her knees, facing him. "Farah's dead?"

He stared at her, and for the first time, she saw fear in his eyes. "I don't know."

"She's one of the people who's missing, then." Terror crawled up her spine while her brain whirled with scenarios. "You said someone other than David died. Who?"

Eddie pursed his lips, put his sunglasses on, and rested his head against the wall.

Ally wiped her sweaty palm on her running pants. "The boys?" she whispered.

"Alive."

She let out a breath only to suck it back in a second later. "Farah's husband, Amir."

He didn't respond.

Her jaw dropped. She could hear the erratic thuds of her pulse against the back of her ears. She stared at him. "He's dead?"

"I..."

She cut him off. "It's the only way they would have been able to get Farah. Amir would have never let her go."

Eddie didn't respond, confirming her theory.

She sat on her haunches as the weight of it all sliced through her. "This is happening because of me? Am I the reason...?"

His head was shaking before she ever finished her sentence. "We don't know anything yet. Which is why you need to disappear."

"I can help get her back."

"You'll get her and yourself killed."

"If it will save her, I'm okay with the other part," she blurted.

She didn't have to see behind his shades to know he currently stared at her as if she were crazy.

Ally cleared her throat and tried to sound rational. "I am the reason all of this is happening. David and Amir's deaths, Farah's kidnapping, all because of me. My parents and siblings are here. If you don't know their motives, then you don't know if they will come after my family."

He put his palm up, silencing her. "Just do as you're told, and *all* of our families will be safe." He rose to his feet and stretched out his hand, helping her up.

"How can you promise that?"

The muscles in his jaw flexed. "Because they have my sister, and I'm going to destroy the motherfucker who killed her husband and took her and her—" He stopped mid-sentence and sucked in a breath. "But before I can do anything, I need you to stop wandering around deserted cemeteries and get your fucking ass to Germany. They can protect you at the base so I can do what I do best. "

"You still haven't answered my question. How do you know they won't come after my family in Philadelphia to get to me?"

"I know them. It would be too messy. They don't like messy."

"Which is why they have Farah?"

He nodded. "From what I've pieced together, they've been monitoring David's cell phone and his work email for information about you. My hunch is they're waiting for the right time to contact you and strike a deal, you for them."

His words chilled her. "Then I need to go to them."

"No," he snapped. "It will only kill her faster. They won't need her anymore. If you really want to help, go to Germany. I know where she is, and you disappearing buys me some time."

She stared in the direction of David's grave. Going to Germany meant leaving him.

"There are lives, living and breathing ones depending on you, and your husband's isn't one of them." He pointed in the direction she stared. "That plot of grass and the box underneath? Those are only his bones. He's not there and never will be."

Her chest tightened, leaving her breathless. Ally wrapped her arms around herself and squeezed. "It feels like he is."

"And what would he say if he were standing right here?"

A second tear escaped down her cheek. They both knew the answer. "You're not playing fair."

"And what about this situation is?" He stepped away from her and waved at the door. "There's a flight leaving today at eleven a.m. to Frankfurt. Your ass needs to be on it. Someone will be waiting at the airport for you and will escort you to the hospital."

# CHAPTER FOUR

## BREAST DESENSITIZATION THERAPY

EIGHT MONTHS POST-RESCUE

*D*ave rested the back of his head on the sofa's armrest and stretched his six-foot-four body across the couch, letting his feet dangle over the other side. He stared at the closed bathroom door and grumbled under his breath. She'd been in there for a good half hour already, and it took every drop of self-control to not check on her. According to their agreement in couple's counseling, he needed to give her space whenever she ran and let her come to him when she was ready.

*Well, fucking great.*

He grabbed the remote control and turned on the television. A newsman with platinum hair popped on the screen, providing commentary about the upcoming presidential elections. That was the last thing he wanted to focus on.

He flipped through channels as his mind drifted to the events which sent her running to the bathroom in the first place. All they were doing was eating their fucking dinner. He'd finished telling her how good the pasta turned out when her eyes glazed over and she left. That was it. Nothing more.

Well, clearly there was more. So he went through their dinner scene by scene in his head. The shirt she wore looked really good on her. She called the shade coral. Whatever name she used, he loved how the color made her tanned skin glow—especially the cleavage peeking out from the top's V-neck. He also appreciated the way it hugged her body. But he kept those thoughts to himself, instead merely stating that he liked the top on her. Maybe he shouldn't have complimented her?

Dave shook his head and focused on his channel surfing until the image of two meerkats having sex popped on. He slanted his head, watching them in fascination.

"Lucky bastard," he muttered before turning it off and tossing the remote back on the table. The digital clock by the television flashed eight thirty. It had been forty-five minutes. He stared at the door for the thousandth time. *Fuck this.* Dave got to his feet and headed to the bathroom, but instead of banging on it, he paced the living room. Once it hit an hour, all deals were off.

"David?"

He paused mid-pace and stared at the still closed door separating them. "I'm here."

"Can you grab a stopwatch, set it for five minutes, and sit on the couch please."

He scrunched his face at the request but didn't question it. Instead, he did as instructed. He sat his impatient ass on the couch while he fiddled with his cell until he found the stopwatch feature. "Ready."

"Don't hit start until I tell you."

Cell on his bouncing knee, he stared at the door, wondering what the hell she had in mind. "Okay."

She came out of the bathroom in the same jeans and coral-colored shirt she wore when she ran in. He focused on her face and the way her nose crinkled up. Something either stank or she was concentrating. His bet was on the latter.

Ally slid the remote control to the side and sat on the coffee table in front of him. She took a deep breath and closed her eyes.

Dave's chest tightened. He hated seeing her like this, and not knowing how to make it better killed him. It used to be he could hug the hell out of her and she'd be good. But now hugging sometimes had the exact opposite effect.

"So I figured out my trigger this time."

He nodded, waiting for her to continue.

"It was you staring at my breasts."

He shifted in his seat as his face heated. "I didn't stare at your breasts."

She raised her brows and smiled. "It's okay. You're my husband and you're supposed to find me attractive."

Dave shrugged and rubbed the back of his neck. "Okay, well maybe I might have stared a little."

Ally nodded and sat up straight. This time he made it a point not to gaze at her chest when she sucked in a breath. "It's unrealistic of me to ask you to not look at my breasts. And since a big part of intimacy is you admiring all parts of my body, it's something I need to work on. So, I want you to stare at my breasts."

Dave laughed. "What?"

She nodded. "For five minutes every day, you'll stare at my breasts. In a few days, we'll up the time to six minutes and keep going."

His mouth had dropped open at some point. He closed it shut only to open it again. "How exactly is this supposed to help?"

"Desensitization. I need to get used to it."

He nodded at the serious expression on her face. She was clearly in therapist mode, which reminded him. "Shouldn't you talk to your therapist about this plan first?"

She shrugged. "I know me and what I need. This is what I need now. So when you're ready, hit start."

Hell if he was going to argue. Dave hit start on the stopwatch and began the breast desensitization session. He shifted in his seat while he focused on the lovely view of her cleavage. She was right; he had noticed them earlier. How could he not? They were his favorite part of her. Well, those and her ass and those legs. A part of him started to twitch in agreement.

*Shit.*

Dave cleared his throat. "So this desensitization thing. You realize no matter how long we do this, it won't desensitize my reaction to your breasts, right? I will get turned on every time."

When Ally shifted in her seat, her chest did, too. Dave glanced at her hands. They were balled in fists. Any arousal he felt started to deflate as soon as he saw her pale knuckles.

He cleared his throat. "Have I ever told you about the naked lady at the hospital?"

"No."

He grinned. "Well, it was a little over a year ago. I was

charting on some of my post-op patients when this woman walked up to me and asked me how I was doing. I looked up to tell her I was doing great and noticed she was naked."

Ally giggled, making her lovely parts jiggle. Dave grabbed a pillow, resting it on his lap. Something told him she'd soon be jiggling a lot more. "She was in her late nineties and stood so close to me that I'm pretty sure her breasts were rubbing against the sleeve of my scrubs."

Again the laugh, and of course the shake. "What did you do?"

He shrugged. "I asked her how her day had been. I figured at some point, they'd come take her away. Just needed to keep her distracted until then. What I'll never forget, though, is she had this one long, straggly piece of hair growing from her left nipple."

Dave smiled at the beautiful sound of her laugh. He put his hands out to show her how long the strand was. "I kid you not, the thing measured two to three inches long and stuck straight up. As much as I tried, I couldn't stop staring at it."

They almost missed the sound of the timer beeping because of her laughter. Dave slid next to her on the table and put his arm around her shoulder, pulling her close. "So at any point will these breast desensitization sessions be with you topless?"

Ally smiled and turned her chocolate brown eyes up at him. "What? Are you wanting to see if I have hair growing out of my nipples?"

He chuckled. "Hadn't considered the prospect. I should probably keep some tweezers on hand just in case."

She jabbed his side with her elbow before resting her head on his shoulder. "I love you."

The act was so natural, so very Ally, the old Ally. Dave's eyes burned with emotion.

# CHAPTER FIVE

## THE ESCORT

FOUR MONTHS POST-DAVID

*A*lly ran from Eddie straight to David's grave. The moment her feet hit the spot, she tossed the backpack to the ground and fell to her knees. From inside the bag, she pulled out her cell and headphones. Her hands shook and the device dropped to the ground. She stared at it as Eddie's caution flowed through her head. The nightmare was far from over, and David's death somehow connected to it all.

Images of her family popped in her brain. As much as they suffocated her, there was nothing she wouldn't do for them. She stared at the black plaque situated on the grave. Even if it meant being away from *him*.

She thought about what Eddie said. Leaving Philadelphia didn't mean she was leaving David. Under the grass laid the physical remains of her husband, not his soul.

"You're not here," she whispered. Saying the words out loud sent a pain so sharp and searing through her ribcage she doubled over, clutching her stomach, breathless. Eyes clenched shut, she repeated the sentence over and over. Her voice grew louder each time she uttered it. The sobs she'd swallowed since his death finally escaped. Through it all, she continued her chant. If she said it enough times, she'd believe it and the pain would stop. Wouldn't it?

An eternity later, her mouth felt like cotton, the tears had run dry, and every muscle in her body ached. She grabbed her cell from the ground and connected it to the headphones. Yes, she could say the words and even accept he wasn't in there, but it didn't make her feel any better. She needed him. To feel his arms around her. To hear him tell her she was going to be okay. But she would never hear those words again.

She scrolled through the phone until she found the playlist he made for her. A second later, the sound she hungered to hear filled her soul.

"Now on to the next song." David's laugh made the tension inside her evaporate. "As many times as I've told you you're strong, it shouldn't be a surprise this one made my list. I'm pretty sure it was written about you. No matter what life shoots at you, there's no doubt in my mind you will find a way out of it."

A sad smile tugged at her lips as the next song came on. He always knew exactly what to say.

~

Ally shifted in the hard plastic airport chair as she scanned the throngs of passengers. Someone sneezed. The sound of it made her jump out of her seat. The woman who sat across from her raised one of her perfectly arched brows. Her cue to chill out. Ally smiled, seated herself, and picked up the magazine she'd dropped a second ago. Her paranoia was getting the best of her. With good reason. Danger would find her, she just wasn't sure when.

Unable to focus, she flipped through the glossy pages. Was running away the right thing to do? Her mind drifted to her family. By the time she'd gotten home from the cemetery, she'd calmed down. But when she told them she'd go, their constant expressions of worry were mixed with guilt. The call from the person who identified himself as the director of the inpatient program at Landstuhl Regional only intensified those emotions. Since most of their clients suffered from severe PTSD-related symptoms, the center prohibited family from accompanying the patient. A trained professional would be waiting at the airport to escort her.

Reya, of course, said "Hell no!" to the idea of Ally going alone to Germany, and her parents nodded in emphatic agreement. Thankfully, Bhai spoke up, used his medical expertise, and shut down the others.

Of course, meeting the transport didn't ease any of their

concerns. Ally looked across at the escort in question. Leanna's french-manicured nails currently tapped against her cell phone as she texted someone. Her dark hair with blue streaks was twisted into a clasp at the nape of her neck. With glowing ebony skin, high cheekbones, perfect almond eyes, designer jeans, heels, and a snug pale pink shirt, she could have easily passed for one of the models in the magazine Ally flipped through.

Leanna bent over, and when she unzipped her purse, Ally noticed the peacock tattoo on her wrist. Tiny blue gems in the intricate design sparkled in the bright airport lighting. A temporary tattoo was not exactly what she expected to find imprinted on a bodyguard. To the average person, the woman appeared to be fiddling with the contents of her bag. In reality, she scanned the vicinity for threat—the action so discreet, no one noticed. Ally let out a breath and leaned back in her chair. Hopefully, Eddie knew what he was doing.

A female voice boomed through the speakers at the terminal announcing the plane to Frankfurt was now boarding. Since the escort didn't move, Ally didn't either. After they made their final call, Leanna rose. Together they entered the plane.

Ally slid in and sat by the window. Leanna took the aisle seat, leaving the spot between them vacant. Even though the flight was full, she knew the middle seat would remain empty. She stared out as the plane rolled down the tarmac.

It sped forward, moving faster until soon it lifted off the ground, angling up higher and higher into the clouds. She watched her life shrink and move farther and farther out of her grasp. A small speck of a lake came into view. Her thoughts turned to the Schuylkill River and the man lying in the cemetery alongside it. No matter how hard she tried to hold on to things, they seemed to fall out of her grasp. She used to think one day she'd look back and would understand why. Since she'd lost David, she never wanted her losses to make sense.

Long after the city disappeared and white clouds replaced land, long after the captain informed the passengers they could move about the cabin, Ally's gaze remained glued to the world of blue and white outside the tiny oval-shaped window.

She ignored the shuffling when Leanna moved into the seat beside her.

"So, I hear you're a therapist."

Ally nodded but kept her gaze fixed on the world outside.

"There's a kind of hypnosis drivers get when they drive long stretches on the highway, what's it called?"

"Highway hypnosis," Ally mumbled.

She patted her shoulder. "That's it. So I'm thinking the same must happen if you stare out into the sky while in flight for too long. "

"I'm not familiar with it."

Leanna laughed. "Keep staring out there. In about fifteen minutes, I will give you a command and let's see what happens." Her purse sat open on her lap, and she rummaged through it. She pulled out a large, clear bag full of snacks and opened it. "Hungry?"

Ally shook her head.

"I bet I can change your mind." She pulled down Ally's table and laid the packets out in front of her as she listed the contents. "I've got dark chocolate, nuts, popcorn, but not just normal popcorn. It's caramel with pieces of chocolate. Healthy crunchy granola, and last but not least, beef jerky. Much better options than little, sectioned boxed crap." She grabbed a handful of the popped kernels. "Airline food screws up my stomach every time. You still sure you don't want some?"

Ally smiled politely. "No, thank you."

"Let me know if you change your mind." The blue gem of her tattoo caught Ally's eye when Leanna dug her hand into the popcorn bag.

"It's very pretty."

Leanna leaned over and rubbed the blue stone. "It's more than pretty," she whispered. "This peacock has a tracking chip in it and monitors my heart rate and blood pressure."

Ally ran the pad of her finger over the lines of the pattern as she described it.

"Eddie is a little..."

"Controlling," Ally finished for her.

"Excessively careful." Leanna laughed. "What I really wanted was the Kydex ring. It does all the same stuff as the tatt but with a small knife thrown in." She rolled her eyes. "But airport security would have peed in their pants over it. So tattoo it was..."

Ally wasn't in the mood for conversation and grabbed her purse from under the seat as soon as Leanna stopped talking. She took out her fully charged iPod and popped the headphones into her ears. Before leaving, she'd managed to download the playlist David made. Starting at the beginning, she hit play and closed her eyes, allowing herself to get lost in the only place she knew she was safe.

# CHAPTER SIX

## THE SEX TAPE

*O*lly pulled her gold stilettos off her swollen feet the minute the elevator began its ascent to the fifteenth floor. She let out a sigh of relief and wiggled circulation back into her crushed toes. One of the many causalities of today's wedding. Thank God she was finally done.

She eyed herself in the mirrored wall of the elevator. Her deep purple sari encrusted with crystals hadn't fallen off once in the seven plus hours since she'd put it on. Considering a large chunk of time consisted of her running around like a crazy woman and then dancing like an even crazier one, she was impressed.

The stylist had secured her hair in a delicate knot at the nape of her neck, and big black barrels of curls cascaded from below the knot. It was fashioned at five in the morning and now, almost twenty-four hours later, not a single piece strayed out of place. Aside from her swollen toes, the only other part of her showing any sign of wear was the smeared eyeliner and faded lipstick. She leaned her back against the cool wall and smiled. The wedding from hell was completed and with it, her obligations to the beautiful bridezilla.

Reya was the diva of the family, and of course, when the diva got married all potential for pomp and circumstance was identified and implemented. Throw the whole Indian girl marrying an American boy into the mix, and it added up to six different social events in the past fourteen days, not including the bridal shower and bachelorette party. Most of the events Ally either threw or helped throw, which also meant time away from her own husband.

She checked the lighted numbers to the right of the doors, two more levels before she got to her floor and to David. A proud smile stretched across her face. The elevator represented her first time in a long time being completely alone, and she wasn't scared. Of course, she spent time in their apartment by herself, but aside from her morning jogs, venturing outside of the safe confines of their building hadn't happened much since she'd returned.

This was an accomplishment, and one she needed to relish. Ally rolled her shoulders back and stood taller.

*Progress.*

She hated the word, but it described her situation perfectly.

Surprisingly, there had been no severe panic attacks throughout the whole two weeks of wedding events, and only a couple of times had she reached for anti-anxiety meds for help. None of this meant the festivities weren't hard on her. Surrounded by hundreds of strangers, she found herself scanning the crowds for the man who abducted her years ago.

Most of the time, she quelled the fear by reminding herself that he was dead and would never hurt her again. The few occasions when her self-talk didn't calm her, David magically popped up by her side.

When she bent down and grabbed her heels from the floor, she noticed her deep maroon, henna-tattooed hands and admired the intricate patterns sketched into her golden skin. She turned her left arm over to inspect the inside wrist where the mehndi artist had scrolled David's name into the floral design.

She smiled. He was magic. Somehow, he knew when she needed him most and with a glance or some whispered words, soothed her. Ally had spent most of Reya's wedding remembering her own to David and the vows they'd made twelve years ago. He represented all the things the priest mentioned in his sermon at the wedding today: patient, loyal, and supportive. David Dimarchi was the best thing to ever happen to her.

The bell dinged and the doors slid open. Ally pulled her hotel room key out from inside her bra and made her way down the hall to her room. For the past few days, they'd stayed at the venue at

David's encouragement. He'd said it made more sense to sleep there than trying to go to their home thirty minutes away.

She quietly opened her room door and let herself in, closing it softly behind her. David left the reception hours earlier, telling her he'd be waiting up for her. She tiptoed into the room to find him sprawled out on top of the covers, fast asleep. Not that she blamed him. Clearly neither had expected her to come in after one in the morning. And yet, a flash of disappointment passed through her. She hadn't had much quality time with him in the past few weeks and missed him.

Ally slid her shoes under the luggage rack at the foot of the bed and admired her sleeping husband. In pajama pants and nothing else, most of his long frame lay chest down and diagonal across the giant bed except for his size-twelve bare feet, which hung over the edge. His head was near the foot of the bed, and his cheek rested on his arm as he snored softly. Next to his face was her iPad, and from the earbuds sprawled beside the device the muffled beats of music echoed.

David had asked to switch iPads with her over a week ago. Ever since then, he'd spent hours messing with it, only to put it away when she complained. Ally picked up the device and considered scrolling through to see what he'd been up to but decided against it. She turned it off, rolled the earbuds up, and placed it on the nightstand beside her.

She crossed her arms and smiled at the peaceful look on his face. As usual, a lock of his wavy brown hair covered his forehead and hung over his eye. She brushed the curl out of the way—one of her favorite things to do.

They had come so far. Just months ago, the prospect of touching him, much less letting him touch her, would have sent terror surging through her veins. The past year since she'd been home had been hard on both of them. After her kidnapping and torture, she returned to him broken and scared. When others would have given up, David stuck to her like glue, holding her hand and whispering the words of encouragement she needed. It couldn't have been easy, especially with how crazy she acted half the time. On so many occasions, she pushed him away. And pushed wasn't even the right term for it, more like shoved. After several of her panic-induced meltdowns, she'd asked him why he was still there. Each and every time he came back, saying he wasn't going anywhere and loved her. There was no question she would always be scarred by her past, but her wounds had begun to heal because of his love and constant reassurance. Now, if she could just enjoy being intimate with him. Her eyes burned with emotion, and she blinked them away. He deserved far better than she could give, and yet here he lay, patiently and relentlessly loving a broken woman.

His eyes still closed, a smile tugged at the corner of his mouth. "Are you going to stand there and admire my sexiness all night?"

Ally shook her head at her smartass husband and sat beside his smiling face. "Haven't decided yet. You look so darn cute."

His brows rose. "Does my cuteness inspire you to get naked? 'Cause if it does, admire away."

David slid closer and rested his head in her lap, invading her personal space. Unlike the past, where the same action would have sent a tidal wave of fear coursing through her, threatening to drown the life out of her, it was now a light ripple, tapping at her.

Luminous green sprinkled with specks of blue stared up at her. He watched her, waiting to see if he'd gone too far. Ally ran her hand through his thick hair. His muscles relaxed and his eyes shuttered.

"Have I told you how incredible you looked today?"

She grinned. "Only a couple hundred times, but you haven't in the past few hours."

"I haven't seen you in the past few hours."

"Good point." She ran her nails gently over the top of his scalp.

His eyes rolled back and he sighed. "I love it when you do that. I've decided you should wear saris in the house at all times, by the way."

Ally stopped playing with his hair and looked at him. "You do realize you say the same thing every time I wear one, right?"

"Mm-hmm. I'm consistent." He wrapped his hand around her wrist and rested her palm against his cheek. "Considering how consistent I am, you probably also know I want to grab one end of the sari and unroll you until you're naked."

She giggled at the image. "Like toilet paper?"

David grinned. "Hadn't thought of it that way, but I'll go with that. Except instead of a brown cardboard roll underneath, I'm going to find a sexy, naked brown woman."

She shook her head. "There are about a million safety pins keeping it together." She traced his lower lip with her fingers, and he kissed them. "And the last time you 'unrolled' me, you ruined my sari."

"I didn't forget." He waved his hand over the growing tent in his pants. "It's not much of a deterrent, though."

There was a time any hint of his arousal would have chilled her to the bone. After months of intensive individual and couple's counseling and a patient husband, many of those fears had eased. As turned on as he was, David would never force himself on her, much less push her for sex. It was one of the many things she loved about him.

"Fuck," David sat up and scanned the bed until he saw the iPad on the nightstand. He grabbed it off the table and fiddled through it. "I have something for you."

He slid the device onto her lap and untangled the earbuds. "So you know how some of the sounds I make when we've tried to have sex are triggers for you?"

Ally stared at the white screen in her lap and pretended to not wince at his words. They hadn't had full intercourse yet because of the noises he mentioned. Sometimes the simple act of him swallowing or grunting prompted a flashback and made her freeze up. He'd worked hard to stop the sounds, but some things, like swallowing and breathing, were impossible to avoid.

David played with the gold hoop hanging from her lobe and kissed her cheek. "Well, I've made you a sex tape."

She laughed as she scrolled through the rows of titles. "A what?"

He slowly worked on undoing the backing of her earring. "A playlist of sexy music you can listen to while we're, you know." He pressed his lips against her neck and planted a soft kiss. "Inserting my gun into your holster. Maybe it'll block out some of the triggers."

Ally laughed at his description and scanned the hundreds of music titles listed, but each time his mouth tugged on her skin, her ability to read dwindled. "How many songs made the cut?"

He bit on her now-naked lobe as he worked on the other earring. "Close to two hundred."

She rested a hand on his cheek, feeling his mouth stretch into a smile. "How many hours do you plan on sheathing your gun?"

"About eight. I didn't want the music to stop midway while we were, ahem, holstered." Both earrings off and on the table, he started removing her safety pins while he kissed the base of her neck.

She leaned her head back and nodded. "Completely realistic and reasonable."

"Completely. Eight hours equals four hundred and eighty minutes." David planted a knee on either side of her, straddling her, while his fingers worked on the tiny buttons of her blouse. "Which means if each gun cleaning took about an average of thirty minutes, you could start the playlist wherever you left off the previous time and still play with my gun about sixteen times before you have to hear the same song twice."

She rolled her eyes. "Thirty minutes per gun cleaning?"

He chuckled and pulled off her blouse, adding it to the pile of pins and jewelry on the table. "If not longer. I mean, it *is* a big gun."

He ran his finger between her breasts and tugged on the top of her bra as he eyed her. "No pressure, if you're not ready. It was just an idea."

Ally's chest tightened. When it came to her, he second-guessed himself so much. She ran the back of her hand against his cheek and smiled when he leaned into her touch. "I think it's an excellent idea, and one we should definitely try out immediately."

~

Naked and utterly content, Ally rested her cheek against David's chest, holding him tight. She smiled. Tonight had been a perfect victory for both of them.

The sexy playlist continued in her ears. A man sang a sweet song asking her to kiss him under a thousand stars until David popped the earbuds out.

He ran his hand up and down her back. "You okay?"

When Ally nodded, his chest hair tickled her cheek. "Very, and you?"

"Amazing. I feel like I should smoke a cigar or something."

She laughed, loving the pride in his voice. It had been so long since she'd heard the tone in him. Although he never said it, she knew it hurt him every time she pushed away.

"So, I'm seriously wanting to call our therapist right now and tell her my penis made you orgasm."

Ally raised her head to see if he was serious and then laughed at the silly grin on his face. "It's two in the morning. I'm not so sure calling her is a good idea. How about we wait until our next session?" She winked at him. "Who knows, we might have more penis-induced orgasms to tell her about by then."

He kissed her forehead and continued with his enormous grin. "Beautiful and smart. Damn, I'm a lucky man."

She blinked to cool the emotion heating her eyes. "I think I'm the lucky one."

Dave put his hands behind his head and nodded. "You really are. Sex tapes aren't easy to make. It takes a special skill. A special kind of brain."

Ally rested her chin on his chest and played with the scattered brown curls running the length of his torso.

"So what's next?" Dave's question had her raising her brows and looking up at him. He shrugged. "I know you have a checklist. What's next on there?"

Ally bit her lip and shrugged. "Well, I wouldn't call it a checklist."

He laughed. "Call it whatever you want but what's next?"

She pressed her face into his chest and braced herself for his reaction. "I think I'm ready to go back to work."

For a good few minutes, he didn't respond. She wasn't even sure if he was breathing until his chest finally rose, lifting her head with it. "What kind of work?"

She closed her eyes. "Counseling at the practice."

When he sat up, she slid off his body and onto her back. Ally stared up at him, watching him rub the back of his neck.

"I lost you because of your job." A familiar shadow of sadness floated across his face. It was one she'd seen at random stretches the past year and a half. "I can't even try to count how many times I've seen the image in the parking lot on the day you disappeared. Your car still there. One shoe. Your purse and a puddle of your blood, but no you." His voice cracked. "I... I can't lose you again."

Ally got on her knees, straddled him, and sandwiched his face in her hands, forcing him to look at her. "You won't. Sayeed is dead. It's all over."

His eyes searched hers. "Your client kidnapped you and took you away. It happened once, it could happen again."

"David, we both need to heal. To learn to trust the world again, like my body's learning to trust you."

He wrapped his arms around her waist and pulled her to him, resting his face against her chest. "Baby, I can't lose you."

Ally held him as tight as he held her. "You won't. Promise."

Neither of them moved for an eternity. Ally waited, giving him the time he needed. Finally, David loosened his grip. "No nights," he mumbled.

She closed her eyes and kissed the top of his head. "Deal."

"No male clients."

"No deal."

His grip on her tightened. "Then no work."

"Be reasonable."

He looked at her with a sad smile. "You're humoring me, aren't you? Making me feel like I have some control in this job decision."

She shook her head. "You do have control. If you say don't go, I won't."

He rolled his eyes. "I hate it when you do that."

He returned his face to his favorite spot, at the nape of her neck. When he spoke, his lips brushed against her skin. "Sometimes at night, I wake up thinking you're still gone and all of this is a big beautiful dream. I have to look over and touch you to make sure you're really there next to me."

She ran her fingers through the back of his hair. "I'm not going anywhere again."

He nodded but didn't respond.

"Ever."

His breath warmed her skin. "You can go back to work if you promise me two things."

"What?"

Soft fingers brushed up and down her spine. "One: we use your salary to buy me a ranch somewhere nice like Seattle, where we can retire early and do something boring like grow fruit or make cheese. And two: After we live a beautifully long life, I die before you. Seeing as how I already had to go through it once, it's only fair the next time around it be your turn."

Ally rolled her eyes at the stupidity of his request. "Deal on the first and as far as the second, you're being morbid, you know that?"

He laughed. "Yeah I know."

# CHAPTER SEVEN

## THE FLIGHT

Four Months Post-David

*A*lly waded her bare feet through the icy waters of the river. Up in the distance, a tall waterfall streaked the side of a small mountain in white. The closer she got to it, the louder the sounds became, roaring like an angry lion. When she rounded the last corner, she stopped to admire the view of the falls rushing from the mountainside into the bank below. The site would've been beautiful but she knew better. The same dream had plagued her for months. Except for the sound of her heart drumming inside her ears, the world went silent.

Something red hung from the top of the cliff, sparkling in the sun. She sucked in a breath as the image came into view. The front of a car suspended over the cliff, lodged in the rocks. She couldn't see the driver, but from the way her chest tightened, squeezing the breath out of her, she knew.

"David!" She sprinted toward it. The icy currents drenched her legs and the bottom of her white dress.

"You can't save him." Sayeed's voice echoed through the trees.

She ignored him and continued to run.

The water deepened with each step. Like angry hands, the rapids slapped against her body, shoving her away. She fought against the currents punching against her stomach and legs. None of it mattered. Because she could see him. His head rested on the steering wheel while the force of the water rocked his car.

Sayeed's laughter filled the forest, grating against her ears. He grabbed her wrist.

"You're not real." Ally tugged at her arm, attempting to break free from his grasp. "You're dead."

"So is he." His laughter grew louder, piercing her heart. "And we both have you to thank." Sayeed gripped her shoulders, yanking her back as the car slipped.

She screamed for David as she fought to break free of Sayeed's grasp. His arms tightened, suffocating the life out of her. When the car slammed into the rocks below, her knees went slack.

"You should have never left me," Sayeed hissed over and over.

Soon another voice joined his. It was a woman's. "It's just a dream," she whispered. Her voice grew louder and louder until it was all Ally heard.

She opened her eyes and gasped for air as she searched for the river, for the forest, for David. Instead, the bright red upholstered seat she sat behind greeted her. She clenched her lids shut. Although drenched in sweat, she shivered from the cold.

"You're okay," Leanna said as she draped a blanket over Ally. "It was a dream."

Ally nodded and tugged the warm fabric close. Her iPod sat on her little table in front of her, and the headphones were wrapped neatly around the device. She slid the electronic into her purse and closed the table. "I need to go to the bathroom."

Ally stared at the back of the brown-haired woman in front of her as she waited her turn for the bathroom. The dreams were right. Everything was her fault. If she had never left the compound, all the lives she'd lost would still be walking the earth, and she wouldn't be thousands of miles in the sky headed to Germany. She looked over her shoulder at her ever-present shadow. Mercifully, Leanna hadn't asked for details about the dream. Nor had she mentioned all the things Ally must have said out loud in her sleep.

~

Ally twisted the Styrofoam coffee cup in her hand while she stared at the back of the headrest in front of her. A movie played on the tiny monitor secured to it, but the thoughts filling her brain had nothing to do with the romantic comedy playing on the screen.

Unease swelled within, and the closer the plane inched to Frankfurt, the more the emotion grew. Her conversation with Eddie left her with more questions than answers. The one answer she did walk away with was everything happening was because of her.

She wondered if going into hiding was the right thing to do. Her mind flashed to Farah and the mystery person being held somewhere because of her. Would Eddie be able to find them in time? What if they were killed? Like Amir. She thought about her former bodyguard. He loved Farah and would have died for her. Her stomach twisted. And he did. Unlike Amir, she was running away when Farah needed her most. The thought didn't sit well with her. How many more people would suffer because of her? If there was some way she could make a trade with the kidnappers, her life for theirs, she'd do it in a heartbeat.

Leanna leaned over and grabbed the cup of coffee out of Ally's grasp before it spilled. "What's up?"

She shrugged, and fixed her gaze at the movie playing on the little screen in front of her. Telling Eddie's partner in crime her concerns about his plan didn't seem like a good idea. "Nerves."

"Nerves I understand, but..." Leanna squinted and stared at her as if trying to read her mind. "This is different."

She picked up the snack bag from her table and pulled it open. "And guilt. I feel like I'm running away."

Leanna gave her hand a squeeze. "You're not. You're making it easier for Eddie to do what he needs to do."

Ally nodded and popped a salty pretzel in her mouth. That's what she kept telling herself. Only time would tell if they were right.

She returned her focus to the movie, and thankfully, Leanna didn't push. In fact, the woman didn't speak to her again until the plane made its descent to Frankfurt Airport. By the time they taxied down the runway, the relaxed Leanna had changed into a serious one.

Before they rose to deplane, the escort handed her a cell. "Keep this on you at all times. Under no circumstances are we allowed to get separated. Understood?"

Ally nodded, slid the device into her jean pocket, and followed the handler off the plane. Tension built with every step she took.

"There's an elevator to the right of the escalators. We're going to take it down." Leanna twined her fingers through Ally's as they exited the breezeway into the terminal.

# CHAPTER EIGHT

## ITALY

TWO YEARS AND NINE MONTHS POST-RESCUE

*A*lly slid into the stone bench and sat cross-legged as she stared at the fountain several yards ahead. In her bag was a travel guide, which explained all the statues in Trevi Fountain and their significance. At some point she'd read it, but for now, she just wanted to enjoy the site. Despite the voices of the hundred or so people around her, the soothing sounds of the water still floated to her ears. Ally admired the giant sculptures of the horses and men and stared in wonder at the perfectly sculpted muscles and features of the figures. Vacationers stood nearby taking turns as they posed for pictures in front of the magnificent stone monument.

Thick gray clouds loomed overhead, shading the crowd from the afternoon sun. On the white stone benches around her, tourists sat enjoying gelatos and other Italian treats while they chatted. Scattered throughout the piazza were freestanding shops selling souvenirs and goods to eager travelers.

Young men who appeared to be in their early twenties weaved through the crowds selling roses and other items from the big buckets they carried. The tour guide described them earlier as migrant workers from Bangladesh and other parts of Asia. Her mind floated to thoughts about the boys she'd left behind. They would be sixteen and seventeen by now.

Since her homecoming, Ally constantly scanned the world

around her for men and women with dark hair and varying shades of golden skin. If they remotely resembled the boys, Amir, Farah, or Nasif even, her heart fluttered. She'd rushed to several strangers, calling them by names that were not theirs.

She shook the thoughts away and focused on the fountain. Memories of her other life were not allowed—not now. She shifted her attention to her melting gelato and scooped another spoonful. She popped the portion into her mouth and closed her eyes, savoring the way the cold, sweet, creamy chocolate dissolved on her tongue.

"Sara Mommy?"

Ally sat up as soon as she heard the words. The voice had been male and deep. She scanned the area filled with people for the source but found no one.

"Mommy!" This time the words were spoken by a child. An adorable little girl about three-years-old. The child lay across the top of the wall of Trevi Fountain, her elbows propped on the marble, and her chin rested on her hands as her parents took pictures. The child smiled and screamed, "Cheese, Mommy!" as her mother clicked away on the cell phone.

Ally shook her head and went back to enjoying her treat. The triggers had decreased through the years, and she wasn't going to allow this one to ruin what was probably the best part of the entire trip to Italy. Her, unafraid and alone in the piazza. She sucked in a lungful of Italian air. The sense of accomplishment and pride flowing through her tasted almost as sweet as the gelato melting on her tongue.

A few minutes later, a man slid onto the bench beside her. She didn't bother looking over; she knew who it was. Instead, she licked the spoon clean.

The deal was David would let her "challenge her fears" for thirty minutes at the piazza. Ally didn't need to check her watch to know it was probably twenty-nine minutes and some seconds by the time he arrived. As much as she played it off to him as a way for her to ease her anxieties, her alone time helped him, too. The idea of her disappearing again wasn't a fear he'd been able to work through yet, and she knew better than to force him.

"*Dammi un bacio*, baby?"

She chuckled at his awful Italian but didn't look over. "I'm a married woman. I only kiss my husband."

"Aw, but this is Italia. Our kisses and our bodies are works of art." His bad accent morphed into more of a French one with each word he spoke.

Ally grinned. "You know, I've heard the same." She filled her spoon with another scoop of gelato. "Which is why I should stick with my husband's kisses and his body. If I tasted yours, I may never go back." As she placed the chocolate in her mouth, lightning struck in the distance, flashing a line of pink and red across the sky.

David slid closer, until their thighs rubbed against each other, and put an arm around her shoulder. "Did you hear that? Even Jupiter wasn't impressed with your answer."

Ally grinned. "It's all a matter of interpretation. I think he's agreeing with me."

He planted soft kisses against her cheek, warming her skin with each peck. "You know the Dimarchi family is originally from Italy."

Ally leaned her head over, letting him trail tiny kisses up her neck.

"Which means you've more than tasted the Italian Kool-Aid."

She rolled her eyes and shoved his shoulder. "Kool-Aid? Really?"

Another roll of thunder cracked overhead.

David shrugged. "Okay, bad word choice. Marsala?"

Ally shook her head and glanced at the dark clouds overhead. Considering they had no umbrella, no car, and the hotel was a twenty-minute brisk walk away, they would need to leave soon.

"Got it." He cupped her chin and turned her face toward his, planting a kiss on her lips. "Cappuccino."

She laughed into his mouth. "Perfect, but we'd better get out of here before your Italian cappuccino gets drenched."

His eyes widened and his grin grew exponentially. "I love the way you think."

Ally tipped his chin, forcing him to look up at the dark skies overhead. "I have no idea where your dirty mind went, but I'm talking about the rainstorm."

They walked out of the piazza hand in hand toward their hotel as large beads of rain fell from the heavens. Five minutes into the walk, the drops transformed into a downpour, drenching them both. David pulled them under the narrow awning of a nearby hotel. Ally's back pressed against the wall. While the roof sheltered her, his back half was still getting drenched. She pressed herself against the surface and tugged him in close. "Squeeze in, there's room."

He kept a hand on the wall on either side of her head and looked down at her. "You're not wearing a bra."

Her cheeks heated. The weather in Rome the past few days had been hot. Since most of the Roman women had dressed sans bra, she decided to do the same and even put on the thickest, darkest colored tee she had just to be safe. The one thing she hadn't anticipated? A rainstorm. Now, as she tugged on the wet fabric of her navy shirt, she regretted her decision.

"This is a great time for us to work on your breast desensitization."

She laughed and put her hands around his neck. "I don't need breast desensitization anymore."

"Well I do, and seeing as how we're stuck here with nothing else to do, why not?"

If her lack of undergarments was visible to him, it would be visible to everyone else who walked by. Ally leaned her head to the side and looked past him. "Or we can look for cabs."

"I can't believe in all these years, I've never seen you in a wet shirt."

Considering they were standing next to a hotel, hopeful taxi drivers should have been parked along the front doors ready for tourists. But of course, when she needed it, there wasn't a single one to be found.

She bit her lip and considered her options. "Maybe we should go inside and ask for them to call us one?"

"Have I ever told you of the first erotic dream I ever had about you?"

She rolled her eyes and slapped his neck. "Did you hear what I said?"

"Not one word." He shook his head and leaned in until his mouth brushed against her ear when he spoke. "You were standing shoulder deep in a pond. And when you started walking out of the water, all you had on was a white T-shirt and nothing else. Your nipples poked out. They looked like they do now."

Ally closed her eyes, savoring the heat of his breath and the way his words warmed all parts of her. "David Spencer Dimarchi, you need to focus."

"Trust me, I am."

A year ago, if he had her backed up against the wall, talking about her breasts, it would have ended with her shoving him and running. And although there were still a lot of things to work on, many of the triggers had diminished, and it was because of him. Even now, as his hands found their way to her rear and his lips pressed against her neck, there was no doubt in her mind he was reading her cues. If her fingers weren't tugging at his hair, and if she wasn't arching her chest into his, or if she said no, he would step back and never question it. That was one of the million things she loved about him.

Ally pressed her back against the wall and crossed her arms, pretending to glare at him. "Are you done? Can we go inside now?"

A slow smile stretched across his face. "First of all, crossing your arms lifts them higher for me to admire." He pointed down at his tented shorts. "And second, we now have another problem."

Ally covered her nipples with her hands, eliciting a groan out of her husband.

"You're reenacting a whole other erotic dream of mine."

"I'm trying to warm them." She studied the unrelenting storm behind him. They'd be stuck in the same spot for a while if they didn't go in and ask for a cab. But first, some things needed to be deflated. "Do you remember the old lady with the hair sticking out of her nipple? Describe the hair to me."

An hour later, Ally lay naked, chest down, on an equally naked David in their hotel bed. Her cheek pressed against the curls of his chest as he ran his fingers up and down her spine. Neither spoke. They savored the silence and their connection. Life was better than she'd ever thought it could be again. She used to believe she didn't deserve to be happy—not after the life she'd lived. Ally let out a sigh.

"I'll take that as a sigh of approval."

She grinned. "I could be thinking about the sexy young cab driver who brought us home."

"Whatever. I guarantee you the driver couldn't have made you scream the way I did. He's not skilled in the Ally ways."

She sucked in a lungful of his cologne, musky with hints of cedar. "You're right. He'll never be my Italian Kool-Aid."

"Exactly."

Ally smiled and let out another sigh.

"So what's next on the list, oh sexy one?" he asked softly.

She pulled herself up and flashed him a questioning look. David's focus went straight to her breasts, which currently brushed against his chest.

"Really?"

"What?" He pulled his gaze away and looked into her eyes with a guilty smile. "They're beautiful."

"What list?"

He shrugged. "The one we never talk about."

Her cheeks warmed. "I don't have a list," she lied.

He rolled his eyes and rested his head back on the pillow. "Of course not. So, let's go over this nonexistent list. Going jogging in the park alone every morning while your husband paces the living room." David stuck his finger in the air and made a check mark. "Driving around town by yourself." Again, his finger swooshed in the air. "Mind-blowing sex. Triple check." This time he air-checked multiple times.

She slid off him, planted her feet on the cold marble, and began picking up their wet discards from off the floor as he went through the list.

"Going back to work. Check. Going on vacation and fulfilling your husband's wet T-shirt erotic fantasy. A big, beautiful check."

Ally paused mid-cleanup and looked over at him. Aside from his hand, the rest of him hadn't moved. "Big beautiful, huh?"

"The stuff that good porn is made of – beautiful."

She pitched his wet shirt at his face and headed to the bathroom.

The bed creaked and soon his feet thumped along the floor as he approached. David leaned against the bathroom counter, his wet shirt in hand. "Well, I'm assuming because I've never watched any"—he flashed a guilty grin—"so I really wouldn't know the difference between good and bad porn."

She shook her head and started hanging wet fabric over the

shower pole to dry. He knew her well; she did have goals, and accomplishing one led to the next bigger one. She smiled at all the things he listed. Those were huge accomplishments, and she'd done them all. Now it was time for her biggest one yet.

He hung his shirt on the shower pole beside hers.

She side-eyed him and cleared her throat. "So you know the checklist?"

"You mean the non-existent one?" David grabbed his boxers from her arm and worked on hanging them.

She leaned against the wall and chewed on her lip. "Yeah, that one."

"I'm listening."

Ally sucked in a breath. "I want us to have a baby."

David didn't answer at first. He sat on the edge of the shower and looked up at her. "You want *us* to have a baby?"

She nodded as he clasped and unclasped his hands.

"It wasn't that long ago when everything scared you. Now we're finally in a good place. One we both like. A baby would screw it all up."

Ally sat beside him and grabbed his hand, giving it a squeeze. "He or she might also make it better. Make our union even stronger."

He stared at the mirror in front of them, locking eyes with her through the reflection. "How much more united can we get? And more importantly, why do you really want a baby?"

She shifted in her seat. "The same reason all women want a baby, and you asked what was on my list." She didn't say the rest because she knew he wouldn't like it. A part of her didn't think she was destined for happiness and having a baby would finally put the fear to rest. And the other part, she hoped it would fill the void she'd had since losing Farah, Nassif, Umber, and the boys.

"A baby sounds great on paper, it really does. But the sleepless nights, the 'it's your turn to clean the shit in their ass' arguments. It's a whole new set of problems we'll have to survive."

"After everything we've gone through, there's nothing we can't handle. You know that." She gave his hand a squeeze. "And imagine if we had a little boy like you."

He wrapped his arm around her waist and pulled her close, contemplating the question. "A mini me?"

In the mirror, she could have sworn she saw his lips twitch. She smiled. She knew him well. "Yeah, a boy like you, brown hair, green eyes, running around drooling at women with wet T-shirts. Or a mini me for that matter?"

He rolled his eyes and stared at the ceiling. "She'd never leave the house. Ever."

# CHAPTER NINE

## GERMANY

FOUR MONTHS POST-DAVID

Sweat dampened the back of Ally's neck as her hands shook. While Leanna scanned the space, she found herself doing the same. On either side of them were gates filled with travelers. Some sat in chairs, others stood in line waiting to board their flights, and still others, like them, exited their gates. A woman's voice on the intercom announced flights in English and then proceeded to repeat the announcement in German.

Leanna led them through the terminals to the main hall where shops and restaurants lined the walls. They weaved their way through clumps of distracted travelers and rolling suitcases.

A few yards before the escalators was a coffee shop. The line of people waiting for their turn to order stretched out of the tiny store. Positioned beside the shop was one of the airport's many bathrooms, except this one had a bright yellow "OUT OF ORDER" barrier written in multiple languages, blocking its entrance. A cleaning cart sat next to the sign. A janitor, a man with brown hair, in teal blue scrub pants, a white long-sleeved polo, and a bright orange vest, mopped the floor in front of the space.

Before Ally was done surveying the area, another janitor, blonde and dressed like the first, ran into Leanna and the carry-on she rolled. She released Ally's hand and managed to catch him before he fell to the ground. While her escort helped him to his feet, the sound of metal colliding with metal resonated through the halls. Ally turned in time to see a cleaning cart speeding down the path toward them. It slammed into Leanna, shoving her face first to the floor and toppling over her. A bucket connected to the contraption spilled dirty brown water. The murky liquid poured out of the wheeled vehicle, covering Leanna and the ground in the process. Canisters of cleaning solutions and other supplies rolled across the walkway. Several of the metal canisters slammed into Leanna's back and head before rolling across the floor.

The blond janitor lunged for the cart, falling on top of it and the woman lying beneath.

"*Es tut mir Leid*," he yelled as he climbed to his feet.

When Ally stepped forward to help, an arm wrapped around her waist and pulled her away. Her back pressed against someone's body. Instinct took over. She tugged at the limb restraining her and stomped her heel into the jean-clad ankle of the person.

His grip tightened, and he shoved a cell phone in her face. As soon as the image on the screen came into view, she froze. The world around her went silent. Only the sound of her heart thumping wildly was audible as she stared at Farah.

She sat on a bed. Her red-rimmed eyes watched the camera, and in her arms, she held a baby. "Fight me and the widow and her child die," a man's deep voice hissed from behind her.

The words were spoken quietly but screamed in her head. They'd known she was on the flight and were waiting for her. Everything had been planned, down to the way he held her. Restrained in what looked like a lover's embrace, no one would think twice as they passed her and the man. Ally forced herself to look away from the phone and watched the scene with Leanna play out in front of her.

Several good Samaritans surrounded Leanna, blocking her from Ally's view. From the way they leaned forward, it was clear the poor woman was still on the ground. *Why isn't she getting up?* Ally stepped forward, only to be pulled back against his hips.

"She's not the one you need to worry about. So listen." He held her close and pressed his cheek against hers. "We are going to keep walking straight to the elevator on the right. If you don't, I will have the widow and her child killed."

Her mind raced as she considered her options. "I'm not

leaving her like this," she whispered. The crowd around Leanna grew. Someone called for a doctor, and a moment later, several bystanders pulled out their phones and made calls.

"She is fine. No one will harm her in front of all those people. Security has already been notified. They will cart her to the airport clinic to assess her for injuries."

When she looked over at him, all ability to breathe, much less speak, ceased. Cold, dark eyes stared back. Eyes she hadn't seen since she was kidnapped years ago. The sight of him sent tremors rocking through her.

He grinned and tightened his grip. "Surprise."

She turned back to the crowd, trying to collect her thoughts. Like a silent movie, memories of her kidnapping five years ago flooded her consciousness. Under the cover of darkness, he and another man had dragged her away from her office. A tremor rocked through her as she remembered the other kidnapper who helped him before. Her chest ached as if the man's hand still cupped her breast. It had outraged Sayeed enough to shoot the man dead on the spot—another image which made her shudder. What was left of his partner's bloodied body spilled all over the floor in front of her. And finally, an image of him, a look of pure hatred on his face while he cleaned the dead man's remains.

Now, standing behind her, he hid his emotions under a smile. He pressed his mouth to her ear. "I wondered if you'd remember me," he said. "Obviously I'm unforgettable."

"You've tormented my dreams since that day." She stayed rooted to the spot, trying to stay focused. "After everything you've done? I'm not going anywhere with you." Ally tipped her chin in Leanna's direction. "Not until I see for myself she is safe."

Fingers dug into her waist, warning her of repercussions by challenging him. "I see Sayeed didn't teach you manners. So let me." He fiddled with the phone still in front of her and handed her ear buds. "Put this on."

"No," she hissed.

He slammed the bud into her ear. Before she could push it out, a woman's soft humming filled her head. Ally's veins turned to ice at the familiar tune. She watched the phone's screen. The walls were pale yellow and the tiled floor, gray. The room had one piece of furniture, a metal-framed bed, and on top of it sat Farah. She sang to the child in her arms.

The mother's lullaby sliced into her chest, leaving Ally breathless. When she was back in the compound, Farah would wake up every night, face wet with tears and sobbing. Each time, Ally sat by her side and sang the same song until she fell back asleep.

She sucked in some much needed air as the screen moved close to the swaddled bundle in Farah's arms. Her legs weakened when the face of the child came into view. Eyes closed, the baby's thick lashes pressed against its cheeks as it slept, oblivious to its mother's pain. A tear slipped down Farah's cheek as she sang, and seeing it made one fall from Ally's eye as well. Farah's thick braid hung like a noose down her side, and she wore a pale blue top with matching pants. She seemed oblivious to the camera and the man taping her as she sang to her baby.

She touched the screen just as it went black. Ally looked up at the growing crowd in front of her and the giant blue golf cart waving a Red Cross flag, which had pulled up.

"Hello, Sara," a man's English voice spoke inside her head through the ear bud. "Beautiful song, isn't it? You don't know who I am, but I am confident we will meet soon."

A woman and two men in lab coats jumped out of the vehicle and ran into the crowd.

"As you see, the widow and her baby are unharmed. What happens to them is entirely up to you. I have sent an old friend to greet you at the airport. Be sure to do as he says, for everyone's sake. This poor woman is already a widow. I am not sure she would be able to survive losing her baby as well."

"Time's up. What is your decision?" the kidnapper asked.

She closed her eyes and said a silent prayer Leanna would be okay. "I'll come."

# CHAPTER TEN

## IT'S SHOW TIME

*D*ave stepped out of the elevator into the hospital parking garage and headed to the right toward his car. It was well after three thirty in the morning, and he'd been in the same scrubs for more than half the day. He didn't have much to complain about. It was a once a month, twelve-hour shift and the rest of the time he worked a standard forty-hour week. Aside from removing an appendix and patching up some non-fatal gunshot victims, his night hadn't been too bad. He stretched his neck to the side until it popped, and then did it again on the other side. Regardless, being clean and climbing into bed beside his wife were top priority on his to do list.

He slid into his red BMW and looked at the text Ally had sent before she went to sleep.

**Have your gun ready. It's show time**.

He chuckled. In other words: Her ovulation window had slid wide open, and she needed his sperm. His friends had warned him how the whole erection-on-demand part of baby making would take all the pleasure out of sex. Dave wasn't so sure he believed them. After all, his wife waited at home for him—naked. The image put a smile on his face.

The sexual festivities were the fun part of the process. Especially now that their roles had reversed, and she followed *him* around begging him to strip naked and fill her up. He sat a little taller. Yeah, he really, really enjoyed that part. It was the screaming, red-faced, eighteen-plus year investment result that sounded miserable. But she swore as soon as he held their baby and saw it smile at him, he'd be singing another tune. Of course he had his doubts, but maybe a baby would make the faraway look she got so often finally go away. It was the one part of her he couldn't touch.

The same look she'd get if he told her about the email on his computer from last week. His fingers gripped the wheel. He'd planned to tell her the same evening it showed up, but then she did something that had left him speechless. She laughed. It was a different kind of laugh than he'd heard from her in a long time. The kind that made his eyes burn with emotion and left him hungry for more. The kind that said she'd finally climbed out of the dark hole she'd been stuck in for way too long. The email would have only tossed her right back in; at least it's what he kept telling himself whenever his conscience kicked him in the balls. Balls which had much more important things to do.

Droplets of rain beaded against the windshield when he pulled out of the parking garage. He turned on the wipers then his radio and headed for home. Dave scanned the mostly deserted road. Philadelphia streets weren't so bad at three forty in the morning. The deep voice of the sports announcer filled his cabin with statistics about the Eagles and their upcoming season, but it was the date the man mentioned that caught Dave's attention. His mouth dropped. How could he have forgotten? He got Ally back three years ago to the day. People died in the process, including the asshole who'd dragged her into hell in the first place. His grip on the steering wheel tightened. She'd almost died—twice. Sometimes he found himself wondering what would have happened if the old man, Nasif, hadn't tracked him down and told him where she was.

He shook the thought from his head. None of it mattered because she was safe and home, waiting to make a baby with him. The corners of his mouth quirked up. Ally was one of the strongest people he knew. Hell, it wasn't too long ago that the prospect of them having sex seemed impossible. Speaking of which, he should have known better than to think they'd need all eight hours of the play list he made. After a couple of times of using it, Ally put it aside and said she wanted to be able to orgasm with him—without the music. His chest puffed up. And she had on multiple occasions. But he wanted her to listen to it, especially the last half hour. He'd put in some serious time and swallowed his pride creating that particular set. Maybe he'd turn it on when he got home during their baby making.

Dave scanned the roads around him and glanced in his rearview mirror. There wasn't a cop in sight, and aside from the distant headlights of the only other car on the road behind him, and the tiny speck of a person on the sidewalk miles ahead, the place was empty. He pressed his foot down on the gas. The engine revved, making his grin stretch.

As he pushed his car to move faster, the figure he'd seen in the distance stepped off the sidewalk and into the path of his vehicle, staring directly at him. Dave slammed on his brakes. The pedal shook under his foot as the anti-lock system activated. His lungs turned into solid masses of ice, and his hands clenched the steering wheel as he willed the man to get out of the way. It was then he got a better view of the person. Eyes the size of hockey pucks stared back through the front window. Familiar eyes he hadn't seen in three years. After an eternity, the car came to a full stop, its bumper barely pressing against the man's legs.

Mouth wide open, he stayed frozen in his seat, his fingers remained glued to the wheel as the realization of what almost happened sunk in. The man pointed at something behind Dave and then ran away. Dave looked over his shoulder in time to see the white SUV before it slammed into him.

～

Ally sat straight up in her bed, drenched in tears and sweat. Terror lay heavy on her chest, making it impossible to breathe. Her body shook. She tucked her head between her knees and worked on taking slow, deep breaths until the panic attack subsided.

Once her lungs calmed to normal, she climbed out of bed and checked the clock. It was close to four in the morning. She hadn't had a panic attack in months, but she should have been prepared for this one. After all, three years ago today she had finally escaped her hell.

Although the cause of the panic attack had been established, she couldn't shake the overwhelming fear still squeezing her lungs. She checked her cell and saw Dave's text.

*He'll be home soon. We'll make a baby and then everything will be better.* The thought eased her. She went to the bathroom.

"Sayeed is dead. He can't hurt me anymore," she whispered

over and over as she splashed icy water against her skin.

An hour later, Ally had thrown on some clothes and paced the living room with her cell in her hand. She'd called David a couple times and he hadn't answered. A nagging sense of doom made her hands unsteady, and no amount of self-talk seemed to help. Until he came home safe, she wouldn't feel right. She needed him home. Soon.

By six, Ally gave in to her fear and left David's boss, Jerry, a message. Fifteen minutes later, she called her baby sister, who lived four stories above her. As soon as a sleepy Rey answered the phone, Ally's doorbell rang. She let out a breath of relief and ran to answer it. Instead of the green-eyed, brown-haired man she hoped to find, her gaze fixed on Jerry and the police.

Her world spun as soon as she saw the look on Jerry's face. At first it turned slow, but the more she stared at his bloodshot eyes and the lines creasing his brow, it spun faster. She shook her head and stepped back, slamming the door in their faces. She didn't want to hear anything he had to say. This was just a dream. A really bad dream.

# CHAPTER ELEVEN

## THE KIDNAPPER

FOUR MONTHS POST-DAVID

ith his arm wrapped around her waist, he guided her through the hall. Sweat beaded her hairline and her body shook, making her trip over her shoes as she walked. The man's grip on her tightened as he steadied her. The voices of travelers around her grew louder. Somewhere out there were people searching for her and Leanna. She tried to catch their gazes, searching for Eddie or another friendly face in the crowd but found none.

She thought of Farah and the baby. "How do I know they are even alive?"

His nails bit into her hip. "Keep talking and they won't be," he hissed.

The elevator loomed ahead, and with every step they took toward it, the faster her pulse raced. Its doors slid open, and a family of four armed with suitcases entered the empty cabin. She looked over her shoulder, searching for Leanna. As if on cue, the phone in her pants buzzed, reminding her of its existence.

With the realization of the phone came another one. They could track her and would know exactly where she went. She thought of Farah and the baby. This could be just the lead Eddie needed to find them. Ally contained her relief. She just needed to bide her time. When they reached the now closed metal doors of the lift, he pressed the down arrow with his free hand while keeping his other glued to her hip. His fingers began to move lower, tugging at one of the belt loops of her jeans. Ally stepped away from him only to be pulled back in. The kidnapper pressed her side to his and cupped her butt and the phone hidden in her back pocket.

The hard edge of the device dug into her under his rough touch. Goosebumps pebbled her skin when his breath hit her cheek from his laugh. Just as the doors opened, he shoved his fingers into the pocket of her jeans and pulled out the phone. In stunned silence, she watched him toss it into the trashcan beside the elevator right before pulling her inside.

As soon as the heavy metal doors slid shut, he released and shoved her aside.

"Where is Farah?" she whispered.

"Shut up and give me your fucking purse," he yanked it from her shoulder and rummaged through it. "When the doors open, we will turn left and walk to the storage room at the far end of the hall. I'll check you for additional items once we get to the room."

"How do I know they're even alive?"

He dropped the satchel to the ground and shrugged. "The same way you know if they're not. You don't." A second later, the doors opened and his arm was once again around her.

They walked down an empty service hallway. Ally wiped her sweaty palms on her jeans and scanned the space. The white door he mentioned loomed a few feet down the empty corridor. People were willing to hurt the ones she loved to get to her, but entering the room did not guarantee anyone's safety. More than likely, it would lead to her death. And without a way to track her, no one would be able to find her. For a brief moment, she contemplated the prospect of running.

He gave her arm a painful squeeze. "Go ahead and run. I've wanted you dead for years. Give me an excuse."

Cold brown eyes glared down at her, promising to make good on his threat. A gift she'd gladly give if it meant all the people she loved would survive. As soon as he unlocked the door, he shoved her inside and shut it behind him. Rolling carts, like the one that hit Leanna, lined the side of the wall. Tall shelves stocked with giant bottles of cleaning supplies filled the rest of the room. Before she took another step, he grabbed the back of her neck and slammed her face first into the wall.

"I can't believe you've been alive all these years. I would have killed you a long time ago if I'd known," he hissed in her ear.

The cool wall did nothing to ease the fiery pain coursing through her cheek and back. Ally planted her palms on the surface as the implications of his words sunk in. They had never been safe. "Now you can, so let them go."

"Not yet." He laughed against her ear. "But I will."

She dug her fingers into the cement wall for support. "Did you kill my husband?"

He didn't answer her question. Pain shot through the back of her head. The intensity of it blinded her, making her fall to her knees. A second bolt erupted at the same spot, this time turning her world black.

~

The back of her neck pulsed with currents of pain when the vehicle ran over a bump. Ally's eyes shot open. Curled up in the back row of a van or SUV, she stared at the gray leather of the seat in front of her. The spot beside her head rustled when someone shifted.

"The queen has risen," the kidnapper said in an amused voice.

Fear gripped her throat. When she shifted, she noticed her legs and arms were not restrained. She kept a hand near the tender spot on her head and pulled herself up. A man sat two rows ahead in the driver's seat, guiding the vehicle down the highway. She turned to face the one situated beside her. "Where are we going?"

He shrugged and pulled out his phone. "Somewhere."

Ally's gaze fixed on the van's sliding doors a few feet from her.

"Before you get any ideas, they're locked, and I brought a friend." He patted the gun in his lap.

Memories of Farah and the video played in her head, and with them came the one question she still had no answer to. "What do you want?"

"For you to shut up." He dialed a number. A moment later, a man's muffled greeting could be heard on the other end. "She's awake." When his eyes locked with Ally's, he slid away from her and covered the receiver with his hand. "She's fine but talks too much." The kidnapper nodded at whatever the man said. "Will do. Just do your part and I'll do mine." A second later, he turned the phone off. "He said to tell you if you don't shut up I get to pick which of your friend's body parts he will cut off first." He winked. "I'm thinking a nipple. She only needs one to feed her baby anyway."

~

The next few hours passed in silence. She spent most of it staring out the tinted window, watching the world fly by. A world she might never see again. Her family back in Philadelphia filtered into her thoughts. They'd endured so much because of her. Thoughts of all they'd done for her the past few months, the sacrifices they'd made to help her heal, sent wave after wave of regret flowing through her. After everything they'd gone through, losing her a second time would crush them. The voices in her head continued. One whispered, what if all she did was for nothing? Instead of saving the ones she loved, what if they ended up dead? She ignored the voice and imagined a better story. A tale in which Eddie followed close behind. Waiting in the shadows for them to lead him to Farah and the baby.

The kidnapper shifted in his seat. His head rested against the windowpane, and his eyes remained closed. The gun still in his lap with most of its grip and the trigger covered under his hand. His fingers flexed and knuckles cracked. His way of letting her know he noticed and would pounce if she gave him a reason. There was no doubt in her mind he would kill her and enjoy the process.

The car pulled into a tiny airport. Other than the handful of large, gray plane hangars looming along the edge of the runway, the area appeared deserted. The perfect place to lock someone away. She scanned them, searching for signs of the young mother and child.

They parked in front of a small white jet on the runway. A thin metal staircase led up to the cabin of the plane. The man stabbed the gun into her side, making her jump. "You have a couple of options. Run and we can play a fun game of Hide and Seek. Who knows?" He looked her over. "You might do such a good job of hiding, you'll get out of here. If so, remember the widow and baby will pay. Or go up the ladder into the jet."

A thin bead of sweat formed along her hairline and dripped down the back of her neck. Her damp hands curled into the leather of the seat.

"Understood?"

She nodded.

The driver jogged around to Ally's side and slid open the van's door. The man beside her shoved the metal barrel against her a second time. This time it rammed into her shoulder blade, leaving her breathless and jerking her forward. "Now go."

Ally climbed out on unsteady feet and scanned the area. A breeze slapped against her skin. The tender area on her scalp pulsed each time she turned her neck. She kept a hand on the spot and surveyed her surroundings. The small runway appeared deserted except for the private jet parked in front of her and the hangars in the distance. She wiped her sweaty palms on her pants and moved toward the jet.

He grabbed her arm and gave it a painful squeeze. "Smart choice." The man propelled her to the steps. "Let's go."

Leather and wood paneling lined the interior of the jet. Individual armchairs and tables were scattered along the spacious cabin. Beside each seat were individual television screens. He grinned as Ally took it all in. "Pretty fancy, isn't it? And it's all for you." He waved his gun along the aisles. "Pick a seat."

Her feet stayed rooted to the spot, unable to move until the kidnapper gave her a shove. She slid into the one closest to the exit watching him text with one hand and carry the gun in the other. "Buckle up, sweetheart. You know the rules."

His cell dinged. After he read the message, he grabbed the television and swiveled it to face her. "It seems we have some in-flight entertainment."

Farah and her baby flashed on the screen. She wore a simple, pale blue tunic with matching pants. She cradled the diapered child against her chest and looked at the camera. It wasn't the baby or the room that captured Ally's attention. It was the mother's eyes, and the way she trembled as if pleading for help. Ally touched the screen, aching to ease Farah's pain. All those nights they spent together in the compound. The same look she'd seen back then in the face of a sixteen-year-old girl was still alive five years later on the woman she'd become. Back then, it had been a younger Farah, huddled in a ball on the floor, rocking as her body shook.

The kidnapper dropped a plastic bag of white powder and a bottle of water on the table in front of her. "Open your mouth so I can give you your in-flight snack."

The sight of it sent a chill through her. Ally sealed her lips and shook her head.

He grinned and picked up the bag, waving it. "Don't worry, we didn't go through all this trouble to kill you...yet. Since you're going solo on this flight, we need you to take a little nap so you're not wandering around trying to kill the pilot."

She eyed the powder. "I don't need it. I won't be going anywhere or killing anyone."

The corner of his mouth twitched. The sight of it made her stomach twist. He shrugged and made a call. "Your passenger is refusing her snack." He winked at Ally and nodded as he listened to the person on the other line. A second later, he pointed at the television. "He said to keep watching."

Ally's lungs transformed into cement blocks when the black screen turned yellow. Farah lay asleep with a protective arm wrapped around the sleeping infant beside her. A shadow fell across the bed. Unable to breathe much less look away, Ally's heart pounded, trying to leap out of her body. She leaned forward, watching a man in a ski mask approach the peaceful pair.

The sleeping mother's eyes popped open, and she fixed her gaze on the intruder. Terror flashed across Farah's face. She pulled the baby to her chest and rose.

"No," Ally whispered. A trickle of sweat slid down her neck. She squeezed the armrests, fixated on the screen. There was no audio, but from the way the mother shook her head and mouthed her words, she was pleading with the man.

Farah clutched her baby and slid back to the farthest corner of the bed; her child's arms and legs waved as she pressed its tiny body against hers. He grasped the baby's legs. Mother and monster played a game of tug of war for the child as Farah continued to cry and plead with him.

A nauseating burn built deep inside Ally's stomach. "Make him stop," she pleaded. "Please."

The kidnapper positioned the phone so the person on the other end could hear them. "Open your mouth and I will," the man on the other end responded.

With a final yank, the stranger stole the baby away. Ally cried out at the sight of Farah falling headfirst to the floor. The mother lifted herself up and ran in the direction of the man and her baby, everyone disappearing from the screen.

Emotion streaked Ally's cheeks. She parted her lips while her eyes remained glued to the empty bed and crumpled sheet on the floor. The plastic opening of the bag brushed against her lips and soon the burn of the bitter powder exploded on her tongue. He cupped her chin and tipped her head back, pouring water into her mouth. Ally gagged as the potent mixture continued its burn down her throat.

"Swallow," he ordered.

She forced the mixture down her throat and returned her focus to the screen, hungry to see mother and child reunited.

"Good job." He patted her head.

Farah sat on the bed, alone. The young mother hugged her knees to her chest and rocked through her sobs.

Through the receiver, the distant sounds of a baby's cries pierced Ally's ears. "I did what you said," she yelled for the person to hear. "Give her the child."

The man beside her pointed at the screen and mouthed the word "Watch."

Farah looked up, a mixture of joy and relief washed across her face. She ran off the screen. Ally swallowed the bitter after-taste of the drug and waited. When the mother reappeared, her baby lay in her arms.

A tear crept from Ally's eye. Farah smothered the tiny face with kisses. "Is it a boy or a girl?"

The ripping of tape filled the cabin. "Why the fuck would I care?" He growled as he restrained her hands to the armrest. "Make yourself comfortable. Once the powder kicks in, you'll fall fast asleep." He grinned. "And don't worry, we'll be together again soon."

# CHAPTER TWELVE

## GOOD-BYE

*A*lly sat beside the hospital bed, her fingers twined through David's. She ached to crawl onto the mattress, lay beside him, and rest her cheek on his chest. Habits that were once every-day occurrences were now dreams, which would never again come true. She stayed rooted in her seat, staring at his face, memorizing every feature. The little brown mole on the edge of his right earlobe. The faint hint of lines had formed in the past few years around the corners of his lips. How his thick, brown lashes appeared even darker against the pale hue of his cheek. She ached to see his eyes. In the right light, specks of gold sparkled in those green orbs.

The people who showed up at her door to tell her the news? She hadn't let them in; her sister and brother-in-law had done the honors. Jerry and the officers sat down with them. Reya kept her arms wrapped tight around Ally while the men explained the fatal accident and how, for reasons they didn't understand, David stopped his car in the middle of the road.

"Basilar skull fracture," Jerry explained. "The force of the collision made the fibers inside his brain stem snap. His death was instantaneous. It's doubtful he felt any pain."

His words were meant to ease her agony but they did nothing. Too numb to speak, Ally clung to her sister as she silently screamed to herself to wake up from the horrendous dream she was having. Thankfully, Reya and Parker did all the talking. They asked the questions. They drove her to the hospital, made the calls. All she needed to do was say good-bye.

She pulled his still warm palm to her mouth, silently begging him to look at her. To stretch those beautiful lips into the smile he saved for her and her alone. To feel his arms wrap around her and pull her close—just one more time. For him to laugh his deep rumble of a laugh. The kind that reverberated through her when her cheek lay on top of his chest. In his arms, she was safe from all the evils in the world. Not a soul could touch her. She was loved.

The heavy crater in her chest where her heart once beat for him pulsed with an overwhelming pain. It choked the breath out of her. She gritted her teeth and wiped her wet cheek against the back of his hand. For the very last time, he'd dry her tears.

It didn't make sense. Why did he stop in the middle of the road? Ally shook the thoughts from her head. Right now, she needed to focus on him. All that mattered was she could still touch him for a little while longer. She kissed against his knuckles and swallowed down the sob threatening to consume her. She had time to figure out the truth, a lifetime to fall apart, and would do both. Just not now, not when this moment with him would be her last.

With his hand still pressed against her lips, she filled her lungs with a deep, calming breath saturated with the scent of his cologne. He looked peaceful, like he was dreaming about something beautiful. Maybe about the two of them together, somewhere far away from the world.

She willed it all to be a dream. An ugly dream. But any time the question of whether he was really dead entered her mind, her gaze wandered to the bandage wrapped tight around his forehead, the beeping of the machines, and the rhythmic flow from the ventilator keeping him alive until the transplant doctors arrived to take pieces of him away.

Ally leaned over and pressed her lips to the corner of his mouth as she'd done a thousand times in the past couple of hours. There were other things she'd done in the past few hours, too. She'd begged for her own death, silently screaming for an end she knew wouldn't come. For some reason, the universe chose to ignore those requests. Life had become some sort of perverse joke, slowly and painfully taking away the ones she loved, and by doing so, stealing parts of her soul. But this time, it took more than a part. It took everything. Her rock. Her hero.

Why him? Why not her? Why was it never her?

A hand gripped her shoulder, giving it a squeeze. Through the fog of her pain, she felt her mother-in-law's lips against her cheek. His parents had finally arrived to say good-bye. Somewhere in the room, the grief of the others had become white noise. Ally ignored them all. Nothing and no one was more important than being with him. Which was for the best. She had nothing to offer them. Her everything was lying before her—never to return.

# CHAPTER THIRTEEN

## THE HOTEL

FOUR MONTHS POST-DAVID

Somewhere in the distance, a faint echo broke through her silent slumber. A voice, a man's, heavy with an English accent. He repeated the same words over and over. "Sara *Bhaabi*, wake up." Instead of doing as commanded, she turned her face and fell back into the darkness.

"How much did you fucking give her?" He penetrated her silence again. This time he sounded angry. "Directions were on the bag. If she doesn't fucking wake up..."

Ally retreated to her peaceful abyss, pushing it all out of her head.

Bright lights flowed through the thin membrane of her lids, invading the darkness. She rested her arm over her face, attempting to block their entrance. The constant shrieking of car and truck horns was harder to ignore. When she rolled onto her side, satin sheets caressed her skin. She stretched her legs and smiled at how relaxed her muscles felt. She opened her eyes, and stared ahead at the enormous window spanning most of the wall. Gold drapes covered the view, and a red upholstered couch sat in front of the fabric.

Ally pressed her cheek into the soft pillow, waiting for David to wrap his arm around her and pull her close, spooning her back to his front. Somewhere in the distance, a horn louder than the rest blared as if telling her she was wrong for wanting him. She paused mid-stretch when the tender area on the back of her head shot ripples of pain through her. Her muscles tightened as the cause of the wound floated into her consciousness. Germany and the kidnapper who'd knocked her out cold. Soon other memories flooded her: The sleeping powder he made her swallow. Farah and her baby. And then David. She stayed rigid, her heart racing, staring at the golden drapes of a foreign land in front of her.

Someone spared no expense to bring her here. Someone male with a deep English accent. The mattress shifted beside her. Ally sat up and looked around the room, not ready to face the figure seated next to her. A dark wood table sat against the wall and next to it a mini refrigerator and dresser. Rich cherry wood paneled the walls of the room. She grabbed handfuls of the satin sheets and rested her gaze on the man seated in the red armchair beside her bed. His long legs stretched out on her bed. The lightest brown eyes she'd ever seen stared back at her in amusement. Brown curls crowned his head and fell loose below his ears. His elbows were planted on the armrests of the chair and his chin rested on the tips of his long, steepled fingers. When their eyes locked, he grinned.

"I hope you slept well."

The sound of him sent shivers up the length of her spine. She tugged at the blanket, not for warmth but to hide the way she shook. In doing so, Ally noticed the unfamiliar, over-sized black tee covering her body and realized she wore nothing beneath it. "Where are my clothes?"

The shadow of a faint beard darkened around the corners of his mouth when his grin widened. "You got sick in flight." He tipped his head at the dresser beside him. "They are here. Cleaned and pressed."

Her grasp on the blanket tightened while her mind screamed to run, but she stayed still. He was well over six feet tall and, from the way his muscles flexed under his snug shirt, much stronger than her. The stranger also had something she wanted: Farah and the baby.

Ally cleared her throat and steadied her voice. "Who changed my clothes?"

He raised his brows while the corner of his mouth twitched as if fighting the urge to laugh. "Me."

She grabbed a pillow and wrapped it around her, eliciting an eye roll from the man who watched her every move. "Trust me, there was nothing attractive about peeling vomit-soaked clothing from your skin." He scrunched his nose. "Let's not even mention the smell. I highly recommend a shower, by the way."

Ally hung her feet over the bed and, with a hand on the mattress for support, carefully stood. Relief flooded her as soon as she took a step. The room did not spin, and her legs easily carried her weight. She rolled her shoulders back, facing her kidnapper. "I'm here."

Thick brows rose. "Yes, you are."

"Let Farah and the baby go."

His smile broadened. "Are you saying you will not bathe until I do? Because it might be the most convincing argument I've heard yet."

She pulled at the hem of her shirt. "You wanted me and now you have me. You have no use for them anymore."

"Not entirely true." He tapped his fingers against his chin. "Do you know what the going rate is for an attractive twenty-one-year-old widow? Let's not even mention the price tag for an adorable, newborn baby." He leaned back in the chair and crossed his arms behind his head. "I'm Shariff, by the way."

Her pulse spiked every second she faced him. Ally walked past him to her stack of clothes and gripped the dresser for support. She needed to stay calm and think. A white binder sat on the table beside her garments. Printed in big script on the cover was a note welcoming guests to the hotel and to Karachi. Acid burned up her chest to her throat. She swallowed it down. "Why are you doing this?"

"Which part exactly?"

She ran her fingers over the binder. "All of it."

"Well, I never got a chance to meet you. And when I finally could, for some reason, I and everyone else was made to believe you and my brother perished in the bombing. And yet, here you are. In the flesh."

Ally wandered to the draped panels and pushed them aside. She counted nine rows of windows between them and the manicured hotel grounds below. Courtyards, ponds, and pools littered the property. Beyond the cement fences were highways and dozens of buildings, some taller than others, as far as she could see. She pressed her hand against the glass. Somewhere out there was Farah and the baby. "Why did you want to meet me?"

"Why wouldn't I? We're family."

Ally looked over her shoulder and watched him type into his cell phone. With his high cheekbones and long, thick neck, the man was handsome. Shariff looked up at her. He cleared his throat, amusement still present on his face. "I take it my big brother never mentioned his good-looking younger brother."

She didn't answer.

The smile faltered. "Of course he didn't. Sayeed was the jealous type, you know. Probably worried you'd love me more."

*Sayeed.* Chills rocked through her at his name. Ally turned to face him and leaned her back against the window, trying to hide the terror brewing within. "Your brother kidnapped, raped, and tortured me. I wouldn't describe my feelings for him as even remotely connected to love." She hugged her arms around her waist and dug her nails into the heel of her palms. "Are you planning on doing the same?"

She scanned him for weapons but found no telltale lumps under his clothes. His pecs flexed under her scrutiny. "Eyes up here, love." When she met his amused gaze, he winked. "I want answers."

"Let them go and I will give you all the answers you want."

Shariff pressed his hands behind his head and crossed one socked foot over the other. "Again with the *let them go* request. This is getting boring. So let's start with a simple question first. Why does everyone think you're dead?"

Ally turned back to the window and stared out at the gardens below. Eddie and the Agency had cautioned her to never tell the truth. They trained her to parrot the story they created, and as much as she hated being away from Farah and the boys, she now understood why. It wasn't about Farah and the baby anymore. There were fourteen boys whose lives rested on the responses she gave. "I don't know."

"Not a good answer. Let's try another. What happened to my brother?"

His words were rushed, impatience seeping into his tone. She rested her hands on the windowpane and counted to ten before responding. "Sayeed never mentioned your existence."

"We have already established that."

*Sibling issues.* "How do I know if you really are his brother, seeing as how he never talked about you?"

"I don't really care if you believe me or not." His feet thudded when they dropped to the floor. She sucked in a breath and tightened her hold on the pane as she watched him approach through the reflection on the window.

Shariff leaned his back against the glass and looked over at her. The smile had disappeared. "You forget. I have someone of yours. Which means my answering your questions are not nearly as important as you answering mine. So tell me, what happened to your husband?" He nudged her with his elbow. "Let me clarify, considering you had two. What happened to my brother?"

Ally met his gaze. "I only had one husband, and he was not the man you call your brother."

Shariff crossed his arms and nodded. "The American you ran away with while my poor brother lay taking his last breath." He waved his index finger at her. "Well, supposed last breath."

"My husband rescued me from hell and took me home. He helped me heal..."

Shariff raised his brow and interrupted her. "And helped you to forget *all* about my brother."

"I will never forget Sayeed or the things he did to me." She kept her voice even and low.

He waved his hand. "Yes, the kidnapping, rape, and torture."

Rather than answering, she stared at the armed security men in blue uniforms who converged together at the edge of the courtyard below.

"He was a bit of an arsehole, wasn't he?" Shariff chuckled. "So, tell me about the day the great arsehole Sayeed died. Is he dead, by the way?"

His eyes burned into her, scrutinizing her every word and expression. "Yes."

"Who had the honor of killing him?"

Cars flew across the highway in the distance, disappearing behind the buildings that blocked the view of the overpass. She kept her face stoic as she watched them escape. "Ibrahim Ayoub. The leader of the As-Sirat."

His lips tightened. "Did you see the killing?"

She shook her head. "Sayeed slammed my head into the wall a few too many times and I blacked out. But when I woke up in Germany, I saw the pictures of his body."

"Ahh, hence the reason you have no memory of what

happened."

Her muscles stiffened as he laughed.

He pressed a hand to his chest and stared at the ceiling. "Thank God. The bastard needs to be dead and stay dead. But tell me something. How is it, contrary to what everyone believes, you are still alive?"

He clearly knew something. It was the *what* that scared her.

"They worried the As-Sirat might come looking for me so they announced Sara Irfani died with her husband."

He tapped his finger against his lip. "The organization fell apart a year after Ayoub died. Why would the Americans have continued the charade? What possible value do you still possess?"

"I wondered the same." She shot him a look. "Clearly they had reason to worry because here I am...with you."

Shariff smiled. "Good point." He walked back to his chair and leaned over to get something from the duffle bag beside it. Foil and plastic rustled when he pulled out a packet of chips and waved it at her.

She shook her head and stared at the world outside while he crunched on a mouthful of the contents.

"Want to know my theory?"

She didn't respond.

"Maybe your death wasn't the only lie to come out of the explosion."

Goosebumps pebbled her skin. She stayed rooted to the floor. "What do you mean?"

The bag rustled when he grabbed a second serving. "Granted, I do think Sayeed has met his maker. There is no way my arrogant brother would have stayed hidden all these years otherwise. But the rest of them, I'm not so sure. What if everyone else is as dead as you and the widow?"

Her heart skipped a beat. She swallowed and looked over her shoulder at him. "The widow?"

He waved a chip in the air. "The widow and her baby from the videos I sent you."

Ally's face heated. "You mean the wife *you* made into a widow."

He shrugged and popped the chip in his mouth.

Her brain buzzed with questions. What did he know? What game was he playing? Ally stared out the window and sniffled. "I miss them and think about them every day. Sometimes I imagine what our lives would have been like if we'd all survived Sayeed." She glanced at him, allowing a tear to slip down her cheek. "Are they alive? Did you take them, too?"

He scowled. The sound of the foil bag crumbling filled the room. "Since we're talking about lies from the past, here's another one. Let's say, yes, big brother was killed. But how do you know for sure Ayoub was to blame?"

She watched as he tossed the empty bag into the trash. "Who do you think killed him?"

Shariff wiped his hands on his jeans. "So many possibilities, including my beautiful resurrected-from-the-dead Bhaabi."

"Stop calling me that. I am not your sister-in-law."

His lip curved up. "According to signed wedding documents, you are." In two steps, Shariff stood in front of her, his face inches from her own. "Now stop deflecting the fucking question or people will die."

Silence filled the space. Ally's pulse raced. She released the breath she held and cleared her throat. "What do you want?"

He closed his eyes. "The truth."

"I don't remember anything from the day of the explosion," she whispered.

By the time he opened his lids, the smile had returned. He scrunched his nose. "You really need a shower."

Her back to the window, Ally didn't move. "I want to see them."

He leaned in closer. "Who?"

"The widow and her baby." She itched to rip the smile off his face.

"You've seen her."

Ally clenched her fists and held his gaze. "In person. I won't help you until I see for myself they are alive."

He quirked a brow. "If you don't remember, you clearly can't help me. Now can you? Did I mention the going rate for a twenty-year-old moderately attractive woman is very high? That's not even considering how much childless couples would pay for a one-month-old orphaned baby. Oh, then there's you." He pressed his finger against the side of her neck and traced a line across her skin.

Goosebumps rose along the path he traced.

"The man who brought you to me. Bashar. He's eagerly waiting to slit your throat."

Ally didn't move and worked to keep the terror out of her voice. "You're a lot like your brother."

His face darkened. "Really?"

"Threats. Blackmail. He had no respect for human lives and used people as pawns for his games."

He nodded. "I can see why you think that." Shariff scrunched his nose and backed away from her. "But aside from those reasons, I am very different from him." He pointed at the open door to his right. "If you want the reunion, you should hurry and take a shower." His smiled widened. "Also, there are some additions to your attire. We'll discuss the rest after you're bathed and dressed."

# CHAPTER FOURTEEN

## BLAME

*O*lly stood along the edge of the riverbank, admiring the mountain looming ahead in the distance. From the edge of its cliff, she noticed a waterfall flowing down into the river below. She sucked in a lungful of cedar and pine and smiled. This had been her favorite spot in the Rocky Mountain forest when she lived in Denver. Every weekend, she'd find herself right here at this spot, making her way to the base of the cliff. Beautiful greens and browns surrounded her while the most perfect blue sky hung above. Birds chirped happy songs. A family of deer wandered by, undeterred by her presence. All of nature seemed to come together here. The world hovered in perfect peaceful balance.

She looked down at her bare feet, in awe at how the rocks didn't dig into her heels. A cool breeze blew past her; it brushed through her hair and made the bottom of her white cotton dress ripple and flow as she walked.

She approached the base of the mountain, noticing a figure standing by the waterfall. She tilted her head and gazed at it as she approached. Her breath caught in her throat. It was a boy. She didn't need to ask; she already knew he was twelve-years-old. He would always be twelve. Tall and thin, he wore a white cotton, short-sleeve shirt, and his navy shorts hung over his bony knees. Her smile turned into an excited giggle. Umber.

He didn't move, just watched her advance. Ally's heart raced and her leisurely walk turned into a sprint. Losing Umber had cut her deep. She blamed herself for the loss. It shouldn't have taken his death to finally propel her into action and go up against Sayeed. In the end, the monster was killed, but so many lives were lost in the process— guilt hung heavy on her conscience.

She pushed the thought away and stretched out her arms, eager to hold him once more.

Umber shook his head. "Nay, Sara Mommy."

*Sara*. Hearing the name again made her stumble over her own feet. Ally fell to her knees. She got up and worked to reach him, but no matter how hard she tried, he remained out of her grasp.

Umber took a step back. The sadness in his gaze poured into her, the weight of it leaving her breathless.

"You can't come here, Sara Mommy."

Although she understood the words he spoke in Urdu, she couldn't understand why he spoke them and shook her head.

"Because you are the reason I am here."

Ally froze, waiting for him to finish. "If you hadn't loved me, I would still be alive."

Emotion dampened her face. "Nay, Umber. Sayeed sent you into the mall. Don't you remember? He gave you the bag of explosives, not me. He told you there was a surprise in the bag for me and said I was in there waiting for you. I didn't know. I would have never let you go in there."

"It's okay, Umber, the bomb wasn't her fault."

She looked over to see an older man, bald with thick-rimmed glasses. The sight of him weakened her knees. The brown suit he wore fit perfectly. He wandered up to Umber, placing a hand on the boy's shoulder. The man who gave his life to protect hers smiled when their eyes locked.

"Nasif, please tell him what really happened."

The old man nodded. "Sara Mommy is right, she would never hurt the people she loves. Not intentionally. But they do all die. It's not her fault she's cursed."

His words ripped through Ally, making the trees around her spin. She grabbed hold of the trunk nearby and steadied herself as she listened to his explanation.

"If I hadn't loved you, I would have never gone after Sayeed for you. He would have never killed me."

She shook her head. "I never asked you…"

He nodded. "No, you didn't. Your heart is too good, but this is what happens when someone loves you as their own. No?"

His words pierced her but she didn't refute them. How could she argue with what she herself believed? "I'm so sorry."

"It is what it is." Nassif and Umber turned their backs to her and began to walk away.

Ally shook in terror. "No! Don't leave me. Please."

"It's time for them to go, Ally." The voice calmed her as soon as it floated into her ears. She sucked in a breath, searching for the source, and when her gaze landed on him, she leaned against the tree to steady herself. Ally watched him approach. In a long cotton shirt and jeans, David walked to Nasif and Umber. His skin glowed with life and his eyes sparkled. She filled her mind with the sight, trying to memorize every part of him because deep down she knew he would leave again.

Ally's heart thudded against her chest as if trying to leave her body and take its rightful place with his. She grabbed fistfuls of her skirt, hiked it up, and rushed to him.

When she tripped on a fallen log, she steadied herself, and returned to her goal—David's arms. But as hard as she ran, she never seemed to get any closer. He stood there, in the distance, staring at her. He didn't smile nor did he appear angry…just sad. A gust of wind shoved against her, forcing her to fall backwards.

"Ally, you can't come here, baby."

She gazed at him, her face drenched and white dress stained. "Please, don't leave me alone."

He shook his head. "It was inevitable."

Ally climbed to her feet. "Your death was my fault, wasn't it?"

He stared at her, not answering, but flashed her a sad smile.

When he turned his back and walked in the direction of Nasif and Umber, Ally shook in terror, and she sprinted. Everything she wanted was by the mountain. Her life, her soul. No matter how hard she pumped her legs, she couldn't reach them. She screamed their names, pleading with them to return, but no one turned back.

"It's your fault, baby. All of this is because of you." David's words echoed through the breeze, growing louder each time. Her tears turned to sobs and the ache in her chest worsened each time he spoke them.

"David, I'm sorry. Don't leave me. Please, don't leave!" she screamed.

In spite of her pleas, the three disappeared into the base of the waterfall. Ally fell to her knees. "Please! Don't leave me!"

As if in a tunnel, she watched the mountain and the waterfall move farther away, the circle growing smaller. She couldn't climb to her feet. She couldn't move. Thick chains wrapped tight around her chest, immobilizing her arms. Ally clawed at them, but the links refused to move until the small circle in which David, Umber, and Nasif existed turned black.

"David," she screamed. "I need you!"

"Di, you're having a bad dream. Please wake up." Her sister's voice floated through the darkness. A voice she didn't want to hear. She fought the chains and screamed for him, ignoring Reya's pleas.

The terror in her sister's words pulled at her, growing louder, and no matter how hard Ally clawed at the chains, she was being dragged in the other direction.

Panting and drenched in sweat, Ally laid there, refusing to open her eyes. If she did, she'd be in her bed. It wouldn't be heavy chains confining her but her baby sister's arms clinging tightly around her.

Reya's lips pressed against her skin as her sister cried for her. "Didi, please open your eyes," she sobbed.

Ally forced her lids open. She blinked a few times as her vision adjusted to the halogen lights in her bedroom. Their bedroom. The one she and David shared until a month ago.

A cool, wet towel pressed against her forehead. When she looked over, her mother sat beside her, her eyes red and cheeks shimmering wet with tears of her own.

Ally patted her crying sister's arm. "It's okay. I'm okay," she reassured her.

Reya lay on the bed with her, her arms squeezing the breath out of her. "Let me go. I can't breathe."

When she finally released her, Ally climbed off the bed and made her way to the bathroom, the one place she knew they wouldn't follow.

"Di."

Ally stopped and waited for Reya to finish.

"It's not your fault. None of it."

She nodded and shut the bathroom door behind her.

～

Ally leaned her back against the trunk of an old tree. She stretched her tired legs across the scratchy patch of earth over David's grave. The soothing echoes of the water and breeze from Schuylkill River, a few hundred yards away, almost masked the sounds of rush hour traffic on the expressway in the distance. Almost. She put her headphones on and hit resume on the playlist he'd created well over a year ago. Once upon a time, he made her promise to listen to the whole thing, and she planned on making good on her promise.

So every morning, she jogged along the Art Museum area until she reached her destination—this plot of land right under the tree. From the worn leather backpack, she pulled out a ziplock bag and stared at its contents—a blue sweater.

She brought the opening of the bag to her face before unzipping it; there was no way she'd allow any of its valuable contents to be wasted. Ally's lungs filled with the smell of cedar, musk, and the faint scent of his soap. She sealed her eyes, savoring it, and for the first time in days, her muscles relaxed. There were other shirts of his in sealed bags hidden away in a suitcase in the back of her closet. She saved them for the hard days, like today. The rest of the time she'd walk into the closet, close the door, spray his cologne on his shirts which still hung on his side, and sit in there, immersed in his fragrance.

Those packages and the playlist he'd made were her most valuable possessions, far more valuable than the pictures or even his wedding ring. They felt and smelled the most like him, and when she surrounded herself in the music and his scent, she could almost feel him holding her. Almost.

"Hey, baby." A voice she'd ached to hear filled her ears. Ally's eyes shot open as she searched the cemetery grounds for him. "I wanted to make this last part of the playlist a bit more special."

"This is a mix of different kinds of songs. Some of them made me think of the person you are today, and others were the ones I used to listen to when I thought I'd lost you. I know it's cheesy, but

I also know you love cheese. So enjoy." The sound of his laugh sliced through her.

The slow beat of a familiar song filled her ears. "You know how you ask me every other second why I haven't given up on you?" The male singer's voice filled her ears. He sang about a woman who was perfect and his promise to always love her. David cleared his throat and recited the lyrics as the song played in the background.

A tear slipped down her cheek, only to be followed by another and then another until they flooded her face. Ally curled up in a ball on his grave with his sweater crushed to her chest, listening to David's promise to never leave her.

# CHAPTER FIFTEEN

## THE REUNION

FOUR MONTHS POST-DAVID

*A*lly tugged on the handcuffs on her wrists. The tight metal dug into her skin, burning her. As painful as the cuffs were, the blindfold and the heavy fabric she wore terrified her more. After she showered and dressed at the hotel, he had handed her a full *burqa*, including the head covering. The sight of the floor-length dress brought back painful memories of Sayeed and the compound. The images and emotions so painful, she shook uncontrollably.

Shariff tossed the burqa on to the bed. "We are going to pay a visit to the lovely young widow and her child you came to see, so the outfit is a must. Oh, and since I don't trust you, you should probably prepare yourself for the blindfold and handcuffs, too. If any of these items are a problem, we can skip the reunion."

It took a while for her breathing to slow and her hands to stop shaking, but once the tremors eased, she slipped the long-sleeved dress over her clothes and covered her head. A mesh window in front of her face allowed Ally to scan her surroundings as they walked through the white marble halls of the hotel. Throughout it all, Shariff kept a firm grip on her arm with one hand and carried a bright red duffle bag in the other. Once they were in the backseat of a black car, he cuffed her wrists to the door and slipped off her headdress.

She sat behind the driver and stared at the back of his head.

His dark hair was cut short, and from the thickness of his neck and round shoulders, he seemed to be a hefty man. Ally gazed out the window at the golden entrance of the hotel. Restrained in a car in a foreign land with two men, she had no clue how the next few hours would play out. Would they even take her to Farah and the baby? And where was Eddie?

She jumped when Shariff leaned toward her. He nudged his chin at the fabric in his hand. "Blindfold."

Everything turned dark a second later when he covered her eyes and tied the scarf behind her head.

Throughout the journey, her senses remained on high alert, her fears plentiful. She tried to breathe through them, sucking in a lungful of the driver's cigarette smoke in the process. Other than the steady stream of cars and blaring of horns that floated into the cabin during the trip, none of the passengers in her vehicle uttered a sound. More than a couple of times, the sharp turns and bumps on the road made her head slam into the window of the door to which she was restrained. After a long while, the car slowed to a stop. It honked, making her jump. The sound of metal hitting metal echoed from somewhere outside, and soon the car lurched forward. The ground beneath its tires was bumpy and gravel crunched under its weight. The vehicle stopped a few seconds later, and the same metal sounds from a minute ago echoed again.

"We're here," he announced while he removed the handcuffs from her wrists. Ally's stomach fluttered and her mouth went dry. She rubbed the bruised area and said a silent prayer for the strength to survive whatever awaited her.

When she reached for her blindfold, he pulled her hands away.

"Not yet. Let's get inside first." Shariff kept a grip on her elbow and helped her out of the car. "You will see again very soon. Trust me."

She wiped her wet palms on her burqa, allowing him to guide her along the pebbled ground. Somewhere ahead, a door opened.

"There's a step coming up. Right here," he warned and directed her into the space. Once inside, the door slammed behind her. The smell of fresh paint mixed with stained wood filled her nostrils. Ally fisted her hands, her pulse thudding against her ears. Things rustled for a while before someone finally grabbed the blindfold and pulled it off.

She blinked a few times, allowing herself to adjust to the light while she massaged the tender area around her wrists. The masked man from the videos sat in the tiny living room on a beige sofa. Her eyes narrowed as she took him in. Tall and lean, he wore jeans and a loose tee with the image of the Eiffel Tower printed across his chest. Beneath the monument's picture were the words "I Love Paris." His eyes were hazel and black strands of his mustache poked out around his mouth from under the mask. She continued to stare at him long after he looked away.

He shifted in his seat, focused his attention on the laptop in his lap before he finally got up, and then walked into the dark hallway behind her. Why did she make him nervous?

Ally jumped when Shariff rested his hand on her shoulder. He gave her a firm squeeze and waved at the closed door across the other side of the room. "Ready?"

She scanned the space. The walls were bare and the area sparsely furnished. A large curtained window was across the room beside the dining table. She noticed three doors: one beside the dining table, one next to the kitchen, and one directly behind her. He grabbed a ring of keys from the counter and headed to the door by the kitchen. "You have ten minutes and then we leave."

Ally weaved her fingers together and squeezed to hide the tremors rocking through her. "Ten minutes. Alone."

He rolled his eyes. "You're not in a position to negotiate."

She didn't say anything, just continued to stare at him as her pulse quickened.

Shariff put the key into the padlock and unlatched the door. "Fine, alone." He opened it and waved for her to enter. "But I will be waiting for you out here."

She sucked in a breath and scanned the same yellow walls from the video. Somewhere in the room was a camera monitoring her every move and word. Ally stepped in and locked eyes with Farah but didn't go to her. She stayed rooted to the spot, surveying the area, waiting for the door behind her to close and lock. From the angle of the videos she'd seen, the camera had to be across from the bed.

"Why did you bring her here?" The masked man in the living room snapped. His words were spoken in Urdu.

"Quiet," Shariff retorted.

The men continued to argue, but their voices dropped so low

she couldn't make out the words. She jumped when a door on the other side slammed shut. Clearly, Eiffel Tower wasn't pleased with Shariff's explanation.

The tail of a black cat clock swished back and forth. Ebony arrows sat in the center of the cat's white belly showing the time. The fixture hung on the wall across from the bed. The perfect height and angle for a camera.

Ally stepped away and focused her attention on the woman seated on the bed, staring at her in disbelief. Her face and arms appeared free of injury. The hallowed cheeks of the eighteen-year-old she remembered had filled in. Although red rimmed, her enormous eyes, which once were sunken, were fuller, brighter. A tear slipped down Farah's cheek and rolled down her face until it fell on the white towel draped over her chest as she nursed the baby beneath it. Her and Amir's baby.

Ally's chest tightened. Yet again, Farah's happily-ever-after had been stolen. She rolled her shoulders back and shook off the overwhelming urge to pull her in her arms and sob. Instead, she smiled and approached them.

Tiny toes poked out from the side of the terry cloth. Two miniature feet flexed and stretched. The young mother pulled down the towel, revealing the feeding baby beneath. Perfectly oval eyes were closed, and the baby's pink lips latched to its mother's breast. "This is not how I wanted you to meet her," she whispered.

*Her.* Ally smiled and sat down beside them. She put her arm around Farah's shoulder while she pressed her lips against the soft, black, mossy hair on the top of *her* head. "I am glad I get to meet her."

"You shouldn't be here, Didi."

Ally rested her head against Farah's. "You shouldn't either."

The baby released her mother's nipple, nuzzled her cheek into Farah's bare chest, and sighed in her sleep.

Ally's eyes burned as she admired the child's bright red cheeks and full pink mouth, along the corner of which still contained remnants of milk. "She's perfect."

When she pressed her finger into the child's hand, soft tiny digits wrapped around her big one, squeezing her tight. A shudder ripped through her as the weight of the situation hit home. This short life and that of her mother's depended on Ally. She closed her eyes and said a silent prayer.

"Would you like to hold her while I fix my top?"

Ally nodded and took the sleeping child, pressing her tiny front against her chest. The baby's chin rested on her shoulder as she supported her back. She pressed her cheek against the infant's soft hair and inhaled the clean scent of powder and lotion.

Once upon a time, she had dreamed of this moment, but her fantasy included a different bedroom, in a different country, with a different man's baby in her arms. How had everything gone so wrong?

After covering herself up, Farah rested her head on Ally's free shoulder, as she used to all those years ago in the compound. "This is my fault."

Ally stared at the wall clock and its wagging tail. "The one thing we've both learned is that some things are beyond our control."

Farah sniffled. "Amir must be searching for us now."

Ally flinched but didn't correct her. She slid the infant off her shoulder and cradled her. A pair of tiny but familiar brown eyes stared up at her, blinking every so often. "She has his eyes."

"He loves it when I tell him that." The pain in Farah's voice deepened the ache in Ally's chest. "We named her Amirah. A combination of both of ours."

Ally cleared her throat. "It's beautiful."

"It means leader. I'm hoping the name inspires her to become one."

Ally smiled.

"It must be killing him to be away from us."

She rested her cheek on top of Farah's head and kept her voice even. "You will get out of here. I promise."

Farah's hair brushed against Ally's skin when she nodded her agreement. "And you will, too. David will come for you. We both know he will not sleep until you're safe."

The void inside her throbbed at the mention of his name. Ally stared at the ceiling and blinked back her tears.

"He is a hero. Like my Amirah's father."

Her gaze fell upon the clock on the wall. Somewhere in the other room, two men watched and listened to their every word, waiting to see what she'd say. "Our husbands will always be heroes. Those men on the other side of the door are cowards, and they will pay with their lives for what they've done."

A few minutes later, keys rattled against the door. Ally stayed on the bed, with Farah leaning against her and the baby in her arms, watching. When it opened, Shariff stood at the threshold, arms crossed. "Your ten minutes are up."

# CHAPTER SIXTEEN

## KARMA

THREE MONTHS POST-DAVID

Seated on the couch in her therapist's office, Ally picked at the plastic label wrapped tight around her water bottle. "Some people consider this world to be hell, and death their only way to find peace. Their only way to find heaven."

"What do you think?" Wendy asked.

While she considered the question, she stared at intricate circles looped together in the geometric rug on the floor. "If you'd asked me four years ago, I'd have told you it was all a matter of perspective. If you choose to focus on the pain and sorrow, then yes, this life would become your hell. If you choose to focus on the beauty and goodness around you, it could be heaven."

"And now what do you believe?"

The space fell utterly silent as she wondered how much to share with the older brunette seated across from her. "I still think it's different for each person, but not so much about perspective as much as karma."

"Karma?"

"Yes. Karma." Ally slipped off her shoes and rested the heels of her feet on the plush cushion of the sofa, hugging her knees to her chest. "Your actions from your previous life will come back to haunt you in your current one. It's the only thing that makes sense."

"So what does your current life say about your previous life?"

She rested her chin on her knees and laughed. "I was a very bad person. Probably a serial killer."

Of course, Wendy didn't laugh, but she did crack an understanding smile. "Couldn't a perspective like this make someone feel they have no control over their own lives?"

Ally returned her attention to the floor rug. If she had a choice, she'd rather be seated in the therapist's chair instead of the client's. Working on other people's pain was a lot easier than dealing with her own. "What did I have control over? The kidnapping, the rapes, the beatings? Losing Farah and the boys? Umber and Nasif?" Her mind drifted to David. "My husband's death?"

Her whispered words were met with silence. Wendy handed her a tissue, but she waved it away and wiped her cheek against the rough denim of her jeans.

"Alisha, you have survived some intense things."

A sad smile tugged at her lips. "That's an understatement."

"So why keep trying? According to your definition, it's all predetermined."

"I've asked myself the same question more times than I'd like to admit." She played with the diamond-encrusted wedding ring, which sat heavy on her finger. "You know what keeps me going?" She didn't wait for the therapist to respond. "If I'm right and this is karma, killing myself might lead me into another miserable existence the next time around. Might as well get all the punishments over with now and do my time."

The leather creaked when Wendy shifted in her seat. "So you keep trying in the hopes it will lead to a better life the next time around?"

A tear slipped down her cheek. She didn't bother wiping it away this time. "I envy the people who are happy and loving the world and the lives they've built."

"What would a better life look like for you?"

"Growing old with David. He wanted a farm somewhere out West. Just us, sheltered from the ugly of this world." Ally closed her eyes. "I should have known that wouldn't be my story." Her voice cracked. Her mind drifted to a life long ago, one she rarely discussed with anyone. She cleared the ball of emotion stuck in her throat and grabbed the bottle of water on the table beside her. "Did I ever tell you about my parents?"

Wendy shook her head. "Not much. You've mentioned they moved in after your husband passed and invade your privacy on a daily basis."

Ally smiled. "Actually, those two are my paternal uncle and his wife. They adopted me after my birth parents died." Her childhood was something she rarely discussed.

"Tell me about your biological parents."

She took a drink from the bottle, relishing the cool liquid flowing down her throat. Talking wasn't something she liked to do anymore. Silence worked much better for her. It was safe and minimized the looks of pity she got when she did share her thoughts and emotions. But this was counseling, which meant processing and healing. "From what I know, both my parents grew up in Delhi with very traditional families, but Mumma was Muslim and Pappa Hindu. Boy met girl in college. They fell in love. Had unprotected sex and got pregnant."

Her therapist's brows rose. "How did that go?"

Ally replaced the cap before answering. "Not well. Their families were angry and swore to keep them apart. So Pappa showed up at Mumma's house one night and snuck her out. They dropped out of college and got married. Pappa got a job with the railroad company while my mother stayed home with me."

"How did it impact you?"

"It didn't back then. We lived in a small apartment in Delhi— the three of us. No extended family and not a lot of money, but I was happy. Really happy." Her voice trailed off as she remembered her little self, running around the apartment in pajamas and braids playing chase with her father. "The world was perfect. Nothing bad could touch me. I want to go back to the little girl. To feeling that way."

"What happened to your parents?"

"I was four and at school when they died. They were on a train and the bridge the train went over collapsed, plunging it and the passengers into the river below. I lost my safe, untouchable world." Ally stared out the window at the parking lot. Each time she'd been dealt a loss, a major life change, it happened without warning.

A car pulled into the vacant spot outside the window, most likely the next patient coming to work on their issues. Hopefully *their* wounds would heal. "A month later, I was in Philadelphia with new parents and a big brother and baby sister." She took another swallow from her bottle and fixed her attention on the woman across from her. "After I got here, I overheard my aunt and uncle fighting. She told him I was cursed and having me around her family and kids would only bring bad things to them."

Concern flashed across Wendy's face. "That's a lot of blame to put on anyone, much less a child."

"True. But the facts speak for themselves, don't they? My parents died when I was four. As an orphan, I learned to accept a new land and a new family as my own. I grew up and married the most amazing man. Then I was kidnapped and tortured. But somehow I learned, again, to accept my new reality and created a new family in Pakistan." Her mind wandered to the day Sayeed died, and the lies she had sworn to tell. "They were all killed," her voice trailed off. Considering they were listed as dead and she would never see them again, and considering how much their loss hurt her, it wasn't totally a lie. "So I end up back here in the States, learning to rebuild, and when I'm finally in a good place, my husband dies in a car wreck."

Ally shuttered her lids and hugged her knees. She left out the part about how she believed the accident wasn't an accident. The last thing she needed was for Wendy to think she struggled with paranoid ideations. The police, CIA, even her family, thought it an unfortunate coincidence that David died three years later to the day Sayeed was murdered. *There was no evidence of foul play.* But Ally's gut told her otherwise. Her gut screamed other words as well. "Sometimes, I wonder. If I hadn't ever been found. If they'd left me in Pakistan, would David still be alive? Be happy?"

"And what kind of life would you have had in Pakistan?"

Ally returned to gazing out the window. "One where I knew everyone lived." She shrugged and looked at the therapist with a sad smile. "Not all people are destined for a happily ever after."

Wendy leaned forward, mirroring Ally's smile. "And you're one of the ones who aren't?"

Ally nodded. "Karma."

# BOOK TWO

# CHAPTER SEVENTEEN

## CHOICES

*A*lly wandered to the kitchen and gripped the marble island. The keys bunched in Shariff's hand slammed against each other and the door while he secured the padlock to Farah and Amirah's room. A bit longer than the rest and brass in color, the key was in the middle of the ring. She shifted her focus to the kitchen counters before he caught her staring.

Ivory granite circled the space around her, bare of everything: dishes, glasses, even a coffee maker. To her left sat a small gas stove, and beside it a white fridge, pristine, unused. Dark wood drawers and cabinets covered the walls of the small room. If she looked inside them, she was sure she'd find them empty as well.

Keys jingled to her left by the sink. He opened a drawer, dropped them in, and slammed it shut. He cocked his head and raised his brows when he caught her staring. Ally looked away and scanned the living room for the masked man, but it was empty. Shariff's shoes tapped against the tiled floor. She gazed ahead, and her skin prickled with each step he took. When his breath hit her bare neck, a shiver of fear ripped through her. Unable to breathe, she steadied herself and waited.

He leaned his back against the island beside her and crossed his arms. From the corner of her eye, she noticed him assessing her. "Well, that was enlightening."

Ally's grip on the counter tightened. "Why didn't you tell her you killed her husband?"

"Because I didn't kill him." His pale brown eyes burned into her.

"You pay people to kill. That makes you a killer."

He shrugged. "I guess it's all a matter of how you define a word then, isn't it?"

"And the fact you didn't tell her that her husband was dead makes you a bastard."

His smile broadened. "Now the bastard label I do accept without question." A lock of her curly hair had fallen out from her ponytail. Shariff played with it and wrapped it around his finger. "And, according to your definition, wouldn't you be one too? I don't recall hearing you break the news of her heroic husband's demise."

She met his gaze. "Do you always lock up innocent women and listen to their conversations?"

"It appears that way, doesn't it?" Shariff rested the base of his elbows on the counter behind him and leaned back farther, his fingers brushing against hers in the process. Ally stepped away from his reach, facing him.

The two stared at each other, one smirking while the other glared. "Well, my fellow bastard? Why didn't *you* tell her that both the heroes she mentioned were dead?"

She kept her face emotionless despite the erratic thudding of her heart. "We all need a seed of hope to cling to. A reason to keep fighting. I couldn't take hers away. And I wasn't lying. She will go home."

The sound of his laughter burned her ears. She narrowed her eyes. "Am I amusing?"

Shariff inched closer and pressed his fingertips against her temple. "Brains..." His touch burned against her skin as the digit slid down her cheek onto her jaw. Ally held her breath when he moved from her face to her shoulder. "And determination." Goosebumps pebbled her skin while his hand brushed up and down the length of her arm. "I can see why my brother was drawn to you."

Ally scooted away and out of the kitchen, rubbing the feel of him off of her. She wandered around the apartment, sensing him close behind. Sayeed and his brother shared a similar taste—her. What wasn't clear was what the younger sibling intended to do about it. "Someone who looks like you can have any woman he wants."

"Why, dear Bhaabi, are you calling me handsome?"

She shrugged and continued past the dining table, resting her hand on the door by the window. "Am I wrong?"

The deadbolt was secured and the knob wouldn't budge.

"Not at all." His legs brushed against her rear and his vanilla and sandalwood cologne filled her lungs. "I get my share of female attention," he whispered against her ear.

She slid past him and moved toward the hall by the front entry, peeking into the bathroom along the way. When she arrived at the closed room at the end, she paused. Would this be where they planned to keep her?

The heat of his body smothered her when he neared. She pressed a hand against the smooth surface of the door and stayed still while Shariff pulled the hair tie from her hair. The strands fell free against her shoulders. Her pulse beat erratically as he ran his fingers through her curls. She couldn't go through the torture Sayeed put her through a second time. It would kill her.

Amirah's distant cries echoed through the quiet home, reminding her of the baby's presence. Ally squeezed the knob and stared at the door. Running would mean leaving behind Farah and the baby. She turned and met his gaze. "So why such a hunger for Sayeed's leftovers?"

Sharif's gaze raked over her face, pausing to linger at the neckline of her shirt. "Sometimes leftovers are the most appealing."

"I'm yours to do with as you please for as long as you want. No argument. No fight." She kept her voice steady, showing no hint of the terror consuming her.

The corner of his mouth lifted. He ran a digit over her skin, tracing the seam of her shirt collar and stopping at the V point of her neckline. "Yes, I am hungry. Very hungry." Her skin prickled when Shariff's finger moved up her neck to the base of her chin, lifting her face. "But." He inched his mouth closer until it brushed against hers when he spoke. "As enticing as the proposition is, I will have to regretfully decline." He looked into her eyes. "Two men have already had you and both are dead. I've no desire to join their list."

Ally leaned against the wooden surface for fear her legs would buckle. "What do you want then?"

Before he could answer, the front door opened. From over Shariff's shoulder, she watched the masked man enter the room. He stopped mid-stride and glared at them, slamming the door to the house so loud the walls shook.

"That." Shariff cupped her chin and made her return her attention to him. "Is a much better question. Why don't we have a seat on the couch so we can discuss it further?"

Ally remained in the hall and watched Shariff disappear into the living room. The leather sofa creaked when he sat on it. He let out an exaggerated sigh. "Brains, determination, and stubbornness. I'm not sure if I should consider those your strengths or your flaws."

Amirah's incessant cries continued from their locked prison. Ally pushed off the door and walked toward Farah's room, only stopping when the masked man took his spot in front of it. They stared at each other, neither one willing to move aside. "They need to go home," she whispered. "What do I need to do to earn their freedom?" Pain flashed in his eyes before he blinked it away.

"The magic question," Shariff answered from behind her. "What can you do to set them free? If you do as expected, they will walk out of here safely in two days."

Ally continued to watch the man in front of her. He sealed his lids, refusing her access to his emotions. "I'm listening."

"Three things. First, where are the boys my brother adopted?"

The stranger's eyes opened, and he fixed his gaze on her. The intensity in them made her take a step back.

Her stomach twisted. "I don't know."

"Unacceptable answer. Let's try another one. My father will arrive in two days to meet you, and when he does, you will confess to killing my brother."

Ally blinked a couple of times and looked over her shoulder in his direction. "Why?"

He tipped his head toward the room with the crying baby. "So those two can live."

Farah's soft voice mingled with the baby's cries as a shudder of fear shot through Ally's spine. "I can do that."

"Excellent." Shariff waved the head covering and blindfold. "It's time to go, so let's get you dressed."

But she didn't move. "And third?"

He climbed to his feet, handed her the items and flashed her a confused look.

"You said three things. What's the third?"

Amusement soon replaced his confused expression. "I will share the information with you when it's time."

# CHAPTER EIGHTEEN

## OUR PAST

Drops of rain hit the top of her burqa as soon as they stepped outside. At first, they were small taps against the fabric. Soon they grew in frequency and weight until they felt like pellets slamming against her. Shariff yanked her hand, forcing her to run. Since her eyes were covered, she allowed him to lead. With her free hand, Ally wiped away the moisture on her head covering and, in the process, pushed her thumb against the blindfold beneath. On the second attempt, the cotton shifted lower, allowing her to see from the top corner of her right eye.

She kept her head lowered and scanned the area. Green grass blanketed the ground beneath her feet. A few palm trees stood tall on the outside of the dark stone and iron fence. The metal barrier appeared to run the length of the front yard. But what caught her eye was to the distant right. White skyscrapers sat side by side, reaching to the heavens. They were identical in shape and size. Rows of tiny windows filled the length of the buildings and what looked like balconies lined the corners. On the roofs of the three, she could see were small structures shaped like orange triangles and around them were trees.

Shariff pushed her into a car before she could assess further. This driver was taller than the last, his thick beard evident when he turned his head and waved at the masked man in the yard. The man outside ran and opened the gates as Shariff climbed in beside Ally. He tossed his duffle bag on the floor and cursed under his breath.

Ally kept her head forward as she watched Shariff out of the corner of her eye. At some point after blindfolding her, he'd tied his hair back and pasted a beard on his face. The snug fitting shirt he wore was also replaced with a long black tunic that hung over his jeans.

Aside from his mumbled curses and the wipers squeaking as they scraped the windshield clean, everyone in the vehicle remained silent during the trip.

Shariff leaned over, and when he grabbed the top of her hijab, Ally lunged away, cowering in the corner of the car.

"I'm going to dry you off."

She covered her face in her palms and pushed the blindfold back into place. "I can't see anything. You have to warn me before you do something like that."

"Well, consider this your warning. I am removing your hijab since its wet. So hold still." He pulled the heavy fabric off her head and ran the towel over her face and hair before adjusting her blindfold. He cuffed her hands to the handle of the door. "Much better. I'd hate for you to catch a cold. You need to stay healthy for the next few days."

Blindfolded in the backseat, the thuds of raindrops, the scraping of the windshield wipers, and the blare of every car horn was amplified. Even the bumps felt more intense, making her jump. The only time Shariff uncuffed her was when he returned the hijab. They exited one vehicle only to slide into another, at which point, the restraints returned to her wrists. Three different cars since they'd left the hotel. A total wardrobe change, including a beard, and aside from the horns of the traffic around them, still not a word had been uttered between him and the drivers. Everyone knew their roles. Except her.

Ally's mind raced. She had two days to figure out the man beside her. So, what did she know so far? Sayeed had a little brother he'd never mentioned, and the little brother didn't care much for his elder sibling. Shariff spoke fluent Urdu but had a heavy English accent. And although he was attracted to her, he seemed to be fighting it, even after she offered herself to him. Could she have followed through if he accepted? Ally sucked in a breath and pushed the question out of her brain. She would do what she needed to do.

A bag zipped and unzipped beside her. The leather seat groaned when he shifted. She listened to Shariff's grunts and the sound of fabric being pulled and tugged, but it wasn't until his elbow stabbed her thigh that she spoke up. "Is there any reason why you're changing your clothes?"

He laughed. "I got wet."

"You got wet about a half hour ago, and we've changed cars since then."

"Such an observant woman you are, and filled with so many questions." He squeezed her knee. "You know what happened to the curious cat, don't you?"

She slipped her leg out of his grasp. "It sounds like that will be my fate regardless of my curiosity."

Shariff didn't answer but tension oozed from him.

"Take a right here," he snapped at the driver.

She honed in on the agitation in his voice. "Wherever we are going is not a place you want to be is it?"

He laughed. "On the contrary, it's a homecoming. Where my mother and I lived until I was six. Exactly where I want to be."

There was a dryness to his words that screamed the opposite. "How long has it been since you've come back?"

"Over twenty-two years."

*Bingo.* "Homecomings are sometimes bittersweet." Ally took his silence to be agreement. "Is your mother waiting for you?"

"Some would say yes." Although he laughed, it sounded cold, hollow. "If you believe in the afterlife bullshit. She passed away when I was a child."

Aside from the soft music playing in the car, silence filled the cabin. So much said without a word spoken. She cleared her throat. "My parents passed away when I turned four. I understand how hard it is to grow up without them."

Shariff released a long, slow breath but didn't respond.

Ally pushed for more. "Is that why you left? Too many memories?"

"The funny thing about memories," he whispered, "no matter how fast or far you run, they follow you. And the darker they are, the quicker they latch on like fucking parasites. So no, it's not why I haven't been back."

She opened her mouth to respond, but he cut her off by

ordering the driver to pull over. The car slowed until it came to a stop and soon the crank of the parking brake clicked into place.

The leather seat she gripped cracked as Shariff slid closer. He removed her handcuffs, and when his fingers pressed against her face, Ally jumped, slamming her back against the door.

"Damn, I forgot to warn you, didn't I?" A second later, the veil was yanked from her head, and soon the blindfold followed.

She blinked a few times as her vision adjusted to the light. Cement walls painted in various colors lined both sides of the narrow road on which the car parked. Hibiscus trees in full bloom softened the cold feel of the fences. Every few yards of the wall were broken up with an iron entryway granting access to the homes behind the fence.

He tugged at the sleeve of her gown. "Remove this, too. We're almost there."

She looked him over. The beard no longer covered his cheeks, and his curls hung loose against his face. She grabbed the hem of the skirt and slid it up her body. Her hands shook as she yanked the heavy fabric over her head. "Who lives there now?"

He grinned. "My Alyah Bhaabi, her son, and her lazy new husband."

A shudder ripped through her. She smoothed out her shirt and hair and pretended to be unaffected by the news. "You brother's first wife and his old guard now live in your old home?"

"Yes."

"And you're not happy about it."

He rolled his eyes. "What makes you say such a thing? I'm smiling, aren't I?"

"You're always smiling."

Shariff waved off her comment. "Not important." He leaned close. "What is important is that we have our facts straight. So listen."

She nodded.

"My father doesn't want the current residents to know why you have been beckoned. So, the story is you're here because he wanted to meet you."

Ally laughed. "Alyah would never believe I came willingly. She knows how much I hated my life with Sayeed."

Shariff pinched her nose. "Ye of little faith. She'll believe you because you're also here to get your share of your late husband's property. It's no replacement for losing my wonderful brother, of course, but it helps ease the pain."

A piece of the puzzle fell into place. "If I, Alyah, and her son all died, who gets Sayeed's inheritance?"

Dark brows rose and a gleam glistened in eyes. "As long as my father lives, he controls it all. But once he passes, it would go to his next living kin."

"You."

He didn't respond.

"You're planning on killing us all," she whispered.

"Don't put words in my mouth. I'm not killing anyone." He flashed his palms in her face. "See? My hands are clean."

Ally pushed them down. "You're the puppet master. If they die, their blood is on you."

He shrugged. "I am only taking back what's mine."

She counted the lives impacted by him, her face heating at the thought of each and every one. "You've killed my husband and Amir. By the end of this week, the toll will more than double. And for what? A house?"

"A *house*?" He leaned close until she was sandwiched against the car door and him. He grabbed her chin, and positioned his face inches from hers. "This is not just about a house. This is about reclaiming what's mine." Angry eyes drilled into hers. "You can either meet my father and confess to being a killer, or sit silent and allow the widow and her child to perish, but you don't get to question my motives. Do you understand?"

# CHAPTER NINETEEN

## BOMB DETECTION

$\mathcal{H}$is nails dug into her chin and his eyes were wide as his grip on her tightened. A shiver shot through her spine. Ally kept her voice low and let him see her shake. "I'm not a killer."

"But you are," he whispered. The smile returned to his face. "You screamed your confession from the treetops the day you killed him."

His words took her back to her final moments in the compound. Held against her will, she had attempted to negotiate with the devil himself, Ibrahim Ayoub. Leader of what was once a powerful terrorist organization, he'd claimed responsibility for the deaths of thousands and was the second most wanted man in the world. She had known better than to think he would let her live when she met with him. Her hope had been to save the boys and Farah. In an attempt to protect the others, she told Ayoub she'd killed Sayeed. Aside from Eddie and the Delta operatives, everyone else who had heard her words was dead—or so she thought.

When she opened her mouth to speak, Shariff pressed his fingers against it. "Of course you don't remember, hurt brain and all. What I don't understand is why everyone thinks Ayoub killed Sayeed."

He let go of her but kept his face inches from hers, eyeing her mouth. "Needless to say, a lot of people are itching to hear the truth from these very lips." He slid back to his spot on the seat and waved at the driver. "Like my father."

The car pulled away from the curb and traveled down the cobblestone road. The farther it went, the more rigid Shariff became. His scowl deepened as he gazed straight ahead. She followed his line of sight and noticed the tall, iron gates looming ahead. A narrow graveled road curved past the entrance and disappeared inside the grounds. Red clay tiles sat on the gabled roof and peeked over the tops of the green trees. A turret stood tall in the center of the building. The top of it was lined with windows.

The car parked in front of the gates and the engine cut off. They had arrived.

Her pulse heightened. "I am not exactly Wassim and Alyah's favorite person. There's a good chance they will kill me before the day is done."

Shariff ran a hand through his loose curls. "Then let's try not to get killed, shall we? My father wants you alive. And your death would be unfortunate for your widow and her baby."

He laughed and patted her head. "Don't worry. Once I'm done talking, they won't touch a strand on your beautiful head."

Two men in navy jumpsuits cracked open the gate, squeezed through, and shut it behind them. Rifles hung against their hips. One was heavyset, and a large white dog on a leash walked alongside him while the other, a leaner guard, approached holding a black object in his hand.

Shariff tipped his chin at them. "The thing he's waving is supposedly a bomb detecting device."

Ally stared at the gun-like instrument as the watchman pulled at the front of it, extending an antenna, and pointed it at their car.

"It was proven an expensive fake years ago." The guard eyed Shariff, who lowered his window and waved back. "Idiots," he muttered under his breath.

The dog sniffed around the car, while the heavyset man shouted questions in Urdu at the driver and Shariff.

After he was satisfied with the answers, the guard pounded his fist on the back of their car. "Open your trunk."

Shariff kept a smile pasted on his lips and leaned to the driver. "Usman, do as the monkey says," he hissed. A second later, the trunk popped. He leaned his face out his open window and waved at the guard. "All you will find are two suitcases. One for me, and the other is Bhaabi's clothes. Now, please, a little respect?"

Ally stayed frozen in her seat. She had returned to the world she fought to escape, and unlike the past few years, none of this was a dream. She stared at the door handle. Once the car pulled inside the gates, she might never get out. The last time, it cost her two years and lots of heartbreak to finally gain her freedom.

One of the watchmen pulled out his phone and called someone while the other searched the suitcases in the trunk. Suitcases she never realized she had. Both guards bent down and peered over at her. The one with the phone took her picture and sent it.

The guard pointed at Ally's door. "*Darwaza khulte hai.*"

Shariff nodded. "He wants you to open your door and get out. Brace yourself. You are about to be inappropriately groped and fondled all in the name of security."

Ally climbed out and stared back at the road they'd traveled as rough hands gripped her shoulders. He pulled her arms out, stretching them as far as they could reach. She clenched her fists and fought the urge to push him away when he patted her back and sides.

# CHAPTER TWENTY

## A WELCOME FACE

*A*lly looked over Shariff's shoulder while he rang the doorbell. Carved into the wood of the tall mahogany doors was an intricate forest scene. From the delicate feathers of the birds in the sky to the complex details in the flowers and leaves in the garden, the artist had not missed a single element in creating the masterpiece. When the doors were closed, as they currently were, a thick-trunked tree formed in the middle. Metal clicked against wood as the locks opened. When the trunk separated in two, the sight of the man who stood between the tree halves made her suck in a breath.

Dressed in jeans, a loose white tunic, and leather sandals, his sleeves were rolled above his elbows. Muscular and about six feet tall, the man's black hair was buzzed short and eyes were dark brown. She stared at the blue tinge of a fading bruise clinging to the corner of his right eye. He didn't say a word, nor did he acknowledge her presence. He didn't have to. She worked on keeping her face emotionless as excitement surged through her veins.

Shariff spoke to him in Urdu, but Ally couldn't focus on his words. For the first time since she'd arrived in Frankfurt, hope fluttered in her gut. Eddie stepped aside, allowing them in. With every step she took, she walked taller and her head lifted a little higher. Ally followed Shariff, ignoring the man at the door. She scanned the foyer. Creamy marble tiles, swirled with grays and silver, covered the floor while soft beige paint hugged the walls. A silver mirror hung over a dark wood console table.

She noticed the way Shariff ran his hand over the table as he entered the huge expanse of a living room. He stopped in front of a large staircase in the middle of the room and gripped the banister, staring at the top floor. Its thick, dark wood rails and long stone rungs made it the centerpiece of the home. The marble stairs ascended up the height of the mansion, branching out into two separate directions.

While she watched Shariff, she felt someone watching her. Her skin prickled. She scanned the room for the source. Hand-carved furniture adorned with richly upholstered cushions brightened the space. Tapestries in deep reds and golds hung against the walls. The furnishings, the carvings, the art, everything about it exuded wealth.

Wassim sat at the far end of the room, in a leather armchair, his dark eyes burning into her. Acid rose in her throat. Ally met his gaze, refusing to look away, and approached him. As Sayeed's widow, she still held a position of power—a fact they both knew. His thick brows lowered, almost forming a straight line, and his jaw shifted from left to right as he grit his teeth.

Dressed in a long white shirt, which hung below his knees, and loose matching pants, his arms rested on the sides of his chair. At five-six, Wassim was average-sized. But what he lacked in height, he more than made up for in his ability to intimidate. It was the reason Sayeed hired him to guard his first wife. Little did Sayeed realize the guard would do more with his wife's body than protect it. Times had changed, and the man before her no longer claimed the title of Alyah's hired guard. He had replaced Sayeed as both her husband and the ruler of the arms trade business his wife's late husband created.

"Such a handsome little guy," Shariff said as he walked by. It was only then she noticed the child seated on Wassim's lap. "Spitting image of my late brother except for the eyes. Those are clearly his mother's. Don't you think, Bhaabi?"

Enormous green orbs stared up at Shariff as the grown man squatted and pinched the child's cheek. "Hello there. I'm your chacha." His plump face tilted and chubby cheeks turned rosy. Brown curls, identical to Wassim's, bounced when he turned his back to them, hiding his face in his father's chest.

"Just like his father," she answered.

Shariff translated her response. Although Wassim said nothing, from the way his jaw twitched, her message had hit the target.

A plump little hand grasped Wassim's ear, pulling it closer to his tiny mouth. The boy pointed back at her as soft words floated through the room, far from the whisper he intended. "Babba, who is she?" he asked in Urdu.

Wassim put an arm around the child, pressing him close, and rested his cheek against the boy's as his icy stare returned to Ally. "No one you need to be afraid of, son. As long as Babba is here, no one will hurt you."

Her chest tightened. His words also hit their target. Only his was a lie. She scanned the space and the men standing around her. So much evil surrounded them, and in the center of it all was a tiny boy with green eyes who had good reason to be scared. They all did.

In the back of the space, an open door led into the hallway. At the threshold stood a woman with the same beautiful green eyes as the child, but this pair was filled with fear. In the three-plus years since their paths had crossed, the sharp edges of Alyah's face had rounded. Her once pale skin had warmed to a soft brown. As beautiful as she was before, she was even more so now.

She wore a short-sleeved paisley *salwar* in pale yellow and matching leggings. Unlike the Alyah of the past, her dark hair was left uncovered, pulled away from her face. A scarf draped around her neck, the edge of which she twisted.

The woman's neck turned a deep red under Ally's gaze. There was no doubt she wished it was all a bad dream. Up until a few minutes ago, Alyah believed Sayeed's second wife had died, and the only people alive who knew about her affair and the truth about the child seated in her husband's lap was herself and Wassim.

"Alyah Bhaabi! You look stunning as ever." Ally looked over her shoulder at Shariff. He leaned against the banister of the stairs, arms crossed, a smirk on his face. "And look at the surprise I brought with me."

Alyah glanced at him briefly before staring back at the floor. "It has been a long time, Shariff."

He laughed. "I know. I have been busy but hopefully bringing Sara Bhaabi will earn my forgiveness? She is a miracle, isn't she?"

"We were told she died three years ago with Sayeed," Wassim said flatly. "How did she survive?"

Ally looked around the opulent home, pretending to not understand the conversation around her. When Shariff started to translate, Wassim silenced him. "Hassan will ask her what happened."

"Wassim would like to know if Sayeed is alive." Eddie spoke in English, but his words were thick with accent.

Ally cleared her throat. "I was told he died in the explosion." She kept her hands clasped and head down as he translated her response to Wassim.

"Who told you this?"

"The American soldiers," she said.

"Did she actually see him dead?" Ally's heart tugged at the fear in Alyah's voice.

After Eddie translated her question, Ally met her gaze. "No. I was hurt in the explosion, and when I woke up, I was in a hospital in Germany with no memory of what happened."

"And everyone else?" Eddie asked.

Ally sucked in a breath. "Dead."

"Liar," Wassim growled. "She has always been a liar. There were over fifteen people with her in the house. And only she survived? Impossible. Unless she had a hand in killing the rest."

Her body tensed. Three other men stood around the room. Although she couldn't see their guns, she was confident they were armed and would do whatever their boss commanded. She held her hands together in front of her and forced herself to stay still.

"He asks how you survived and no one else did?" Eddie translated.

"I don't know. I went back to the States after recovering from my wounds."

"She hated us all. The woman is here only for money," Wassim snapped upon hearing her response. "She should be dead, not standing in my home."

"The length of her life is not your decision to make, Wassim. And,"—Shariff stretched out his hands—"as far as this *home* is concerned, it is not yours. It is my father's. He will arrive Sunday so he can talk to her personally and hear the story for himself." He walked to her side and crossed his arms. "Let me be very clear to all of you. She is my bhaabi. My brother's wife. As such, *everyone* in this house will treat her with the respect she deserves. If she is hurt in any way, you will have to answer to not only me but my father. Understood?"

Wassim's scowl deepened, but he did not respond. A heavy silence fell upon the room as most glared and one smirked. "Now, will someone see to it that a nice room is prepared for her?"

Eddie nodded, grabbed her suitcase, and disappeared up the stairs.

"Excellent." Shariff wandered over and picked up the child from his father. The little boy looked between the lap he left to the face of the man who currently held him, as if trying to decide if he was happy with the change. "You're not scared of me, are you?" he asked the child in a singsong voice.

Ally remained rooted to the floor, willing the child to cry and run away. Unfortunately, the toddler grinned and shook his head.

Shariff laughed. "Smart boy. We are going to have a lot of fun together."

# CHAPTER TWENTY-ONE

## A DISHONORABLE DISCHARGE

*W*assim and Shariff walked off, discussing preparations for his father's arrival and leaving Ally and three of the guards alone. They were dressed the same, in jeans and long tunics. None of them stared at her, but she knew they were keenly aware of every breath she took. She looked over at the two people who did overtly stare at her—Alyah and her son. The child leaned against his mother's legs while he surveyed Ally. He tilted his chin and looked her over as if assessing her threat level. Once he'd deemed her safe, he raised a plump hand and pulled up four fingers. "*Mera naam Aadam hai. Main teen saal ka hu,*" he announced in Urdu.

"He says his name is Aadam. And that he is three," Eddie said while he descended the stairs. She walked over to the child and squatted to face him. His green eyes were pale and lighter than David's but they still reminded her of him and her chest ached. She stretched out her hand and grabbed the four fingers he still held out, giving it a squeeze.

"Hi, Aadam."

He stared at their connected hands curiously before letting out a giggle. The sound made her heart melt.

"Come, Adi, let's get some food." Although she said the words sweetly, the tension in Alyah's voice echoed through the room.

He ignored his mother's words about food and gave Ally a

hug. She disregarded the way the guards and Alyah stiffened and wrapped her arms around the tiny body. Emotion heated her face, and she made a silent promise to protect the child, even if it meant revealing the secret his parents would kill to keep hidden.

As soon as she released him, Alyah picked him up and retreated down the hall. "Let's go see what they've made for dinner," she said to her son as they disappeared. One of the men followed the mother and child out of the room.

Ally stayed on her knees, the warmth of his touch still lingering on her skin. Two days. She had two days to figure things out. She looked over her shoulder at Eddie. He stood by the stairs, arms crossed. But she wouldn't have to do it alone.

Ally sat on the private balcony connected to her room. For the first time since she woke up in Karachi, she was alone. It appeared no one wanted her company. Not that she minded. Her shoulders ached from the weight she carried. She stared at the barely touched plate of food in front of her. Fresh bread and bowls of lentils and mutton filled the dish. Alyah had always been an excellent cook. Her mutton had been one of Ally's favorite dishes, but eating was the furthest thing from her mind. There were so many other things she needed to figure out.

A faint summer breeze ruffled the sleeve of her shirt. Swirls of oranges, blues, and reds streaked across the horizon. She had always considered the setting sun as a promise of a new day. A shiver ran up her spine. Except now those promises no longer filled her with hope—more a sense of dread.

She rubbed her arms and stared at the courtyard below. A large stone water fountain of a white elephant sat in the center. Aadam squealed and ran toward it, his mother close behind. In her hand, she carried a plate of food, and while he looked for treasures on the ground, she filled his mouth with dinner. Alyah gazed up at the balcony where Ally sat. When their eyes locked, the scared mother looked away.

She rose from her plastic seat and took her dishes into her small bedroom. Eddie placed her in the farthest room on the third floor and, from what she could tell, far away from the mother and son. To her right was her private bathroom. Diagonal from it, her bed. The servants had laid out fresh linens and a peach coverlet embroidered with tiny flowers. A built-in closet, with wood the color of rich caramel, occupied the length of the wall beside the bed. The cabinets were the same as the two doors and the stand beside the bed. Inside the closet, women's clothes she'd never purchased were neatly arranged. She had already showered and taken the liberty of changing into one of the loose-fitting outfits.

A knock on the door startled her, almost making her drop her plate. She put a hand on her chest and slid the dish onto the bedside table but kept the fork in her hand.

"Sara Bhaabi, it's your doting brother-in-law." As saccharine as his words were, there was nothing sweet about him. His voice gritted against her ears. She tightened her hold on the utensil and opened the door.

His grin dropped slightly when he looked her over. "It appears your clothes are a little big on you."

Ally adjusted the wide neck of the red tunic. "I must have lost weight during the flight."

He chuckled. "Would you like to have a tour of the home and the grounds?"

"Do I have a choice?"

"Always." He winked and glanced down the hall. "By the way, it appears we both have our own guards following us around. So you may want to hand over the fork before they catch sight of it."

She leaned over in the direction he peered, noticing two men a few feet away. They stood side by side against the wall, one much taller than the other. The shorter one was clean-shaven, revealing his younger features. He stared at his phone, but she knew he watched her every move. The thick hair on the other man's head and beard was a mix of black and silver. He crossed his arms, tilted his head, and made no attempt to avert his gaze from hers. She stepped back into the safety of her quarters.

Shariff took the utensil from her hand and wandered into the space. Ally hovered by the entrance, unsure of who was more dangerous—the men in the hall or the one lurking around her room.

"Quaint," he said as he surveyed the bathroom and the patio. He tossed the fork to the floor and waved at the still open door. "Let's have some fun. Close the door."

The hair on her neck stood and goosebumps erupted across her skin. "I'm not sure Wassim would appreciate you being in a closed room alone with me."

The bed creaked when he sat on it and patted the spot beside him. "Which is exactly why you're going to come in and shut the door."

Ally closed it as ordered but did not join him.

He shrugged and bounced. "Wassim is a judgmental arse who will run and tell my father, another judgmental arse, everything. Why not give them something substantial to share?" The headboard slammed against the cement wall. "Excellent."

She leaned against the door, cringing as the thuds grew louder and faster. On the other side of the wall, two guards listened to the same sounds. "Are you almost done?"

Shariff chuckled. "A couple more minutes. Wouldn't want them to think I'm having a dishonorable discharge. Could you throw in a moan or a scream or something?"

She ignored his request, opened the door, and left the room. Both men remained in the same spot she left them, but now they were on their phones, one texting while the other pointed his device's lens at her. Shariff walked out of the room, pretending to adjust his clothes and fix his hair.

Her face heated at the proud smirk he flashed the men and at the camera recording him. Ally headed down the hall. "This is not a game," she hissed when he grabbed her wrist.

Shariff pushed her back against the wall and pressed his body against hers. "You're wrong."

Every muscle in her body froze except for her heart, which pounded hard against her chest.

"This. Is. A. Game," he whispered. "And no one is forcing you to join. So either play or leave." He kissed her cheek. "Just be sure to consider the consequences of your actions before you walk."

She dug her nails into her palms but didn't move.

"Well? Are you leaving?"

"No," Ally choked out.

"Excellent." Shariff released her, fixed the collar of her shirt, which had fallen off her shoulder, winked at the guards and the phone, and walked to the stairs.

The taller guard lowered his device and punched some keys while he wrinkled his nose and shook his head in disgust. She sucked in a breath and followed Shariff down.

"Let's start with the courtyard, seeing as how Alyah Bhaabi

and my nephew are there," he said from over his shoulder.

On the bottom floor, Wassim sat with his men huddled around him, staring at the mobile device in his hand. A tense silence fell across the room as soon as she and Shariff appeared. Most averted their eyes from her except for Wassim. He stroked his beard and curled his lip, refusing to lose their staring match. Hate and disgust filled his gaze; all of it aimed at her. Shariff hummed a tune and patted the man's shoulder as he walked past, but even then Wassim continued to track her.

Ally looked away and followed Shariff outside. The early evening breeze cooled her heated skin as soon as she exited the house. She filled her lungs with the air and tried to calm her emotions. Too much was at stake to allow her anger or shame to get the better of her. Yes, the man in front of her was in control, and everything was going according to his plan. A plan she needed to figure out by Sunday.

She paused mid-step and stared at the child Shariff approached. The heels of Aadam's bare feet kicked against the base of the fountain as he threw pebbles into the water. His mother sat beside him. She whispered a story to him and popped food in his mouth every so often. The attractive smile on her face was not one Ally had ever seen before. Alyah looked up and when she caught sight of them, her smile faded and body stiffened.

"Chacha!" the three-year-old screamed through his mouthful of rice.

Shariff laughed and waved. "Come. Let's show Sara Mommy around."

The knot in her belly tightened.

Ignoring his mother's commands to finish his meal, Aadam slid off the fountain, slipped on his sandals, and ran to his uncle.

"No. It's late. He needs to eat and get ready for bed," Alyah snapped as she headed for her son.

Shariff picked him up and wiped a smudge of food off his chin. "It's barely five. Let him come along, Bhaabi. I promise to bring him back soon."

Aadam wrapped his arms around Shariff's neck and hid his face in his shoulder. "Please, *Ammi*. I want to go with Chacha and Sara Mommy."

The bitter taste of acid burned Ally's throat. She silently prayed for Alyah to sense danger in the man holding her son and take Aadam away. Far away.

"It's fine. Let the child go." She looked over her shoulder at Wassim, who stood at the door. He waved at someone in the room with him. "Hassan."

Eddie appeared behind him.

"Go with them."

He nodded and walked outside.

Shariff stiffened. "No need. We are going to the well. I will keep him safe."

Wassim shook his head and waved for his guard to follow. "It's not you we're worried about. Hassan will go along."

Shariff turned to Ally, his scowl visible under the smile plastered on his face. "Apparently, it is not safe to walk the grounds with you alone," he translated and waved toward the path down the forest. "Shall we?"

"You shouldn't be with her, Shariff. She is not what you think," Alyah hissed as they walked past.

Her words didn't bother Ally. She had a feeling they may have helped more than hindered. Unlike the suits and short hair donned by Sayeed, he chose jeans and left his locks long. Shariff seemed like someone who wanted to break the rules set down by his father; he was the rebel of the Irfani family.

They wandered down the walking path into the gardens. Trees of various shapes and sizes stretched out above them, their leaves reaching for the clouds. Along the trail, roses and hibiscus bushes clustered together in various spots, forming beautiful groupings of colors. After a while, Aadam climbed out of Shariff's arms and ran ahead on the pebbled trail.

Ally walked beside Shariff in silence, pursuing the child a few feet ahead of them. Aadam's brown curls bounced as he moved. When he found a rock, an insect, a bird, anything he considered fascinating, he shrieked. His screams sent bursts of adrenaline through her already-anxious system, making her jump toward him. Each incident ended the same. He'd turn those enormous eyes up at her and show her his most recent find before moving along in search of another.

He was beautiful, and his laughter so infectious, a couple of times she forgot the danger and allowed his excitement to fill her, until she remembered the man pretending to be the doting uncle beside her.

Shariff side-eyed her. "What?"

"How do you sleep at night?"

His laugh echoed through the forest. "Curious about my sleeping arrangements?" He wrapped an arm around her waist and pulled her close. "If you're not careful, I might start thinking you really do want to get in my pants."

She fought the urge to pull away. Partly because she needed to understand him better, and partly because Eddie followed close behind, tracking their every move. Shariff pressed his mouth to her ear. "The man behind us is listening and will report it all back to his boss, so watch what you say."

Ally nodded. When she tried to step away, he held on tighter. "And for the record, I sleep quite well. You're welcome to join me and see for yourself."

She twisted out of his grasp and moved a few feet ahead. "So tell me the story about this house," she said loud enough for Eddie to hear.

Shariff caught up with her, his smile a bit tighter than a few seconds ago. "It was built over thirty years ago, after my parents married. Since my father spent half the year here doing business, he wanted to have a nice home when he came to town."

She glanced over at him. "Your father only lived here half the time?"

"Yes." He grabbed a flowered branch from a tree along their path and broke it off, handing it to her. "Smell this."

Tiny, white flowers bloomed along the thin limb. She didn't have to get too close for the blossoms' fragrant scent to fill her sinuses.

"It's a neem tree. My mother had several of them planted along the gardens."

She took the branch and pretended to admire the flowers. "Where were you the other half the time?"

"Here. Running around these grounds. Playing Hide and Seek under this very neem tree." He stopped beside the trunk and traced his hand over a heart carved on its trunk. "My father, on the other hand, was with his other family in Kabul."

Ally walked on, shadowing the child who ran several feet ahead. His resentment of his brother now made more sense. Shariff only had a father six months out of the year. "How does a boy running around Karachi end up with an English accent?"

He caught up with her again. "After my mother passed, I was sent to boarding school. I've lived in England ever since."

She watched him from the corner of her eye. For the first time, his mask had lowered and a flash of pain passed across his face. "How did she die?"

"You know those lovely stairs we descended back in the house?" He pointed over his shoulder. "I watched my big brother, your late husband, push her down them."

Ally paused mid-step and turned to face him, unsure of how to respond.

"Chacha!" Aadam hollered. Shariff winked, grabbed the branch from her hand, and walked ahead to attend to the child.

She glanced over her shoulder at the expressionless guard trailing. He directed her with his eyes to continue.

She found uncle and nephew staring at a hole at the base of a tree. Shariff dug the branch into the entrance, explaining how it was the home of the chipmunk the child had seen. Once Aadam was satisfied with the information, he moved on.

How much pain and anger brewed under the smile Shariff donned? She'd already seen glimpses of it, but clearly not the true intensity of his emotions. He watched a brother he barely knew kill his mother. Then he was sent off to boarding school, ripped away from probably the only home he knew.

Shariff twined his fingers through Ally's as they followed the child. "What did your father do about Sayeed?"

He shrugged. "Nothing. According to him, she tripped. His precious son wasn't capable of doing such a thing."

"So to shut you up, he sent you away to another country?"

His smile tightened. "He visited a few times, but he had another family to consider." Shariff waved his hand as if to swat her words away. "It made me stronger."

Now he wanted restitution. Punishment for the pain he'd suffered, but his memories of the home weren't all painful. Ally stared across the pink and orange foliage of the hibiscus bushes beside them. "Coming home must make you feel closer to your mother."

"It does, actually. More than I realized." Shariff looked her over. "You mentioned your parents were killed when you were young. What happened?"

He gave her palm a squeeze. Ally focused on their connected hands. She needed him to align with her. "The bridge their train traveled on collapsed. Two weeks later, I left my home in India to live with my uncle in America."

He shook his head. "We seem to share the same story, just a different continent. They treated you well?"

"No," she lied. Although she had some challenges with her aunt in the beginning, they were her rocks, and somewhere out there, they worried about her. Her face heated at the way their last conversation had gone. Her family spent the time telling her they loved her and were worried about her. She spent it pushing them away.

Shariff's reassuring hand gave her another squeeze. "The ugly skeletons in our closets are plentiful, aren't they?"

The exact reaction she hoped for. Ally nodded her response to him and walked ahead to catch up with Aadam.

Once the happy child was within her reach, she slowed her pace. He ran to her and wrapped his tiny hand around hers as they strolled along the path together. The feel of his warmth, the sound of his laughter, fused him to her. How could Shariff or anyone else even consider hurting this child? It was a question she needed to investigate further. She released Aadam's hand and waited for his uncle. When Shariff was beside her, she grabbed his arm, pretending to work on dislodging an invisible pebble from her shoe. "So, Sayeed took your family when you were six, and now you're going to take his?"

He leaned in close. "I never said such a thing. I'm only reclaiming what's mine."

Ally considered her words before uttering them. "Why does reclaiming what's yours have to mean killing others?"

Shariff shot her an angry look. "Keep your voice low," he hissed.

Her stomach twisted. "He's just a child," she whispered.

He waved her words away and pointed ahead. "See the crumbled mess over there?" Aadam tapped his hand against the curved bricked platform Shariff mentioned. "It's a well. When I was a child, a servant's son fell into it."

Her breath caught in her throat and her hands clenched. Too short to see over its wall, the toddler stood on his tiptoes and grabbed on to the ledge to pull himself higher. One of the bricks he gripped crumbled, falling to his feet.

Shariff crossed his arms and watched, as if waiting to see what the child would do. "It took most of the day before someone finally found his body floating in there. Parsa, the poor mother, was such a mess for years."

Ally rushed forward. She reached the child before he made a second attempt to climb and lifted him into her arms. Aadam wrapped a hand around her neck and leaned forward over the edge, looking into the black waters below. She kept a firm grip around his body while he pointed into the darkness and rambled about the water and the plants growing inside it. Any doubt she had that Shariff would hurt the child vanished. The man was indeed related to Sayeed.

Shariff grabbed a nearby metal pail and dropped it into the mouth of the well. The child craned his neck, searching for the source of the splash. His uncle held the rope connected to the pail out for him. "Want to pull?"

Reluctantly, she let the squirming boy climb out of her arms and onto his feet. He grabbed the tightly wound cord. Unsure of the man's plans, she kept a firm grip on the child's shirt.

"This spot used to be one of my favorites when I was young." Shariff poured the pail of water onto the ground. An elated Aadam stretched his sandaled foot into the stream and stomped in the puddle.

Ally edged closer to Shariff and whispered, "He's done nothing wrong."

"Neither did I." He tossed the pail back into the well and began to pull up another bucket full of water.

"You're still alive. He won't be."

Shariff poured the contents of the pail down in a steady stream. Aadam ran out of her grasp and positioned himself under the falling liquid, drenching himself. His uncle laughed at the happy but wet child. "Who knows? He may prefer death. There were many times I wished for it."

Her muscles tense, she watched the child's every move. "Why now? If this was your plan, why didn't you reclaim your things when Sayeed was alive?"

Shariff put the pail on the ground and shook his head at the wet, giggling child. "I'm always late. It's one of my character flaws."

The child pulled at the shirt glued to his skin and begged his uncle to do it again.

"His father's dead. You can't punish a dead man."

Aadam picked up the empty bucket and turned it over onto his head. Squeals echoed from under the container.

"Who said it's a dead man I'm trying to punish?"

She nodded her understanding. "You're punishing your father?"

Shariff didn't respond. He took the bucket off the child and picked him up. "Stubbornness, by the way, is my other flaw. Once I make up my mind, it's hard to convince me otherwise. Come, let's get him back home. He's all wet. We wouldn't want him to die from a cold." He winked.

As they walked back down the road to the house, Ally thought about Alyah and Wassim's secret, wondering if the truth might save them all. "What if he's not Sayeed's? Wouldn't that be punishment enough?"

He rolled his eyes. "Making up lies will not change anything. My father believes this is his beloved son's child. Nothing and no one on this planet will change his mind."

The child wiped his wet face against Shariff's shirt and pointed up to the sky while he talked about airplanes to his uncle.

"He could be Wassim's. For all we know, he could have been conceived shortly after Sayeed died. Have you had him tested?"

"Getting desperate, are we?" Shariff moved the long, wet curls out of Aadam's face and pulled at one of the ringlets. "We have the same hair and the same interests. Watch." He looked into the child's eyes and grinned. "Tell Sara Mommy what sound airplanes make," he said in Urdu.

The child beamed and waved his hand in the air, making engine sounds. Shariff laughed. "See, we both love planes. What more proof do you need?"

It was exactly what she worried would happen. He looked too much like Sayeed for them to question his paternity. Her eyes burned. "None of what happened was his fault."

"We all pay the price for our family's actions, don't we?" Shariff's face darkened. He took in the house looming ahead. "You know the old saying about the sins of the father."

# CHAPTER TWENTY-TWO

## TWO HUNDRED SECONDS

*T*he tension in Ally's body eased the moment she walked into her room and locked it. She leaned against the door and rubbed the throbbing of her temples while she processed the conversation with Shariff.

He wasn't like his big brother. Sayeed had one motivation: power. Shariff's obsession was more complicated. He wanted to fix the hand dealt by his family. He was right; it wasn't about a house. His desire centered on punishing his father for choosing Sayeed over him. Which, in his twisted brain, meant killing the old man and everyone involved, including Aadam. For all their sakes, she needed to convince him it would never ease his pain, only make it worse.

She sat on the corner of her bed. But there was another layer. Abandoned by his family at an early age and left to grow up in an institution, a part of him still hungered for a familial connection. It explained why he possessively called her "his bhaabi" every chance he got. Even the hand holding he did. She was his.

From the corner of her eye, a dark shadow moved. When she looked up, Ally stared into the hungry gaze of a man standing in her bathroom. Her heart leaped to her throat as the guard from the hallway stepped into her room. A large mole covered his right temple and his thick beard stretched when he grinned.

She rose and stood tall, trying to hide the tremors rocking her.

"How did you get in here?"

He didn't answer.

When he took another step, Ally inched toward the door. She knew the expression on his face, had seen it a hundred times before in Sayeed's. It wasn't just lust; it was an angry hunger. One he believed only she could quench. She ran for the exit, but he stepped ahead, blocking it with his body.

He grinned, waving his long fingers at her, beckoning her. "Please, run to me. I want you to pull me away from the door. I think I would like that."

She stepped back, pointing at the entrance behind him. "Go." It was a simple word. One most people around the world understood. "Go!" she yelled a second time.

When he lunged at her, Ally jumped out of his reach and tripped over the foot of the bed, falling on the floor.

"You are a bold one, aren't you?" His grin widened. "How bold will you be underneath me?"

She slid backward toward the patio as he approached. He was a tall man. His long arms stretched out in anticipation of her attempts to escape. He pointed to her with his index finger and flicked the digit up. "Take your shirt off. I want to see what you showed Shariff earlier today."

Ally climbed to her feet, her back to the door. Her heart thudded an erratic beat as she felt for the knob. "Go, and I will not tell Wassim you ever came here." She unlocked it and twisted the handle while keeping her attention on the man in front of her.

He laughed and shook his head. "I don't understand you, but if you are threatening to tell Wassim, don't worry. He sends his love."

She turned and opened the door at the same time. Before she could run out into the balcony, he slammed his body into hers, shoving her face first against the wooden surface. The entrance rammed shut from the force of him, and the knob dug into her groin, leaving her breathless.

Ally put her palms on the flat surface and pushed off only to have him grind harder into her. The door's brass handle stabbed into her side and she cried out in pain.

With his hips, he secured her midsection in place and grabbed her wrists. Fire coursed through her shoulder blades when he yanked her arms over her head and restrained her two hands with one of his.

"Let me go!" she screamed as she slammed her head back, trying to make contact with his.

A salty hand slapped across her face, covering her mouth and pulling her neck back until her head rested on his shoulder.

"You enjoy spending time alone with Shariff in this room." The sharp bristles of his beard pierced into her skin when he kissed her neck. The mix of scotch and cigarettes on his breath suffocated her. "In your bed." He continued to press his lips against her while he spoke. "Going for walks alone with him."

She kicked backward while she tried to bite into his palm. In return, he dug his fingers into her cheeks. Pain coursed through her jaw, making her ears ring.

"I hope you fight me like this the whole time." His beard scraped her cheek as he spoke.

She twisted her body, trying to free herself of his grasp. He shoved his hips harder into hers, his arousal digging into her back. "This evening when you were outside, the sunlight went through your shirt. I liked what I saw."

Hot tears fell from her eyes when he sucked on her neck. *Not again.* The words screamed on repeat in her mind. A sob escaped her lips. Restrained and held against her will. Yes, it would happen again. A loud crack resonated through the room. A second later, the guard's grasp on her loosened until finally he released her.

Ally's legs buckled and she fell to her knees. She looked up and gasped when her gaze landed on Eddie. He stood with an arm wrapped around the man's chest and the other around his head. The guard's body sat limp in his grasp, his lifeless eyes wide.

Ally climbed up on unsteady legs as terror rocked her, watching Eddie lay the man on the floor.

"Look away." He ordered while he took his sandals off. He tossed them at the closet and then proceeded to take off his shirt and pants until he wore nothing but white briefs. He reached for a metal rod lying across her bed.

Unable to speak, Ally gasped for air and leaned against the wall for support.

He raised the rod over his shoulder and stared at her. "You need to close your eyes," he whispered.

She couldn't move, couldn't think. The realization of what

almost happened sent wave after painful wave of hysteria coursing through her.

"Alisha, close your eyes. Now," he growled.

She nodded and turned her face, shuttering her lids. The thud of metal slamming into flesh and bone filled the space. Bones crunched and cracked over and over. Every now and then, the pipe echoed when it hit tile. Mingled in with the sounds was the metallic smell of blood, which filled her nostrils. The warmth of the liquid seeping between her toes burned her skin. Ally swallowed down the rising bile and covered her ears to block it all out. Long after the noises ceased, her body continued to tremble.

Something warm splattered against her neck. She took her hands away from her ears and opened her eyes. Eddie stood in front of her, shaking his blood-soaked hand at her, coloring her clothes and skin with spots of red. She stared at him, avoiding the body crumpled a few feet away.

He handed the wet pipe to her, "Take this." She gripped the handle, still warm from his touch, and pointed it out in front of her. Tiny strands of black and gray curls were glued in the thick red fluid flowing down the pipe and covering her hands. Nausea filled her.

"Count to two hundred and then scream for help."

She lowered the pipe so the blood would flow to the ground and rested her back against the wall behind her while the room spun around her.

"Look at me."

Ally stared into his hazel gaze. "I need you to listen," he said slowly.

She nodded.

Eddie grabbed his shirt from the bed and wiped all remnants of the man off his face, neck, and hands onto the fabric. "After you're done counting, you will unlock that door, and scream until people show up. Okay?"

Ally nodded again.

He took the wadded fabric and proceeded to clean the rest of his body. "You killed him, understood?"

Eddie lifted his leg from the puddle and wiped it and his foot down. "He was in here waiting for you and you told him to leave. He pushed you in and locked the door." He then worked on the other leg. "You grabbed the rod and defended yourself." He put on his pants, slid on his clean sandals, and stared at her, waiting for her to respond.

Ally continued to nod.

He opened the far door to her closet and tossed the balled-up clothes inside. "You found the rod in the guest bathroom, and you took it and kept it hidden under your bed just in case."

Eddie hesitated at the closet door and looked her over. "What did I say?"

"I killed him. I hit him on the head with the rod and killed him."

This time Eddie nodded. "And I wasn't here."

When she hugged her waist with her free hand, more of the man's blood smeared against her red shirt, soaking into her skin. "You weren't here."

By the time Ally looked back up, he was gone and she was alone. For the next two hundred seconds, she stood beside the crushed remains of a dead man. When she got to the magic number, she finally looked at the remains on the floor and screamed.

# CHAPTER TWENTY-THREE

## QUESTIONS AND ANSWERS

or the past hour, Ally sat on the edge of the bed, staring at the floor by the patio. Spotless. As were the walls and the sheets. The old curtains on the back door were ripped away and replaced with fresh ones. Even she was clean. And yet, the warmth of his blood burned her skin. The smell of his death lingered in every breath she took.

If she stared at the spot by the patio hard enough, she could still see him, flat on his back, blood and matter flowing from the gashes in what was once his head. She blinked away the image and crawled to the corner of the room beside the closet. Curling into a ball, she huddled on the floor, her back pressed into the corner, working on taking slow deep breaths. Ally forced her lids to stay closed but the images continued to consume her.

She hugged her knees, waiting for sleep to arrive and provide much-needed respite. But it refused to answer her calls, possibly because she couldn't stop glancing over at the spot, waiting for the dead man to return. At some point, exhaustion finally won, lulling her to sleep. When she did, she found she was right; he did return—in her dreams, and this time he was not alone. The man carried the metal rod covered in his blood, and behind him, Sayeed watched, nodding his approval.

Before the weapon slammed into her head, Ally popped her lids open and jumped to her knees. She slapped the air, fighting away the imaginary danger. She blinked a few more times before finally allowing herself to breathe.

The only sound in the room was her gasping for air. Ally sat on her haunches and rested her damp face in her hands. "It's just a dream," she whispered.

She worked on calming herself, only to suck in a breath when a shadow moved in the room. Ally froze. Her head still in her palms, she peered at the white marble around her, until her gaze landed on the jean-clad legs of the man kneeling in front of her. Her nails dug into her skin as she considered her options. The rod wasn't in the room anymore. They'd taken it when they cleaned up. She thought about the padlock she'd fastened to her door. A guard had handed it to her after they cleaned the room. Considering it fastened from the inside, there was no way anyone could have unlocked it. Which meant...

"It's me," Eddie whispered.

She released the breath she held at the sound of his voice. Ally took her hands off her face and slid back to her corner on the floor, hugging her arms around her knees. "How did you get here?"

"Through the closet." He sat back on his haunches and stared her down. "Are you okay?"

Uncontrollable tremors rocked her body. She grit her teeth and nodded. "Yes."

He eyed her, clearly not believing her answer.

She put up her hand. "I'm fine. Just give me a moment. This is the first time I've felt safe since everything happened. I think it's all hitting me at once." Her voice shook as much as her body.

He pressed his fingers against the bruises below her hands. "I noticed these when you showed up at the door yesterday. What happened?"

Ally stared down at the red welts around her wrists. "Shariff handcuffed me in the car."

Eddie's eyes darkened.

"Tell me how you ended up here while I work on my breathing." She sucked in a breath and began counting.

He nodded his understanding. "I have a contact in Kabul who works for Sayeed's father. After Farah disappeared, I reached out to him. He told me something was going down. Said the old man was preparing to come to Karachi. Breathe out now."

She nodded, blew, and continued her slow repetitions,

allowing his voice to calm her.

"He hadn't left the country in over a decade, so clearly whatever it was, was a big deal. One he needed an English-speaking translator for. Apparently, he was also getting the house prepped for a new resident, a child." He rose and grabbed the blanket from the bed, draping it around Ally's shoulders as he talked. "After I took care of the guy he hired, I stepped in."

Her body finally calm, she wrapped the fabric tight around her and thought of Aadam. His grandfather planned to steal him away, and his uncle planned to kill him. Somehow, she needed to help the child.

Eddie slid down beside her and rested his arms on his bent knees. "Better?"

She nodded. "Thank you."

"Don't thank me yet. You're still in danger."

"What are we going to do?"

He leaned his back against the wall. "I'm going to get you out of here tonight while it's still dark."

"No."

Eddie continued on as if he didn't hear her. "There's a spot in the back of the yard where you can safely climb over the fence."

Ally reached out and squeezed his hand. "I'm not leaving."

Silence filled the room. His fingers flexed into a fist under her grasp.

She let go and tried to explain. "I am the reason he kidnapped Farah and Amirah. And I am the reason he killed Amir and David. He needed to lure me here. Your sister and the baby are his guarantee that I will stay and comply. If you want me to leave, you need to find them and get them to safety."

Eddie turned his focus on her. He clenched his teeth so hard the muscle along his jaw flexed. "What the fuck do you think I've been trying to do this entire time?" he hissed.

"I know you have." Ally grabbed his hand a second time and squeezed. "It's the only reason you're here, and it must be killing you that you haven't found them."

He didn't respond, but the muscles in his hand relaxed. His thumb rubbed against her injured wrist.

"If you sneak me out of here and they die..."

He rested his head against the wall and let out a sigh. "It's a risk I have to take. *Everyone* in this building wants you dead. Tonight was the first attempt."

She knew neither of them would back down from their decision, so she changed the subject. "I saw them."

His fingers fisted again, and his eyes slammed shut. "Has he hurt them?"

She shook her head. "So far she and the baby have been treated well."

Eddie let out a breath and pulled his hand out of hers. He ran his fingers through his short hair. "All this time, I had no clue if she was dead or alive."

The pain in his voice stabbed at her. She hugged the blanket to her body and continued, hoping her information would help. "The man who kidnapped me five years ago. His name is Bashar. I'm pretty sure he helped kill Amir and took Farah and the baby."

"I know."

Her brows rose. "You knew?"

"I mean I didn't know until yesterday. When you showed up at the door, I realized things hadn't gone according to plan. I snuck out and tracked down Leanna."

The mention of the escort's name sent relief flooding through Ally. "She's okay? I didn't know what else to do. I had no choice but to leave her and go with him."

Eddie nodded. "We know, and she's fine. She ended up with a concussion and a highly bruised ego." He grinned. "Which is a good thing because she tracked down the janitors who helped Bashar and got them to talk. Turns out he's been holed up in Germany for the past four years and had hired them to do some jobs here and there."

A shudder went through Ally at the mention of the men in the airport. "How did they know I was going to be on the plane?"

"Someone bugged your house. Leanna found about three months worth of tapes in Bashar's home."

Ally's chest tightened. Her thoughts turned to her family and the danger she'd put them all in. "My parents still live there."

He nodded. "Leanna's already had them sweep your place clean. Your family is under their watch. I'm not worried. It was you Shariff and Bashar were after, not them."

She stared at the wall ahead. "Did they kill Amir? And where are the boys?"

Eddie rubbed his palms on his knees. "Farah and Amir lived in Dresden. The janitors helped kidnap my sister and niece. Amir got in the way and ended up with a bullet in the head. They claim Bashar pulled the trigger."

"Bashar wants me dead. He killed Amir because of me." So many lives damaged because of her. "I think he had something to do with David's death too," she said in a low voice.

"Leanna tracked him and the half dozen or so aliases she found in his house." Eddie's voice remained without inflection as he scanned the space. He was in work mode. His brain trying to put all the pieces of the puzzle together. "Turns out he was in Philadelphia a little over four months ago. Even found footage of him with another man."

None of what he said surprised her. "Was he the one they have on video, running away from David's accident?"

Eddie shot her a look. A look that made her pause. He cleared his throat. "Not Bashar, but the guy he was with, yes."

"Do you know who it was?"

Eddie stared at the wall across the room. "Yeah, but first tell me everything you know."

Considering he wanted to find his sister, the request made sense. For the next fifteen minutes, Ally described in detail the incident at the airport, to waking up in the hotel, the burqa Shariff made her wear, her time with Farah and the baby, the multiple car changes, and how Shariff altered his appearance. Through it all, Eddie stayed next to her, listening to her every word, interrupting her every now and then for clarification.

Ripples of tension flowed from him. "Tell me what you know about the house she is being kept in."

Ally closed her eyes, trying to remember. "It's a new home. I could smell fresh paint and wood stain. Two bedrooms. One bath. Hers is the one by the kitchen, and they keep the key to Farah's room in the kitchen drawer to the left of the sink. There's a small grassy front yard with a black metal gate. The iron on the gate was shaped like ivy. There were other houses on either side of it. And in the distance, there were three white high-rises. Maybe about twenty stories tall? They had these orange pyramid-looking structures on their roofs."

"That helps. I'll call in a favor to see if we can find aerial footage of the vehicle you came in today, and we can do a scan for those buildings. With as many spies in the sky that we have, they should be able to backtrack the car to the house."

She shook her head. "You won't be able to. We changed cars twice on the way here, and he even changed clothes in the process. He said he doesn't trust anyone."

He leaned his head back and let out a soft growl. "Motherfucker."

It was an excellent description of Shariff. She thought back to the conversation she had with him in the garden. "He hasn't said so, but I think he's going to kill Aadam as some perverse way of hurting his father. I have to..."

"Do nothing," Eddie snapped. His lips flattened into a thin line. "I'm not sure you're grasping the seriousness of this situation." He put up a finger. "David and Amir are dead." A second digit joined the first. "Farah and her baby are locked up in some room I can't seem to find." A third was added. "They were waiting for you at Frankfurt, and Leanna, a trained agent, was attacked and left unconscious." A fourth digit flipped open. "A man died in this very room a few hours ago." He added a fifth. "And finally, if I hadn't been here"—he aimed all five fingers at the spot where the guard's body had laid—"that asshole and his horny buddies downstairs would have drilled their dicks into every hole in your body until the sun came up, and then killed you. I know this because that's what they said they'd do and all before they took a sip of their morning coffee."

His words stabbed into her, making her stomach twist. She blinked and stared at his hand and the five fingers he now waved in her face. "And most of this in under twenty-four hours," he continued. "You can't do a damn thing about any of it. So what we're going to do is climb down that closet hole and sneak you out of here tonight."

Time had run out. She'd avoided the argument as long as she could. She climbed to her feet and stared down at him. "Until I know Farah and the baby are safe, my leaving is not an option," she whispered. "I am not the person you need to worry about. Just find them and get them out of Karachi. I can take care of myself."

He rolled his eyes. "Do you really think my sister would let me leave you behind? And for that matter, your husband..."

"Is dead," she finished. Ally's face heated but she kept her voice low and calm. "And he can't do a damn thing to help either of us."

Eddie ran his fingers down his scalp. "Clearly your heart is in the right place, and thanks for that." He stood and planted his hands on his hips. "But you're not trained for this. Which is why I need to get you out of here tonight."

Ally stepped closer until her face was inches from his. "I'm not a dog. And you're not allowed to pat me on the head and send me on my merry way." She jabbed a finger into his chest. "If I leave, Shariff promised to sell your sister and her baby. Do you want them hurt?"

The vein on his neck pulsed. "No."

"Then let me help you."

He grabbed her finger and scowled. "Help me do what? Swoop in on your invisible jet and use your golden lasso to free my sister from her evil captives?"

Eddie's words stung but she didn't retreat. She watched the way the skin above his collar turned deep red. The color crawled up his long, thick neck. He released her hand. "The only problem with your plan is the fact you don't have super powers."

"I think you should leave."

His light brown orbs stayed fixed on her, and he didn't move. In fact, she couldn't tell if he was breathing. Finally, the corner of his mouth curved up. "I'm all you've got, and you're asking me to leave?"

"I don't need your help." Ally kept her voice void of the uncertainty within. "I need you to go find your sister. And if you don't leave now, I'm going to open the door and scream for help."

"Is this some crazy suicide mission you're on?"

"In a way, yes." Her face stung from the implications of his words. "My husband is dead. Amir is dead. And if your sister and baby are hurt... It. Will. Kill. Me."

He slammed his eyes shut, and his chest rose as he sucked in a breath. "You don't belong here, Alisha."

"Neither do they, Eddie. But here we are. Look at me." He complied. "Use me."

His shoulders slumped. "If your husband were alive, he'd surgically remove my balls and staple them to my head if he knew I was even considering this."

She smiled. "Yes, he would."

# CHAPTER TWENTY-FOUR

## RAZAA

Eddie rubbed the back of his neck and paced. "Okay."

Ally released the breath she held. She seated herself on the bed and patted the spot next to her. "Tell me what you know."

He situated himself on the edge of the mattress beside her and turned to face her. "After Amir was murdered and my sister and niece disappeared, I did some digging. Turns out David sent Farah an email the day before she was kidnapped, asking her to meet him."

She tilted her head in confusion. "He's been gone for over four months and your sister was kidnapped a few days ago."

His head bobbed. "Exactly. Dead people don't write emails. And then I searched deeper and found one she sent him a week before he wound up dead."

Ally's breath hitched. "David never told me."

"I figured as much. He didn't respond to it, either." Eddie tucked one of his legs under him and leaned forward. "Your husband did everything right. Farah messed up by reaching out to him. But I don't think she led Bashar to you. It was the opposite. Her email to David led Bashar to her."

Her hand covered her mouth. "Because he already knew where I lived and was monitoring us."

"Exactly."

Ally scooted across the mattress until her back hit the wall and stretched her feet out. "Then why wait until now to make a move?"

"Not sure. What I do know is I ran a scan of all yours and David's accounts about a year ago, and they came up clean for spyware etc. When I ran it again a few days after his death, I found fingerprints."

Tension thudded against her temples as he talked. Ally pressed her fingers into the spots and shook her head. All this time, they'd been in danger and didn't even know it.

"Something else I don't understand is how my sister tracked down David and why."

A smile tugged at Ally's lips. "When we were stuck in the compound, I had Farah memorize David's contact information. In case she ever got away and needed help, I knew David would do whatever he could for her."

He looked over at her, a flash of hurt shot across his face. "If she needed help, why didn't she ask me?"

"She was about to have a baby, Eddie. Emotions are high during the third trimester. With all those men around her, she probably felt very scared and alone and needed a mother or sister. Speaking of which, you didn't answer my question earlier about the boys. How are they?"

"Fine."

Ally shot him a look. Something felt off. "Shariff keeps asking me about them and where they are, so I'm assuming they are somewhere safe."

He nodded and cleared his throat. "How's Farah holding up?"

The question made the pulsing in her head intensify. "She thinks David and Amir will come and get us out of here."

The space filled with silence.

"She doesn't know?" he whispered.

Ally's eyes brimmed at the memory. "I couldn't tell her. She needed to believe they were still out there." She thought about the man who stood outside Farah's room, monitoring her every move. "There was someone else there. He wore a mask."

Eddie stiffened. "What do you remember? Heavy, skinny, tall?"

"Tall and skinny. Maybe a beard or mustache under there. I

got the feeling he knew me and didn't like me."

His eyes stayed glued to her. "Young?"

"Possibly. The way he carried himself seemed younger, but I'm not sure." She eyed him. "You know who it is, don't you?"

He cut her a look as if weighing the decision. "After the explosion three years ago, the orphans were sent to live with different families."

Ally leaned toward him, not sure she heard correctly. "What do you mean different families? You said there were living with Farah and Amir. Who did you separate?"

Eddie clasped his fingers together and cleared his throat. "All of them."

A stunned silenced fell between them. He had avoided her questions about the boys and, when she'd been direct, provided one-word responses. Now she knew why. She cleared her throat and kept her voice low. "Those boys grew up in the same orphanage. They were adopted *together* by Sayeed. They *only* had each other all their lives, and you ripped them apart?" Her gaze fixed on him. "Why would you tear them apart?"

"Because of my sister, I had no choice." He lowered his head. "With the kind of security clearance I have, a first-degree relative, who is a foreign national and resides in another country, is considered a liability by the Agency and would cause questions of loyalty. So it was best to not say anything about Farah and let them split everyone up."

The pulsing in her temples intensified. "Do you know how traumatic it must have been for them to not only lose the only father they ever had but also be separated from each other?"

He nodded. "Better traumatized than dead, like Amir. If they had been with my sister, what would have happened to them?"

His words chilled her.

Eddie rubbed the back of his neck. "I did what I needed to do to keep everyone safe. You can be as mad as you like. But we need to work together, and it also means you need to know the rest."

The pounding spread from her temples to across her forehead. She worked the tense area and braced herself. "The rest? What do you mean the rest?"

"One of the boys disappeared about a year ago."

Her brain went straight to the man in the mask. "Who?"

"Razaa."

Ally's heart broke as soon as Eddie uttered his name. The strongest and most assertive, he was the natural leader and kept an eye on the rest. She'd seen firsthand his deep love for his family, his brothers, her.

"They sent him to live with a family in Istanbul, but things didn't go so well. The couple who took him in said he was sullen and angry all the time, and they weren't surprised when he disappeared."

"What have you done?" She thought about the man in the mask from the day before and the way he stared at her. She'd seen anger in his gaze; a testament to how hard his life must have been out in the world alone.

"I tried to find him. I got a lead he was under the care of an asshole in Qatar, known for rescuing kids like him and promising to take care of them but in reality using them for labor. The unlucky ones end up prostituting themselves all over the world."

Ally lowered her head in her hands, and an overwhelming ache for Razaa rocked her. She'd failed him. Failed them all.

"Someone who looked like him was spotted with a group of migrant workers in Madrid, and then Istanbul a few months later. But every time I followed up on a lead, they were gone. A few days before David's accident, a group of them was smuggled through San Diego into the US. From the videos I've seen, he and Bashar were with them."

She removed her hands and glanced at Eddie. "You think Razaa had something to do with David's death?"

He shook his head. "I don't think, I know. He was the hooded figure running away after the accident."

Her lungs turned to ice, trying to make sense of it all. "Razaa is not a killer."

"Funny thing to say, considering Sayeed trained him to kill."

There were so many unknowns in this equation, but this was not one of them. She shook her head. "Doesn't matter what Sayeed trained him to do. It doesn't even matter that you took him away from his brothers when he needed them most. I know him."

Eddie flashed her a knowing look. "If I recall, there was another kid you knew real well, and he turned out to be a suicide bomber. I'm thinking you might be a little biased on the good kid label."

"Umber didn't know about the bomb. He thought he was meeting me in there," she snapped.

"Sure, and this one didn't know either, right? He doesn't know he's holding my sister and niece against their will. He doesn't know he's killed Amir and David."

Ally thought back to the days in the compound. Umber was the smallest and weakest of the group. Often, when he was picked on by the other brothers, Razaa stepped in, making the others back off. Until she knew what was going on, she was going to cling to the boy she remembered. "So how did he end up with Shariff?"

"My guess is he must have bought Razaa."

*Bought Razaa?* Ally leaned her head against the wall and looked at the ceiling as she fought the tears. This was not the time to cry for him. She cleared her throat and worked on staying focused. "What do you know about Shariff?"

Eddie nodded. "What you know, they have the same father, Rizwan Irfani, but different mothers. Rizwan's made a fortune off selling Afghani jewels on the black market. When Sayeed got old enough, he talked Daddy into expanding his business to a whole new type of trade—people.

"Sayeed ran it for a few years until he got bored and moved on to the weapons industry. From what I'm understanding, since Shariff is such a people person, Rizwan let him take over the human trafficking part of the company."

Bile rose up her throat, and her face twisted at the bitter taste of it all.

"Clearly there was no love lost between the brothers."

"Sayeed killed Shariff's mother," Ally answered.

"Not surprising."

She nodded. "He pushed her down the stairs. Shariff told his dad, but he didn't believe him and sent him off to boarding school. He ended up losing everything and now he wants revenge."

"By killing his entire family. I get that. But what's your role in all this?"

She rubbed the pounding ache in her head. "I got the impression I'm the reason his dad's coming to Karachi. He's hoping if I'm alive that maybe Sayeed is too."

"Considering the old man hasn't left his men or compound in Afghanistan in over a decade, Shariff's using his father's hopes as a way to lure him here. A great opportunity to have everyone together and kill them all. Basically using you as bait."

She didn't respond. So much needed to be done before Rizwan arrived.

"But I've seen the way he looks at you," Eddie continued. "It's not only bait he wants to use you for."

She stared at the mattress and didn't deny the statement. Nor did she confess that her body was something she would offer to Shariff if necessary.

Eddie climbed off the bed. "I need to reach out to some friends and see if they can use the information you gave me to find Farah. In the meantime, you need to do me a couple favors."

Ally looked up at him.

"Here." He pulled out a padlock and key from his pocket and handed it to her. "Swap this one out for the one Wassim left for you. Seeing as how they have an extra key to theirs, it's not going to do you any good. There are latches on both sides of the door. When you leave the room, put it on the outside. When you're in the room, put it on the inside. Use it at all times and always keep the key on you. Understood?"

Ally laid the lock on the bed.

"Trust no one. Talk to no one. I'll figure out the rest."

She traced her finger over the cold metal shackle. "Get Farah and Amirah out of there. You don't need to come back."

"Alisha, look at me." He stood by the open closet door and stared down at her. "I'll be back by morning. Understood?"

She nodded.

He lowered himself to his knees and slid a thick chunk of the concrete floor to the side, revealing the bright light of the space below.

Her pulse heightened at the thought of being alone in the house without him.

He sat on the edge and hung his legs over it. "Stay away from Wassim. He wants you dead. You know the kid's his, not Sayeed's. But you killing his favorite guard was the exact opposite outcome of what he'd planned. Stick close to Shariff. Considering he's using you to lure his old man out, he needs you to stay alive...until tomorrow anyway."

A shudder ripped through her.

And then he was gone. The cement block made no sound as it returned to its spot. She walked over and eyed the floor before closing the closet.

Ally spent most of the night pacing her bedroom. Could Razaa have been involved in David and Amir's deaths? The fourteen-year-old she remembered wasn't a killer, but at the same time, life events changed people. He had gone through some intense trauma the past few years. Her chest tightened. Unnecessary trauma none of them should have ever had to endure. But a killer? He looked up to Amir, worshiped the man.

There had to be more to this story. If there wasn't, then Eddie was right and he killed David. A shudder went through her. If Razaa was a killer, she'd deal with the consequences when the time came. With Eddie off to find his sister, she had other issues to address. Like how to keep Aadam safe.

She walked around the spot where the guard died and peeked out the patio curtains. Dawn streaked the black sky with orange and yellows. Most of the house still slept. The key word was most. One person would be awake. And it was time they had a chat.

# CHAPTER TWENTY-FIVE

## THE LIE

*D*ressed in loose jeans and a pale yellow tunic, Ally left the safety of her bedroom. She snuck down the quiet halls, her senses heightened for lurking danger. When she descended the stairs, she moved close to the banister and gripped the rail. Another woman had fallen down the very steps she currently took, and more than one of the home's residents would love for Ally to have the same fate. At the bottom, she stared around the dark, empty living space and approached the hallway in the back of the room.

Rays of golden light poured out from an entrance at the far end of the corridor. Alyah typically arrived before the servants. If Ally was right, she would be in there preparing for the day. She sucked in a breath and walked toward the kitchen.

Richly engraved mahogany doors, some closed and some open, lined either side. The savory scents of caramelized onions and garlic mixed with the nutty aroma of spices filled her nostrils, and the sound of vegetables chopping filled her ears. She slipped inside the open door to the kitchen.

Deep brown cabinets lined the walls above and below the white marble countertops. A table sat in the far corner. Dressed in a rose-colored salwar *kameez*, Alyah stood with her back to Ally, cutting vegetables. On the gas stove, a large pot sputtered with oil. Only after she scanned the room for others did Ally let out the breath she held; they were alone. She closed the door behind her and locked it. One chance was all she had. If she failed, the consequences would be deadly.

"You're early. Peel and chop all those onions for me while I finish with the okra," Alyah said as she worked.

From the dish drainer, Ally grabbed a cutting board and a knife. She took her supplies and the basket of onions and set up beside the woman.

Alyah paused mid-cut, staring at the onion in Ally's hand before returning to her task. "I knew you understood Urdu." Although her words were calm, the knife she used shook while she worked the blade over the green vegetables. "Why are you here? Why couldn't you stay dead and let me live in peace?"

Ally worked on removing the waxy layers from the root and didn't respond.

"When I saw you yesterday, I was thinking 'Why is she back? She was never happy with us. She was finally free.' Only one answer came to mind. Is money that important to you?"

Ally smiled in spite of herself. Although right about the first part, Alyah couldn't be more wrong about the second. No amount of money would have brought her back.

"Wassim will gladly pay you whatever you want to make you disappear," Alyah said as she worked on the okra.

The vapors of the onions burned Ally's eyes. She rubbed the tears on her shoulder and continued to remove their skins. "Your husband tried to make me disappear last night. It didn't work."

"I don't know what you're talking about," Alyah snapped.

All four of the roots peeled, Ally grabbed one and cut it into paper-thin slices. "Your husband sent his guard to kill me last night."

Alyah's knife slipped, almost cutting her own finger. "Do you really think I would believe you? Tariq was a good man. Loyal."

"Loyal enough to kill for him." She sniffled from the sharp burn of the vapors.

Alyah laid down her knife and turned to her. "What do you want?"

She shrugged and worked the blade through the membrane of the root. "Things I can no longer have." Ally considered her words. "I had a husband who loved me very much. Sayeed took me away from him and forced me to live in hell with you. Those were the most miserable years of my life."

"Would you like for me to cry for your pain?"

Ally laughed and reached for another onion. "No. I know your life has been miserable too. Which is why I am here to warn you." From the corner of her eye, she noticed the way Alyah's hands squeezed together. "Tomorrow, Rizwan is coming but not for the reasons he claims."

Alyah grabbed the tray of cut okra and dropped the processed vegetables into the pot on the stove. Oil spurted and popped as soon as the pieces fell inside.

"He wants to find out if you and Wassim had a sexual relationship while his son was alive," Ally paused, waiting to see the woman's reaction.

Alyah's hand stilled. "What did you tell him?"

Ally cleared her throat. "The truth," she lied. "But it is not only my word. Do you remember the guard Sayeed assigned to watch over me?"

Her nervous laugh sent a wave of guilt through Ally. "Amir is dead," Alyah hissed. The poor woman's hands shook as she opened each tin and scooped spoonfuls of the seasonings into an empty bowl by the stove.

"As dead as I am." Ally said in a soft voice. She wished her words were true for Farah and Amirah's sake. "He saw what you two were doing. Took pictures in case he would ever need proof. You can ask him about it tomorrow when he arrives." She watched the way her shoulders stiffened. "Once Amir, Rizwan, and the doctor arrive, they will want to talk to you both and run medical tests on the child to make sure he really is Sayeed's."

Alyah turned to her, her eyes bright red. "Why are you doing this?"

"Like you said," she smiled. "Money."

The poor woman closed her lids and turned back to stir the pot on the stove.

Guilt sat heavy on her chest, but if it kept Aadam alive, the lies and the pain would be worth it. Ally walked to her side, grabbed the bowl of spices, and poured them into the vessel Alyah stirred. "But I have no ill will toward you and don't want to see you or your child harmed in the process. Which is why I am warning you, Shariff plans to kill you, Wassim, and your son if the medical reports find the child is not Sayeed's. And we all know what the answer will be."

The vegetables turned a golden yellow as soon as the seasonings mixed with them. Alyah dropped the wooden spoon into the pot and busied herself with cleaning the countertops.

"I tried to talk him out of it. Asked him to kick you out, but he says his brother would want vengeance." Ally turned the fire to low and put the lid on the pot. "He asked me not to tell you. It was supposed to be a surprise. If I were you, I would take my son and leave before the morning. If you feel Wassim is a good husband, take him with you. If not, leave him behind and know he will be dealt with."

Someone knocked from the other side of the locked kitchen door.

"If you're lying? What then?" Alyah whispered.

She dug her fingers into her palms at the question. "If I'm lying then you will come back and Wassim will kill me. But if I'm telling the truth, you might be a homeless widow, but you and your son will still be alive." Ally cleared her throat. "If you decide to tell Shariff that I shared this secret with you, you will have to deal with his questions sooner than later. Oh, and if you and Wassim try to kill me in the meantime, it will only prove your guilt." Before Alyah could respond, Ally unlocked the door. The seeds had been planted. She hoped they'd take root soon.

One of the servants stood in the hallway. She wore the brightest orange top Ally had ever seen. Ally smiled at her and left the kitchen.

# CHAPTER TWENTY-SIX

## THE RING

*A*side from the brief run-in with Alyah, everyone avoided Ally. While they didn't overtly stare, their eyes burned into her back when she walked by. Considering they believed her to be a killer, she wasn't surprised. When the jumpiness became too much, she escaped to the one place she felt safest—the bedroom.

She stood in the far corner of her quarters, the key to the secured padlock in her jean pocket, and scanned the space for the hundredth time. Both the door and the patio were sealed. Aside from the possibility of someone climbing into her third floor balcony and breaking through the glass, there was no way anyone could get inside, unless it was Eddie.

Once she deemed it safe, she allowed herself to think about her conversation in the kitchen. Hopefully, Alyah not only believed her but would take her child and run. Telling her the truth would not have worked. Alyah would have laughed in her face and called her a liar. Instead, not only had she used what the woman already believed, that Ally was greedy and selfish, but she also gave her an escape from Wassim if she needed one.

When exhaustion overwhelmed her and her legs buckled, she leaned her back against the wall and slid to the ground. She ran her hand over the still crumpled blanket on the floor beside her. After wrapping it around her, she stared at the closet door behind which Eddie had disappeared. Before she could delve deeper into thoughts of the next day, sleep overtook her.

~

A cool breeze tickled her skin when it moved past. It permeated through the sheer fabric of her crimson sari, waving it like a flag behind her as she walked. The night sky sparkled with stars, illuminating not only the earth around her but also bouncing off the gems stitched into the silk of her garment. The pebbled ground cut into her bare feet with every step, but it didn't deter her. Her attention was fixed on one thing—the building a few yards away.

Ivory stairs led up to the entrance. A pair of giant arched doors sat in the center of the structure, framed on either side by thick pillars. She didn't care it was closed, nor did she care about what the building contained. It was the person standing in front of the doors she focused on. He stood with his back to her, facing the entrance. His black suit fit his tall, lean body perfectly. She grabbed handfuls of her skirt and lifted it as her walk transformed into a sprint.

David turned, watching her, a smile on his face. He leaned against a marble column, arms crossed, while she climbed the steps. Once on the same level as him, she stopped. Out of breath, she let go of her skirt and stared. Each lock of his brown hair sat in place, his eyes clear and reflecting the moon's light; his smile tugged at the ache within her that she knew would never end. She took a cautious step toward him, fearing he'd move away, and when he didn't, she took another and another until their bodies were a hair's breadth apart. Afraid to touch, Ally tried to memorize every part of his face, the woody smell of his cologne, the way his breath hit her cheek.

The soft tunes of a ballad she hadn't heard in a long time filled the silent space. "Dance with me?" she whispered.

A knowing look flashed across his face. "One day."

She watched his beautiful his lips move as he spoke.

"Why not now?"

His laugh was a cool wave flowing through her; a wave she prayed wouldn't stop. "It's not time yet, baby."

She stared into his eyes, her heart thudding against her chest, trying to find the words to convince him otherwise.

As if reading her mind, he nodded. "You have a lot more left to do."

Ally blinked back her emotion and shook her head. "I can't. Not without you."

David backed away. "You've got this. And I'm here. I'm always here."

Ally reached out to him, only to grab air. "Don't go."

He moved farther from her. "Go back, Ally. Do what needs to be done, for them, for you, for me."

The doors behind him opened, and when she tried to grasp his hand, he moved yards away inside. The room was a long hall. Arched walls painted orange grew longer and deeper the more she rushed toward him.

"Don't chase me. When it's time, you won't have to run." His words echoed through the building.

She stood frozen, watching her soul fade away. "Touch me," she whispered.

"Ally." The pity in his voice pierced her, and she fell to her knees.

"Just one time. I need to feel you." She stretched out her arm, but he retreated out of her grasp. It was as if everything inside her ripped out of her at once. "Please."

David made no attempt to reach for her. He continued to shrink into the dark hall of the building behind him until only a tiny shadow of him remained.

"Give me something," she sobbed. The world faded into the blackest of nights, but she didn't care. Ally stayed on her knees, her hand outstretched, her body aching for him. She tried to call out to him, but she couldn't speak much less breathe, her lungs like heavy steel. Gasping for air, she watched helplessly as the building and David shrunk in the distance.

Warm skin pressed against her palm, sending a surge of heat through her. Strong fingers twined with hers, filling the cavity where her soul once resided. She tightened her grip on him. His firm touch calmed her, evaporating her pain, the terror. She didn't move, for fear he'd pull his hand away. Ally stayed there. In the dark. With David. Praying he'd never let go.

"Breathe," the voice urged.

She did as instructed but the tears refused to stop. Although she ached for him to hold her, to promise he'd never leave again, she knew she asked for the impossible. This was a dream. A beautiful aspiration from which she never wanted to wake. She pressed his hand against her cheek, savoring David: his strength, his love, all of it, allowing him to fill her lungs, her veins, nourish her body. For the first time in over four months, she wasn't drowning alone in her darkness.

In the distance, something hard slammed against a wall. A voice she didn't like called out to her. She shook her head, knowing her time with him was about to end. When his hand pulled away, she didn't stop him. The knocking grew louder until she could no longer ignore it. Ally opened her eyes and blinked as she adjusted to the afternoon sun streaming into her room.

"Sara Bhaabi, open the door," Shariff yelled from the hall.

She stared at her palm, which still held the warmth of David's touch and pressed it against her cheek.

"Sara Bhaabi, are you there?"

When she rose to her feet, something fell from her lap and jingled against the marble floor by her foot. She bent down and picked up the silver ring. Its heavy metal band was cold against her skin. The piece was one she had never seen before. She glanced over at the closed closet door. *Eddie?*

The ring consisted of three thin, corded ropes stacked together. A small diamond square sat on either side of the band. She pressed the pad of her finger against one of the diamonds and sucked in a breath when it started to slide.

The knocking grew incessant. "Bhaabi, the guard is with me, and if you do not open the door now, I will have him break it down."

Ally slid the ring onto her finger and rushed to let them in.

# CHAPTER TWENTY-SEVEN

## THE SEARCH

*W*hen she opened the door, Shariff and the guard stood on the other side. Neither of them waited for her to grant them access. Instead, they stormed past her, scanning the room.

The constant smile was gone from his face. He grabbed her arm, surveying her face. "Are you okay?"

She nodded. "I'm fine. Just a bad dream."

He ran his hand through his loose brown curls, and his chest rose when he sucked in a breath. "I heard about what happened last night."

The guard rushed into her private patio. "No one thought to wake me up and share it with me," Shariff growled.

Eddie appeared about five minutes later. "Took you long enough. Check the bathroom," Shariff snapped and walked over to Ally. He placed his palm on her cheek, peering at her face. "Are you okay? Did he hurt you?"

She fisted her hands and resisted the urge to jerk away from him. "He waited for me in my bathroom, but no, he didn't hurt me."

The patio door behind her slammed shut making her jump. Shariff dropped his hand from her. "Check the rest of the room."

The guard went to her bed and searched beneath it.

Her heart raced at the thought of him looking in her closet. "They don't need to. I'm safe now. I fell asleep and had a bad dream."

Shariff wandered to the corner by the armoire and picked up the crumpled blanket she'd left, tossing it on her mattress. "On the floor?"

She didn't answer. Eddie walked to the closet and gestured for Shariff to move. Her muscles relaxed.

Shariff sat on the bed, stretching his legs across the mattress. "And the screaming?"

Ally raised her chin, meeting his gaze. "A bad dream about strange men invading my room and looking through my things."

An amused smile tugged at his lips. He shook his head and waved at the guards. "Enough," he ordered in Urdu. "You two can leave. She's clearly fine."

The other guard left but Eddie rooted himself by the closet, his arms crossed. "Wassim has ordered I monitor her at all times." He spoke his words in English.

Shariff's mouth dropped. "You can't be serious. It was one of your own who tried to hurt her in the first place."

Eddie pulled out his cell phone. "Would you like for me to call him?"

He waved it away and crossed his arms on his lap. "Well, my dear Bhaabi, it appears everyone here is either trying to kill you or are afraid you will kill them." He jutted his chin in her direction. "And from the way you're standing, with good reason."

Ally looked down at her clenched fist pressed against her chest. The hand David held in her dreams. She cleared her throat and hugged it closer. "It hurts from last night."

"Considering you single-handedly beat a man to death with a metal rod, I'm surprised it's the only part of you that hurts. Now hurry up and get ready because we need to leave."

She eyed him suspiciously. "Where are we going?"

"Somewhere away from this nonsense." He smiled at Eddie. "I think I will hang out in your room, Bhaabi, while you get ready. Wouldn't want you to kill or be killed between now and the car."

~

Ally stood at the bathroom sink. Icy water flowed from the faucet over her fisted hand and down the drain. She pried her fingers open and let the liquid wash away the heat within and with it the dreams of David. Just as she couldn't contain the water, she couldn't hold on to someone who no longer existed. As much as she wanted to believe it was real, he hadn't touched her. Her mind gave her what it thought she needed to survive. She pressed the damp hand against her face. And her mind was right. Seeing and touching him, even if only an illusion, was exactly what she needed.

She slid off the ring she found earlier and played with one of the square diamonds on the side. Like before, it slid. As the distance between the gems shrunk, the end of the middle rope popped out. The farther she slid the square, the longer it stretched, forming a small arc much like a cat's claw. Once the squares were side by side, they clicked, and a thin, beveled blade popped out from inside of the claw. She pressed her finger against the steely edge, feeling the way it cut into the thin membrane of her skin. Ally threaded the jewelry over her knuckle; she waved it around getting comfortable with how it worked in case she needed it. Could this be the ring Leanna mentioned on the plane? The one she said not only worked as a knife but a tracking device. When she moved the diamonds apart across the band, the blade slipped back inside the claw and the rope slid into place between the other two, creating the three roped layers of the ring. She threaded the piece on to her fingers and returned to the bedroom to find Eddie still standing in the corner and Shariff leaning against the wall texting someone. He looked her over. "Ready?"

Once she slid on her shoes, she headed for the door. "I'm ready."

"Hold on." Shariff grabbed her elbow and turned her. With her back to him, she gazed at the closet. Shariff's fingers pressed against her hips. "I am going to have to make sure you're not hiding anything," he whispered.

Instead of fidgeting with her wedding ring, her thumb traced the edge of the band, which sat heavy on her right hand. Would he notice it? Her gaze fell on Eddie, standing stoically in the corner. "What would I be hiding, and where would I keep it exactly?"

Shariff's breath blew against her cheek when he laughed. "You managed to sneak a metal rod into your room last night and kill a man. I don't want to spend the entirety of our trip worrying what my outcome might be. Arms out."

Before she could comply, his hands were already feeling around the waistband of her jeans. When his palms moved lower, a shudder ripped through her. Ally sucked in a breath and stared ahead while his hands cupped her backside. When she tried to step away, he pulled her closer.

"I'm not done." His voice was husky.

She clenched her fists and stared at the white of Eddie's knuckles. Ally rolled her shoulders back. She was not alone, and even if Eddie didn't intervene, there was only so far Shariff would go with an audience. Ally grabbed his wandering hands and pulled them off her. "Don't do this."

"All I am doing is searching you, and the sooner I'm done, the sooner we can get out of here."

When his hands cupped her breast, the façade of strength she worked so hard to show cracked. The heaviness of his palms against her chest, the way he squeezed, all of it, triggered not only pain but also memories she had worked hard to forget. Images of her arms and legs tied to the bed as Sayeed ripped into her flooded her mind. Her body shook while her knees weakened.

Eddie must have noticed her reaction. The muscle on the side of his jaw twitched, and he took a step forward. The way his eyes stayed fixed on Shariff, his clear intention to harm the man who held Farah and Amirah, flipped a switch in Ally's brain. If she didn't do something, he would.

She turned to face Shariff. His hands immediately returned to her breasts. "Those were your brother's favorites, too."

His fingers froze.

"He liked it when I fought him." His nails dug into her skin. "Is that what turns you on?" She smiled. "Or would you rather I stripped and got on my back?"

He slammed his eyelids shut. "Neither." He dropped his hands and cleared his throat. "I like my women begging for more, not begging for their lives."

# CHAPTER TWENTY-EIGHT

## THE SHADOW

*A*lly wiped her clammy hands on her shirt and followed Shariff down the stairs. Unlike the early morning when she descended, the bottom floor now filled with bright sunlight and activity. The sounds of a television blaring floated up the three levels of the home.

Like the morning, all eyes fixed on her, eyes filled with anger and disgust. The hair on her neck stood. There was no question each and every one of the men, aside from the one who walked behind her, plotted her death; especially, now that she'd killed one of their own.

Wassim rose from his seat and pointed at her. "That woman is no longer welcome here."

Shariff laughed as he descended the final steps. "Would you like for me to call my father, and let him know you are about to kick out his dead son's widow from his home? A woman he is traveling all the way from Afghanistan to see?" He stopped at the base of the stairs and pointed his hand at her. Ally stood a few steps behind him, holding on to the banister, pretending not to listen. "But before I make the call, tell me, what business did your guard have sneaking into her room last night? I'm sure Babba's going to want to know the answer to that question as well."

Wassim's brows rose and he flashed a knowing look. "Tell your father she is a woman of no character. She's been here barely a day and has invited many men into her bed."

Shariff's back stiffened. "So she seduced him and then killed him? Is that your story?"

Ally's grip on the wooden railing tightened.

"We all know who was in the wrong last night, don't we? As for myself, yes, I entered her room just now. With your guard, mind you, assuring my bhaabi it was safe to come out, and promising her that, unlike the bastard from last night, everyone else here knows their limits and would treat her with respect."

Shariff waved for her to follow. "Come, Bhaabi, let's go for a walk in the courtyard while we wait for the car."

He led her down the same gravel path they'd traveled the day before. His shoulders were stiff and every pore of his body oozed tension. She waited until they were a good distance from the house before she cleared her throat. "What happened back there?"

Shariff tipped his head backward at Eddie, who walked a few yards behind. "Wassim likes to wave his unimpressive dick around and expects everyone to bow to it."

Ally nodded. "He doesn't intimidate you?"

"Not in the least." He chuckled and poked her with his elbow. "Granted, I haven't seen his dick, but I am sure even if I did, I would still be left unimpressed."

She thought about Wassim's son. Somehow, she needed to attach him to the child. "Aadam seems to adore you."

Shariff's shoulders lowered as some of his tension dissipated and smiled. "What's not to adore?"

"You seem comfortable with him as well."

"I'm good with kids."

She stopped by a tree and sat down with her back against its trunk, waiting for him to explain.

"The boarding school I grew up in had students of all age ranges."

She grabbed Shariff's hand and gave it a tug, encouraging him to sit beside her. The crunch of the gravel a few feet away let her know Eddie stood close by. Ally didn't need to read his mind to know he wouldn't be happy with the way she behaved with Shariff. But this was not just about her life. She looked up at Shariff and patted the ground next to her. "They didn't separate you by age?"

Shariff slid beside her and leaned against the trunk of the tree. "They did for schooling, of course, and sleeping arrangements, but those of us who had nowhere to go on the weekends and holidays spent our breaks together."

She imagined the boy he once was, waiting for a father who never came. "It must have been hard." He looked at her as if not understanding. "Seeing everyone leave with their families and knowing you would be left behind."

Shariff stared off in the distance. "It was better than being with my father and his family." He rested his elbows on his knees. "Anyway, it was rather fun. We became our very own dysfunctional family."

His hand brushed against hers. Ally glanced at her ring that sat inches from his touch. "Do you keep in touch with the kids from the school?"

"Ha! Like I said, we were a dysfunctional family. We ran as far away from each other as possible."

She put her hand in her jean pocket and worked on slipping the band off her finger. "The thing about family, blood or not, is they know your history. They know the pain you've gone through. Sometimes they contributed to the pain, and sometimes they experienced it with you."

"Very true."

After shoving the band to the bottom of her pocket, she pulled the unadorned fingers out and placed them on her lap. He seemed to be enjoying the conversation. There was no sign of irritation or tension. She leaned forward. "I've heard good things about boarding schools in general, but I've also heard some bad things."

Somewhere in the courtyard, Aadam's laughter filled the grounds. Shariff side-eyed her. "Bad things like?"

"Like sometimes children are abused either sexually, physically, emotionally. Sometimes by the adults and sometimes by other kids."

He didn't respond but she noticed the way he stiffened.

"I hope yours was one of the good schools, and I hope your story wasn't the same."

Shariff grabbed a rock from the ground and tossed it at a tree. "We all have stories, no? It's what makes us who we are."

While he threw his stones, she watched him. Each pebble was flung farther and harder. She'd pushed too far. Ally cleared her throat. "How long has it been since you've seen your father?"

He laughed and picked up a piece of a crumbled brick, tossing it as well. "Last year. I have to go to him, always. He doesn't leave Kabul." He picked up another rock and then another, throwing them at some invisible target ahead. "But the ninety-year-old bastard texts me once a week."

She handed him another piece of the brick. "If this place means so much to you, couldn't you ask him for the house?"

He stopped mid-throw and wiped his hand on his jeans. "Babba gave it to Wassim as a wedding gift for taking care of Alyah and the child. The lazy bastard does nothing but sit on his ass all day and he gets everything."

She eyed him. "While you do all the work and get nothing."

"Exactly." Shariff grabbed her hand and twined his fingers through hers. "And my father has promised him many more gifts as long as he takes good care of his son's beloved child." He kissed the back of her hand. "So even long after his death, Sayeed is still the favorite."

She stared at the locked fingers and considered her words. "The things your brother did to me could have easily turned me bitter and angry. I had to work hard to remember I was good. Once I started looking, I noticed all the good people around me. They gave me hope. They were the only reason I survived."

With the pad of his thumb, he traced the veins on the back of her hand. "Such an idealist."

"Maybe." She shrugged. "But it's better than the alternative. You have a choice: let go of the anger and live your life in spite of the past or allow your past to consume you."

"It's too late for that. I am beyond consumed. I've been digested and crapped out."

She shook her head and honed in on the sadness in his voice. He was a child, abandoned, who believed himself unworthy. "I don't believe you. You're a good person, Shariff," she lied. "And you deserve good things, good people. No matter what trauma has happened in your life, you've already shown you're not like your brother or your father."

Shariff cocked his head and stared at her but did not respond.

"I see it in the way you are with Aadam, even with me. Like in the bedroom, you wanted me but respected my wishes. In the same situation, Sayeed would have—and did—rape me."

His grip on her hand tightened. "Don't misconstrue manners

for good character, Bhaabi."

"You're better than Sayeed."

"It's not hard to be better than him, is it?" He leaned his head back on the tree and laughed. "What if I am aspiring to be worse than him?"

"You'll never get your childhood or your mother back. And no matter how hard you try to right this wrong, it will never be enough."

Shariff rose to his feet and reached out his hand for hers. He pulled her up and nudged his head behind him, reminding her they had company. "True. But it will feel damn good to make the old man hurt."

His words sunk in. She had been wrong. He didn't plan to kill everyone tomorrow. Just everyone his father valued. "Will it?" Ally scanned over her shoulder. Eddie stood a few feet away, staring at the ground and following their every move.

"You have no clue how good it will feel." Shariff tugged at her, leading her along the path.

She pressed her hand against her jeans until she felt the hard outline of the ring. "Closure is a funny thing. We all seek it, but the sad reality is that oftentimes it is not found in the ways we think it will be."

"Closure?" he whispered. "You're wrong. I don't want closure. I want pain. I want to see him suffer."

"He lost his wife, had to send his youngest son away, and then he outlived his oldest son. I think he may have suffered already."

Shariff shook his head. "You have to be able to love someone before you can suffer for them. He never saw me or my mother as his own."

She thought about Razaa. "I did not give birth to the boys Sayeed adopted, but I loved them as if they were. They were part of the good that kept me hoping. I wonder about them all the time."

His brows rose at the mention of the boys. "Do you?"

She stared out in the distance and softened her voice. "All the time."

If he knew about them, he showed no indication. "Have you looked for the boys?"

Ally stepped over the thick tree root protruding from the

ground, keeping her gaze low. "I had no way of tracing them."

"I find it hard to believe, considering your little widow found you."

"I didn't know she had." She glanced over at him, feigning surprise. "I wish she hadn't. Her search ended up costing us our husbands' lives. It's why we are both stuck in this mess with you."

"Stuck?" He planted their intertwined hands on his chest. "That hurts me."

"You didn't have to kill them. I would have helped you if you'd asked me."

"Who said I did? And..." Shariff tipped his head toward the gate as a car pulled up on the drive outside. "Our car has arrived."

The guards by the entrance went out to talk to the driver, their dog and bomb-detecting device in hand. A second later, Eddie stood at Shariff's side.

"You, my shadow, will not be coming with us." He patted Eddie's shoulder and walked away.

"Wassim's instructions—"

"Have no power once we leave this house," Shariff snapped before Eddie could finish.

One of the uniformed men lowered his head while the other glared openly at her.

"Mind your manners," Shariff roared at the guard.

She slid into the backseat of the car and pulled the ring out of her pocket, slipping it back on. Ally stared out the window at Eddie. Their eyes locked for a brief second before he looked away. The connection lasted long enough for him to nod his head. A nod so slight no one else noticed.

Shariff continued to hound the guards. "Don't look at her again. Understand?" Then he pointed at Eddie, "Tell Wassim we will be gone for a few hours." He slid into the car and slammed the door before anyone could respond.

She rubbed the back of the ring, hoping it contained a tracking device and hoping they were on their way back to Farah. The car revved its engine and backed away from the drive. It pulled over and stopped a few streets later, next to the gates and hibiscus bushes from the day before. He pulled out the black fabric from the duffle bag on the floor, unfolded it, and waved it at her. "Shall I do the honors, or will you?"

Everything turned black the instant the blindfold slid into place.

He helped her slip the burqa on and then rubbed her wrist. "Do I need to tie your hands together or can I trust you to behave?"

"Depends. Where are we going?"

"Somewhere safe."

"That doesn't ease any of my fears."

He laughed. "At the moment, by my side is the safest place you can be."

# CHAPTER TWENTY-NINE

## THE GIFT

*U*nable to see, Shariff held her arm and guided her through the space. Like the day before, they changed cars, but this time he kept her uncuffed. A door opened and shoes squeaked against the hard floor. No one spoke. He propelled her inside the building; somewhere nearby a door slammed shut. A few minutes later, Shariff pulled the burqa and the mask off her. Ally blinked and stared around the room. A sink sat in the corner of the bedroom and a glass mirror hung above it. A pile of clothes lay on the floor against the wall and on the top of it a pair of men's briefs. She glanced at the closed door across from her before looking at the rest of the space.

He waved around the room. "You were clearly not expected but it will do. So make yourself comfortable. You will be in here for a while."

A baby's hungry cries filled the air. Ally looked at Shariff, knowing exactly where he'd taken her. "Let me stay with them."

He laughed and headed for the closed door. "I would need to trust you for that. Seeing as how I don't, hidden metal rods and beating men to death and all, here is where you'll stay."

"Please, let me..." The door slammed in her face. Before she could reach for the knob, metal slid into place and keys jiggled, locking it. A few minutes later, the front door closed as well. The engine of a car in the driveway revved, and soon he was gone.

Ally sat on the bed, fiddling with the ring and gazing at the door. In the past half hour since he left, Amirah's cries had grown louder and more hysterical. When it became unbearable, she ran to the door and banged against it. "Anyone out there?" The only response came from the screaming infant. She slammed her knuckles against the surface and pressed her ear against the smooth wood. "Is there something wrong with the baby?"

Although no one answered, something squeaked against the floor. "I want to know if Farah and Amirah are okay."

Razaa didn't respond, but from his footsteps, she assumed he paced the area outside her door. She rested her forehead against the door. "Please. I might be able to help."

The baby continued to wail, pausing to take a breath and start again.

His footsteps disappeared, leaving only the child's laments as company. Ally grasped the handle and jiggled, but it didn't budge. A few minutes later, the footsteps returned and along with it, the metal clashing of keys.

"I am going to open the door. You will walk with me to the other room, and I will let you in. If you try anything, I will shoot you. Understood?" Razaa commanded.

His words chilled her but not because she believed he'd hurt her. The fact he allowed it meant something was very wrong. "Yes."

"Step far away from the door."

Ally rushed to the other end of the room, her chest tight as tension coursed through her. When it opened, the young masked man stood at the threshold, a gun protruded from the waistband of his jeans.

"What's wrong with Amirah?"

He shook his head. "It's not the baby. It's her mother." He rested a hand on the gun's handle and stepped to the side, granting her exit.

She hurried to him and paused at the doorway, in front of him. Razaa stared ahead, not acknowledging her. Ally opened her mouth, trying to find the right words.

"Go!" he snapped.

She nodded and moved on with Razaa close behind. The cries grew louder as she neared the locked bedroom.

His hands shook while he unfastened the lock. As soon as it clicked, he pulled the door open and waved her in.

She stepped into the room, the door shut and locked behind her.

Ally's attention went straight to the bed. In a diaper and nothing else, Amirah lay in the middle of the mattress. Her face bright red as she screamed, and her arms and legs flailed. She scooped up the baby and pressed her cheek to her own as she swayed and hummed to her. While she tried to calm the child, she scanned the room for the mother.

She sat in the corner on the floor, rocking herself. Her body shook as she sobbed.

"Farah?"

She looked up at Ally, emotion glistening against her cheeks. "I fed her, cleaned her, everything. She won't stop crying."

From the looks of it, it wasn't just the baby who couldn't stop crying. Ally held Amirah tight and continued to bounce until finally, after a long while, Amirah fell asleep. Afraid to wake her, she walked over to Farah and smiled down at her. "It's okay, Farah."

Her vacant gaze stared out across the room. "Nothing's okay, Didi. Because of my mistakes, we will all die. I've destroyed everything."

She sat beside her, careful not to jostle the exhausted child. "She is going to be okay. Both of you will go home."

"Home? What home? There is no home without him. And he won't be there." She fixed her gaze on Ally. "He's dead."

Her throat tightened. It hurt too much to confirm her fears. Ally grabbed her hand and stared at the floor.

Farah rested her chin on her knees. "It's okay, Didi. I know," she whispered. "He's dead because of me." Her words trailed off as the sobs took over.

～

"I think I'm cursed," Farah said. The tears had long subsided, but the women were still on the floor. Farah's head rested on Ally's shoulder; a towel covered her chest, hiding the nursing child.

A sad smile tugged at Ally's lips. Those were thoughts she understood all too well. "It feels like that sometimes, doesn't it?"

Farah's hair rubbed against her cheek when she nodded.

Ally stared at the cotton hanging over the nursing mother's body. The edge of it fell over her lap, covering most of it from view. She tucked her hand under the cloth and rested it on Farah's knee. "Whenever you feel that way, look at this beautiful gift Amir left for you." With her thumb, she worked on slipping the silver band off her finger. "You can't see him, but he is here watching over the two girls he loved more than his own life. And as hard as it is to stay hopeful, you have to for him. Don't let his death be in vain, Farah."

The woman stiffened as soon as the ring dropped into her lap. "You can't give up. You have to live. To fight for her. The way he fought for you so many times before. Protect his daughter at all costs."

Farah's fingers brushed against hers from under the towel, and Ally knew she was slipping the ring on to her own hand. She smiled and patted her head. "You will continue being the strong, proud woman your husband believed you to be, and by doing so, you will raise his Amirah to be the same."

Ally pressed her cheek into Farah's cheek, and whispered into her ear. "A gift from your brother. We will get you both out of here. I promise." She climbed to her feet, reaching her hand out to her. "Now, you need to go to bed and get some rest."

# CHAPTER THIRTY

## THE TRUTH

*F*arah lay curled up on the mattress, Amirah snuggled up against her belly. Ally stared at the two of them, praying she would be able to keep the promise she'd made to get them out. Her thoughts shifted to the man in the living room. It was time they talked. She sucked in a breath and knocked on the door, waiting for the masked Razaa to arrive.

The gun still sat in his waistband, and he moved aside to let her out. She stepped out of the room and looked over her shoulder at the sleeping pair. So much would happen by the next day, and she worried she'd never see them again. The door slammed shut as she watched. She scanned the empty living area. Shariff had not arrived yet.

"You may have more crying spells from her. She is a new mother, and there are a lot of hormones running through her body," she said as he locked the door. "Then for husband to be killed, and she and Amirah to be locked away from the world, it is a lot for anyone to deal with."

He put the keys in his pocket and nodded, his hand still resting on the gun in his waistband.

Ally reached to touch his masked face as he stepped away from her. "You don't have to hide from me anymore. I know it's you, Razaa."

He stiffened but didn't respond.

She smiled. "My sweet Razaa, who loved to eat *ledus* and play cricket."

"I'm not your anything," he snapped. "Back to the room."

She headed to the other side of the house. "I know it's you," she said over her shoulder. "The way you walk. Your eyes. You're my Razaa."

"Don't call me that," he growled.

"What happened?" She didn't have to fake the sadness in her voice. The question did make her sad for him. "The Razaa I knew was loyal and kind. He would never have hurt the people he loved." She thought about the fourteen-year-old boy she once knew, not the seventeen-year-old stranger standing a foot away. "I used to be one of those people you loved. I'm hoping I still am."

"You don't know anything." His words were spoken softly, but the pain in his voice cut her.

A tear rolled down her cheek. She paused at the entrance of the hallway that led to her room and leaned against the wall, staring at him. "True, I don't know anything about what's happened to you, but I do know how much you loved Amir and he, you. He was your hero. My heart can't believe you would have killed him."

He stared at the room down the pathway and didn't respond.

She pointed at Farah's door. "As for Farah, she was a big sister to you all those years. She sat beside you and took care of you even when you were sick. Why would you keep her and her baby locked away in here and make them hurt like this?"

"Nobody was supposed to get hurt," he whispered.

"Then help her. She's hurting."

Red-rimmed eyes welling with emotion stared at her. "Who helped me when I hurt?"

"Who hurt you, Razaa?"

He laughed. "You."

She nodded. "That's why you hate me." The weight of guilt had always sat heavy in her chest, and now that she knew they had been split up, the guilt consumed her. His words were intensifying the grip it had on her. "I'm sorry. I should have never left you and the boys."

"No, you shouldn't have. But you didn't want us, and I have learned to accept the fact."

"That's not true, Razaa."

"Stop. You asked, now you need to hear the answer so you can understand why I hate you."

Tears spilled down her cheeks.

"I hate you for pretending to love us when you really didn't. I hate you for tearing my family apart and ruining my life. But most of all, I hate you for killing our father." He inched closer. His breath blew against her face when he spoke. "You see, I heard every word you said to Ayoub. You told him you killed Babba and how you were going to sell us, like we were animals. You never cared for us, so please don't talk to me about love."

She raised her hand to touch him, but he stepped away from it. "No, Razaa, it's not what happened. I would have never sold you. Everything I did was to protect you."

"So many lies." He leaned against the wall across from her and shook his head. "If I ask you something, can you tell me the truth?"

She nodded her head. "Anything."

"Did you even think once about me?" He pulled off his mask and tossed it on the floor. "And after you killed him and took everything, did you care how much I suffered while you lived your happy new life in America?"

Tears drenched her skin as she looked at him. A beard covered the cheeks of the man in front of her, but he was still the same boy she loved and risked her life for.

"Every single minute," she whispered. Ally sucked in a breath. "Losing all of you was one of the hardest things I've ever gone through."

"Stop lying!"

She shook her head. "I'm not. What you think happened wasn't true, Razaa. I wasn't the one trying to sell you."

He ran a hand through his thick black hair but didn't argue.

"Sayeed trained you and your brothers so he could sell you off to the As-Sirat."

Razaa rolled his eyes. "Unfortunately, he is not alive to explain your version of events to me."

"He lied to you about so many things..."

"Stop it!" His fist slammed into the wall. "Go." He pointed to the room at the end of the hallway. "I've heard enough."

Ally stared at him and didn't move. "Did he tell you what happened to Umber? Did he tell you he gave him to Ayoub as a gift?" She rushed through her words, willing him to hear them all. "He sent the poor boy into a mall with a backpack full of explosives. Your beloved father sent him to his death."

He pulled the gun out from his waistband and waved it at the awaiting bedroom. "It's time to go."

But she didn't move. "I know you don't know who to believe," she said. "And I know what you heard made me sound like a bad person, but you have a computer in the living room."

"I can't look at you. Go to the room now."

She nodded and walked slowly into the room. "Go search the Egyptian mall bombing from three years ago and look for pictures of the bomber. It's Umber."

The door slammed shut before she finished. "His death was the reason I killed your father. I saw the picture of Umber on the news the day he died." She pressed her hands against the wooden barrier and talked louder. "His face haunts me to this day. They put it all over the news and called him a terrorist, and all I saw was a scared little boy."

She heard nothing but silence on the other side. "No matter what you think of me, Farah and her baby are innocent. Let them go. You have me. I'm the one who killed your Babba, not them." She omitted the part of how it was Farah who actually filled Sayeed's body with bullets. Regardless of the shooting, it was Ally who'd poisoned him. If anyone should claim responsibility for the man's death and deal with the consequences, it would be her.

Something slammed against the wood she leaned against, the force of which pushed her head back.

"I've heard enough," Razaa growled. His sneakers squeaked against the floor, and a few seconds later, the front door slammed shut.

She closed her eyes and prayed he'd believe her.

# CHAPTER THIRTY-ONE

## NEW CLOTHES

*A*lly sat on the floor with the back of her head leaning against the locked bedroom door. Razaa stormed out of the house hours ago and had yet to return. She let out a nervous breath. Eddie would have been furious if he knew she had talked to either Alyah or Razaa. In the past few hours, she'd talked to both. To one she lied and the other told the truth. All of it in the hopes of saving them. She couldn't change the pains of their past, but if she was lucky she could help them have a future.

Alyah never believed Ally possessed a good bone in her body. Telling her anything to disprove her theory was a waste of everyone's time. Hopefully, the tale Ally weaved would scare Alyah enough to send her and her son into hiding by the morning. If she didn't, Ally wasn't sure how any of them would come out alive tomorrow.

Then there was Razaa. The boy had become a man. A man that if Eddie got his hands on...

Ally pushed the thought away. Anything could happen, and she hoped he was somewhere researching Umber and the information she gave him. She let out a long sigh. He was involved in all of this. Somehow, he had a hand in David and Amir's deaths. She wanted to hate him, but the only person she hated was herself. Ally rested her head in her hands. If Razaa realized the truth... If any of that boy she once knew still existed within him, he would help Farah and the baby. With any luck, the realization would happen before Shariff returned.

Those hopes plummeted the second a car pulled up the drive. She rose to her feet when the vehicle's door slammed shut. Someone entered the home, but unlike Razaa's, these shoes didn't squeak. The footsteps wandered around the house before heading in her direction. By the time her door unlocked, she'd positioned herself at the foot of the bed, hands in her lap, waiting.

Shariff stood at the entrance, a shopping bag in his hand. "I leave you alone for a few hours, and when I return, my guard is missing in action. Did you manage to kill him as well?"

She shrugged. "Murdering guards seems to be one of my superpowers."

He laughed and sat beside her, putting the tote he carried between them. From inside, he pulled out a clear plastic bag of chips. He ripped open the package and tipped it in her direction. "Hungry?"

Her stomach growled, but Ally shook her head and continued to stare out the open door.

Shariff popped a chip into in his mouth. "You can leave if you want. I never forced you to stay."

She rolled her eyes. "Promising to kill or sell the people I love if I leave is the same as chaining me to the bed."

"Chain you?" He laughed and tossed another chip into his mouth. "I'm not a fan of all the bondage stuff. I tried it a few times. Too many sharp objects and too much planning involved. Want to know what I find attractive?" He grabbed the bag between them and poured the contents on the floor in front of her. "A well-dressed woman." Brightly colored fabric, each in individual clear plastic bags, lay around her feet. "Hence, I picked up some new things for you."

She didn't move, instead stared out at the front door for Razaa to return.

Shariff picked up one of the items and dropped it on her lap. "New jeans. They should fit you better than the ones you're currently wearing."

He grabbed a royal blue piece and stacked it on top of the jeans. "A new *kurta* that won't look like you borrowed someone else's shirt. This one should fit you in all the right places."

One by one, he identified the clothing and added it to the

stack until the tower of packets almost tipped over. Ally grabbed them before they fell and laid the stack beside her. "I will be dead by tomorrow. Why bother buying me a new wardrobe?"

He scrunched his face. "You don't know for sure you will die. And even if you do, it's more reason to spend your last day looking your best. Which reminds me." Shariff picked up the remaining packet from the floor and pulled out a peach fabric. When he held the dress out for her to see, the matching shawl and pants to the outfit fell across her feet.

The piece was silk with embroidered flowers across the bodice, its sleeves sheer. She eyed the delicate roses weaved into the chest of the outfit, but more than the fabric, she noticed the way he looked at her eagerly awaiting her reaction. In so many ways, he remained a child, hungry for affirmation.

Disappointment flashed across his face when she didn't give him what he wanted. He laid it across her lap. "You have to look nice when you meet your father-in-law for the first time." He grinned. "I know he's very eager to lay his eyes on you."

Her stomach twisted. She could only imagine what the man who spawned the two brothers would be like. Ally stared at the embroidered fabric in her lap, honing in on the bitterness in his voice. "I'm sure he's just as eager to see you?"

He chuckled. "The old man made no attempt to visit me in over fifteen years, but now when there is a possibility his dead son might not be dead, he's had a sudden urge for a family reunion."

Shariff picked up the sheer shawl from the floor and pressed it tight against her chest. He leaned over, his face close to hers. "Beautiful." He dropped the fabric in her lap and ran his hand up her arm, slowly making his way to her bare shoulder. "When I saw it at the store, I imagined it on you." Goosebumps pebbled her skin as his fingers moved over her. "And then I envisioned taking it off you."

She raised her chin and held her breath while he traced her collarbone. "You need to make up your mind, Shariff. One minute, you're telling me you don't want your brother's leftovers. The next, you're sharing your fantasies of undressing me."

"I know." He rested his forehead against her temple and sighed. "My two heads are at war with each other. One screaming to stay away and the other screaming to sink himself inside you."

She clenched her fists around the scarf in her lap as a shudder rocked through her.

Shariff wrapped his arm around her hips and slid her body closer. His lashes brushed against her cheek when he blinked. "Those two typically play nice together, but over you, it's been an ugly battle." His breath hit her skin. She fought the urge to push him away and wipe him off her.

"Speaking of fantasies, last night I had the most lust-filled one about you." Shariff ran the pad of his thumb over her lip. "And we were fabulous together. Want to hear about it?"

Ally swallowed the terror and shook her head.

His hand wrapped around her neck and traced up and down the length of it. "I'm starting to wonder if I had you, maybe these fantasies would stop."

Her heart pounded an erratic beat. She wound the sheer scarf around her hands until the fabric was tight and imagined it wrapped around his neck, crushing the breath out of him. "A taste of me is not going to be enough. It's not usually how things work."

He laughed and pressed his lips against the corner of her mouth. "For some reason, that intrigues me even more."

She shuttered her lids as he kissed along her jaw, moving down her neck. Just as Ally raised her hands and prepared herself, the front door opened. She dropped her palms back in her lap and watched Razaa.

The mask had returned. He entered the home and slammed the door shut behind him. He stared around the house until his eyes locked with hers. His gaze shifted between Ally and the man currently kissing her neck.

Shariff pressed his lips on her cheek, making a loud smack before he moved away. Even then, he kept a possessive hand on her back. "Where did you disappear to?" he asked in Urdu to the young man.

Razaa walked to them, his hands stuffed in his pockets, and jutted his chin at her. "She wouldn't stop talking."

Ally shifted in her seat. Would he tell Shariff about what she said?

Shariff laughed, while his fingers brushed lazily up and down her spine. "Yes, it is a problem I'm having with her as well. She is a woman of a thousand questions."

Razaa stood a few feet from them and crossed his arms. "Most brother-in-laws do not touch their bhaabis the way you are."

Shariff's hand stilled. He rose from the bed and scowled at him. "I am not like most. Now am I?"

Ally sucked in a breath as he approached Razaa. Shariff walked past him and stopped at the doorway. "It's time to go, Bhaabi. Everyone at the house must be wondering where you are. And Razaa, pack up the clothes on the bed for me."

The young man nodded and did as he was told. Ally remained glued to her spot, looking up at him as he put the packets in the shopping bag. Razaa avoided her gaze. A few dots of red stained the pale yellow collar of his tee.

"Did you hurt yourself?".

Other than a slight pause before returning to his task, he showed no indication he heard her.

Ally cleared her throat and spoke loud enough for both of them to hear. "Can I say good-bye to Farah and the baby before we go?"

Razaa's gaze met hers, but he did not answer.

"Thirty seconds," Shariff said from down the hall. "And I will be standing in the room the whole time."

By the time they entered Farah's room, the mother stood in the middle of the space, the baby in her arms. Her gaze darted between Ally and the man standing behind her.

Ally went to her and wrapped an arm around the young mother's shoulder. "I will be back for you two," she whispered.

Farah pressed her cheek into Ally's. "Don't worry about us. Please be careful."

Ally nodded and wiped a tear off of Farah's cheek before walking out of the room.

# CHAPTER THIRTY-TWO

## TRUST NO ONE

*A*lly spent the drive back to Wassim's not only shrouded in darkness but also in silence. Again, the constant honking and the voices of people along the roads were loud, but the passengers in the vehicle were not. The only sound inside the cabin was the beeping of a cell phone.

"Shariff?"

"Hmm," he mumbled as he typed on his phone.

"Why do we keep switching cars, and why do you keep changing your clothes?"

"Changing clothes?"

She shook her head. "That's the same response you gave me yesterday when I asked."

He rested his hand on her knee. "Sweet, beautiful Bhaabi, if you don't like my answers then stop asking the question."

Ally bent over and felt the floor of the car until her fingers touched the duffle bag. She lifted it up and dropped it on what she hoped was his lap. "My eyes may be covered, but I'm not deaf. I can hear the zipping and unzipping and the shifting as you put things on and take them off. Why go to so much trouble?"

He let out a long exaggerated sigh but didn't respond. The bag thudded on the floor by her feet.

She cleared her throat. "Unless you're worried people are

following you."

The grip on her knee tightened.

"Who's following you, Shariff?"

"You continue to amaze me," he said. "It's no wonder you managed to kill my brother." His finger traced circles on her thigh. "As to your question, let me explain something I learned a long time ago." He slid close and whispered in her ear. "Trust no one. Not even my sweet, beautiful Bhaabi who has already killed two men."

She stayed rigid long after he returned to his seat and the beeping on his cell phone resumed. A little while later, the car pulled to a stop, its gears groaning when the driver put it into park. Shariff pulled the cover off her head. Ally blinked a few times, adjusting to the bright afternoon sun. Her stomach growled, making Shariff laugh. "You should have eaten those chips when you had the chance."

She didn't answer but looked out the window at the same narrow street and the same hibiscus bushes. Unlike the other times, this drive was shorter and took at the most twenty minutes. Clearly, there was an urgency for him to get back to the house. An urgency that took precedence over his trust issues.

"No worries." He pulled on the sleeve of her burqa. "As soon as you take this off, we can go inside and get you some dinner."

The car rolled up to the gate a moment later. As usual, the guards came out, and after they completed their routine bomb inspection, the vehicle entered the grounds. Ally pretended not to notice their scowls when the car drove past.

Apparently, Shariff noticed the glares as well. He cleared his throat before he opened his passenger door. "You should probably stay in your room with the doors locked the rest of the day. They don't appear to enjoy your company as much as I do."

Ally nodded but didn't respond. She was too busy watching Aadam and Alyah sitting on the porch. Heat prickled the back of her neck. Why were they still there? She wiped her sweaty palms on her jeans and followed Shariff inside.

The musical ballad to a soap opera played on the television in the living room, but there was no one in the room watching it.

"Hello?" Shariff said as he wandered around. He shot her a puzzled look and peered into the hallway. "Anyone home?"

Ally stayed near the front door, unsure of what danger lurked inside.

A few moments later, one of Wassim's men appeared. "We are in the back room, having dinner. Wassim Bhai asked you to join us."

She knew better than to think the invitation extended to her and, even if it did, had no desire to see any of them. Ally headed for the stairs.

"Bhaabi."

She paused at the step.

"I will send you a plate to your room." She nodded and made her way to safety.

~

Ally sat on her private balcony overlooking the courtyard and nibbled on her dinner. The security dog from the gate scurried around the giant water fountain below while Aadam chased after him. The sight of them ruined her appetite. Things weren't going the way she'd hoped. Maybe, just maybe, Alyah planned to disappear during the night, without drawing too much attention. Either that, or she didn't believe a word of their conversation, and she and Wassim were plotting Ally's death.

Aadam's squeals drew her out of her thoughts. The happy child pursued the dog, trying to wrap his chubby arms around the furry beast. Every time he came within hugging distance, the animal leaped a few feet ahead and glanced back, wagging its tail for the child to pursue. The game lasted for a while before finally the dog allowed Aadam to catch him, rewarding his efforts with sloppy wet kisses.

Soon the boy was on his back while the dog stood over him, licking his face clean. The courtyard erupted with Aadam's giggles and squeals. For a brief moment, the tension of the past few months melted and Ally laughed. As soon as she heard the sound escape her lips, she stopped.

How long had it been? Her mind wandered to David. His smiling face filled her mind. Once upon a time, they planned to have a family of their own. Her chest ached. It wasn't only her heart she'd lost four months ago. Her hopes, her faith, her future were all destroyed in one morning.

She sipped her water and tried to swallow the guilt rising in her throat. Apart from her dreams, he had only been a fleeting thought in the past day or so. It was the longest he'd gone from her mind since his death, longer than she liked.

Life was strange, hers stranger than most. Whenever she believed she was in control, it changed paths, thrusting her in directions she never desired. All she wanted was to go home, to the only man who ever made her feel loved or safe. A home that no longer existed. She pressed the glass against her face to ease the heat building beneath the surface.

A bead of condensation rolled down the side of the vessel. Her mother had asked why she didn't cry in front of the family. She wiped the moisture away with the pad of her thumb before it fell from the cup. The day she lost David was the day she realized her pain would never end. The only person she could cry in front of. The one who always knew exactly what to do, and how to make the pain stop, was gone. Which was why she made it a point to seal off the cracks of her walls as soon as they formed. If the cracks weren't sealed and the walls crumbled, she wasn't sure the tears would ever end.

Women's voices and laughter filled the grounds, pulling Ally out of her thoughts. With their workday over, the servants congregated by the water fountain, ready to go home. They patted Aadam's head as they walked past and headed down the driveway to the gate. The woman with the bright orange top, whom Ally had seen in the kitchen, stood with the group. She moved slower than the rest as they strolled and soon fell several feet behind the others. The road curved and disappeared under the tall shade trees. While the rest continued down the path, the orange top stepped off the drive and slipped into the trees. A minute later, she appeared, rushing down the road with something in her hand.

Ally stared at the spot from which she emerged long after the woman disappeared. Another shadow moved among the trees. She tracked the figure until it came into view. Shariff.

# CHAPTER THIRTY-THREE

## THE CHAT

For the past few hours, Eddie drove around the neighborhood, conducting reconnaissance of the area and its residents. The community of homes was new, with several empty plots awaiting construction. This worked to his benefit because all the floor plans were online; including the one for the house he intended to break into. The building in which he hoped to find his baby sister.

After he realized Shariff had her, he'd contacted a friend and cashed in a favor. But even with all his high-tech devices and his eyes in the sky, his friend couldn't trail the asshole. Alisha had been right. Irfani was slick and changed cars and appearances multiple times, making him hard to track. The person who finally helped him find the house was the one person he'd wanted far away from Karachi—Alisha.

The sun set over an hour ago, blanketing the perimeter in darkness. Shrouded in night, he hoisted himself up the stone wall in the back of the property. Once he could see over it, he studied the yard before hopping on to the empty lawn.

He pulled out his Walther PPK and flashlight from the back of his jeans. In his dominant hand, he kept his gun cocked, his index finger resting on the trigger. With the slightest of pressure, the weapon would fire. He held the back of the unlit light against the knuckles of his armed hand, prepared to blind any potential threats if need be.

With his tall frame low to the ground, he crept across the lawn until he arrived at the one-story building. Eddie pressed his back to the wall and slid along the length toward the door, peeking into the windows as he moved. He knew Alisha and Shariff were no longer on the premises. Arial footage indicated they'd left the property hours ago. What hadn't left the house was the ring Eddie gave her. He knew her well enough to know the only reason she'd leave it behind was if there was someone else she thought needed it more than she did. In this case, that someone would mean his sister.

From Alisha's descriptions, his sister and niece occupied the bedroom closest to the kitchen. The one with the boarded-up window. He also knew a camera monitored the room twenty-four seven. He'd tried to tap into the live feeds from the device they used but couldn't access it. Once he entered the building, he needed to grab them and get out before anyone watching the live feed noticed.

Bright yellow light streamed through the fibers of the curtained window at the end of the wall. Two shadows moved on the other side. Eddie slid close to the light and listened for voices but heard nothing. He leaned in and peeked through the thin slit on the curtain before gluing his back to the side of the wall again. His brows lowered, and he blinked a few times as he processed what he'd seen.

He snuck in another glance and this time watched for a little longer before pressing against the bricks a second time. Farah sat on the sofa and not only was Razaa by her side, the motherfucker's head rested on her shoulder. They both appeared to be crying. His niece, nor anyone else for that matter, was visible in the room.

Eddie's trigger finger flexed. He'd learned long ago, things were never as they appeared. This was clearly such a situation. He crept beneath the window and made his way to the patio door. When he gripped the knob, it turned easily. His eyes narrowed. It wasn't locked. Soundlessly, he rotated the handle and sucked in a breath. One chance was all he had. If he fucked up, they'd pay with their lives.

Before he blew out the breath he sucked in, he shoved the back door open. He'd already scanned the space, stepped in, and used his foot to close the door behind him by the time asshole and Farah were on their feet.

"Bhai."

Seeing the smile on her tear-stained face sent a surge of adrenaline through him. But it wasn't time to celebrate. Asshole took a step back. Eddie pointed the gun at his head. "On your knees. Now," he hissed.

Farah moved in front of the man and extended her arms out. "It's okay, Razaa. He's going to help us."

Asshole who currently used his sister as a human shield stared at Eddie from behind her head. A fresh cut ran along the man's left cheek. The muscles in Eddie's jaw twitched. "Farah, he might be your forever friend." He kept his gun steady and moved around the room for a clearer shot. "But to me, he's the bastard who kidnapped you and Amirah." Eddie saw no signs of a weapon on the man but he couldn't be sure. He jutted his chin at him. "And you. I'm the one with the gun, not her, so get on your fucking knees and put your hands behind your head before I put a hole in it," he growled.

His sister nodded her approval at Razaa, at which point he lowered himself to his knees and complied. From the back of the room, a baby's wail erupted.

Farah looked between the open door from where the cries originated, to the man on his knees, to Eddie. "She is hungry and I need to feed her. Promise me you won't kill him."

Eddie circled the man on the floor and approached him from behind. "As long as he does what I tell him, he will live." *For now.*

"What happened to your face?" Eddie asked the kid after Farah disappeared.

Razaa stared at the ground. "Your sister."

The reply made Eddie grin. By the time Amirah's cries were silenced, he had cable-tied Razaa's wrists behind him and cleared the other rooms for potential dangers. A handgun sat on the kitchen counter. He grabbed it and sat on the couch beside the target. He planted the newly found weapon on the cushion beside him and kept his PPK aimed at his head. "So, Razaa let's have a chat."

# CHAPTER THIRTY-FOUR

## THE PATH TO SUCCESS

*T*he early morning sky remained pitch black when the *Azaan* from a nearby mosque floated through the walls of the house. Ally closed her eyes and absorbed his soulful call to prayer. When he spoke about the path to success, she hung her head. As far as she knew, Alyah was still in the house, and since Eddie had not paid her another visit, Farah was still locked away somewhere. To top it all off, time was running out. Her path to success seemed more and more like a mirage.

Ally's chest tightened as her lungs transformed into rigid steel. She sucked in some air and released it slowly, fighting through the terror choking her. The thud of footsteps approaching her room intensified her panic. There were no more options. If she didn't change Shariff's mind, they would all die. Goosebumps pebbled her skin when he knocked at her door.

*It's show time.*

A tear slipped down her cheek as David's catch phrase floated through her head. She sucked in another lungful of air and imagined him wiping the tear away. She had no idea how the day would end, but the possibility of her soul reuniting with his by the time the sun set floated into her mind. The thought calmed her.

"Bhaabi, good morning. It's your favorite brother-in-law." The fake peppiness in Shariff's voice ground against her ears.

She wiped the thin film of perspiration from her forehead and rose from the bed. With unsteady hands, she unlatched the lock and opened the door. Shariff stood before her in the hall, his usual designer jeans and tee replaced with a tailored silk kurta in ivory. The fabric clung to his broad shoulders, accentuating his muscular chest, and fell well below his knees, revealing the slim matching pants below. Delicate gold embroidery wrapped around his Nehru collar and around the cuffs of his bunched-up sleeves. Long curls, which typically hung loose, were tied back tight and his face freshly shaved.

As usual, a smirk stretched across his face, but what caught her attention was the rage brewing in his eyes. She pretended not to notice and raised a brow, looking him over a second time. "Impressive. What's the occasion?"

His grin widened but did nothing to soften the intensity in his gaze. "So many things." He glanced over his shoulder at the two guards standing against the wall and then back at her. "All of which we need to discuss. Now."

She tightened her grip on the knob. "Let me get dressed first."

"By all means." He took a step forward as she slammed the door in his face and locked it.

Shariff's laughter chased her to the bathroom. "Be sure to wear the peach outfit I picked for you," he said through the wooden barrier.

Ally tied the drawstring of her snug cotton leggings and inspected herself in the mirror. Delicate golden thread formed intricate designs over the peach bodice, sleeves, and scarf. The embellished fabric fit snug against her chest and waist, flaring out in layers of peach and gold silk to the floor, hiding the tight pants beneath. Although the outfit's pale sheer fabric was lined with silk to conceal her breasts, the way it clung to her chest had the opposite effect. The long sleeves were left sheer, showing off the bare arms beneath.

She twisted a few locks of her hair around her fingers and checked her makeup for the thousandth time. It wasn't Rizwan she hoped to impress—it was his son. But how far would she go to do so? With a palm on her stomach, she looked herself in the eyes through the mirror. *Anything for Farah and Amirah.* It was the idea of what anything would entail that scared her.

The light rasping at the door made her flinch. She was stalling, and clearly, he knew it. When she opened it, Shariff stood with a hand on either side of the threshold, looming over her.

"It looks better on you than I imagined." While his hungry gaze roamed her body, she took in the two guards standing behind him.

As usual, they avoided her gaze. Like Shariff, they also dressed up for the visit. Their jeans and tees were replaced with clean and pressed traditional attire. One held a plate overflowing with fruit and sweets while the other carried a tray with a carafe and cups.

The corner of Shariff's mouth lifted. "Do I need to feel you for weapons before we enter?"

Sirens roared in her head, shrieking danger, but she fought the reflex to look away. "Where in this outfit would I have space to hide a weapon?"

"I'm not quite sure." His attention lingered over her hips and breasts before finally meeting her eyes. "But it would be exhilarating to find out."

She stepped aside, granting him access. After she shut the door on the guards, she turned to find him standing behind her.

He grabbed her hips, pressing her body to his.

Her head clouded with memories of Sayeed and the trauma she endured. A battle of emotions raged within; fear for herself and a need to protect the others challenging each other for dominance. Focusing on the latter, she locked the fear away into the far recesses of her mind. The repercussions of her decisions, she'd deal with later. Instead of moving away, she brushed the back of her hand against his cheek. Shariff closed his eyes and rested his forehead against hers. "You are a dangerous woman, Bhaabi."

Before she could respond, there was a loud knock at the door.

He let out a breath and stepped away from her. When he opened her door, the guards stood at the entrance with their trays. He ran a hand over his tightly pulled back hair and smiled at her. "It may be wiser if we sit outside on your patio and cool down."

She swallowed hard, forcing herself to stay on task. "Is that what you want?"

When she took a step toward him, he raised his hand. "For now."

Ally stayed on the lit terrace while Shariff led the men out of her room. The food sat on the center of her tiny table with two chairs on either side. She leaned against the railing and stared out into the courtyard. A soft breeze caressed her cheeks and played with her hair as it swept past. Lamp posts were scattered around the grounds, illuminating the darkness with their yellow glow.

Shariff approached behind her, but she didn't acknowledge his presence.

"Do you do that often?" he asked as he slid beside her.

She gripped the metal railing and reminded herself of her mission. "Stare at the sky?"

He laughed. "No, slam doors in men's faces."

"Only if they are related to you."

"Not everyone related to me is an arsehole." He put an arm around her waist and stared out at the sky. "It is lovely, isn't it? It takes me back to better times."

The anger she saw in his eyes earlier seemed to soften. "Times when you were here with your mother?"

He nodded. "On nights like this, she and I used to sleep out on the terrace. It was only a sheet, a pillow, and the two of us with the stars and the moon."

Ally ran her hand over the cool iron bar of the railing, honing in on the sadness in his tone. "They say the first few years are the most crucial in a person's development. That it impacts the way they see themselves and the world around them for them rest of their lives."

Shariff hadn't stiffened, nor had he pulled away, so she continued. "Your mom loved you. She showed you how valuable you were."

"And then she died. Like your parents." He gave her waist a squeeze. "It's hard to remember one is valuable in a world where so many make it a point to devalue you, don't you think?"

The motorized gates to the home opened, drawing their attention. A shudder ran down the length of her spine. She stiffened when the gates slammed shut. Soon tires crunching over the gravel filled the otherwise silent morning. Shariff's fingers dug into her hip and from the corner of her eye, she noticed the tight smile on his face.

It wasn't until the car rolled up the driveway and parked that she finally broke the silence. "Your father?"

He shook his head. "He's not expected for another half hour."

If it wasn't Rizwan, then who? A movement from below caught her attention. Alyah rushed across the roundabout. A sleeping Aadam lay in her arms, his head resting on her shoulder and a bag dangling from her wrist.

Ally's fingers squeezed the smooth iron bars of the balcony.

"Alyah Bhaabi," Shariff yelled.

The poor woman almost tripped on her shoes at the sound of his voice. The fear on her face when she looked up at them made Ally wince. She willed them to get in the car and leave before anyone stopped them.

"Where are you going this early in the morning?"

Alyah opened the passenger door and laid the sleeping child in the backseat. After her son was secure, she stood by the car door and flashed a tight smile at them. "I have some last minute purchases to make before your father arrives."

"Excellent," he said dryly. "But why isn't Wassim coming with you?"

She shook her head. "He has too much to do here to prepare for the visit."

Shariff feigned understanding while his tone screamed something more. "Why not leave the sleeping baby at home?"

Alyah shook her head and gave instructions to the driver, who sat patiently inside the vehicle.

He leaned over to Ally. "She's going off to buy things this early in the morning. Nothing is even open yet."

Ally shrugged but didn't trust herself to respond.

A woman hurried outside to the car, carrying a tote bag. A chill shot through Ally at the sight of her. Unlike yesterday's bright orange, today she wore floral yellow. Alyah took the bag from her, tossing it onto the floor of the backseat.

"Parsa." Shariff waved at the woman in yellow below. "You should go with them to make sure they return on time. I'm sure Bhaabi could use your help."

She squeezed the cool metal of the bannister so tightly it cut into her skin.

When Parsa attempted to get in the car, Alyah said something to her, which made her stop. The woman stepped back, shot

Shariff a look, and disappeared into the house. A few minutes later, the car drove away with Alyah and Aadam.

It wasn't until after they vanished beneath the trees that Ally was able to breathe again.

"Crazy women," he muttered and then squeezed her elbow. "Come, let's have some breakfast."

She listened for the gate closing before she unwound her fingers from the railing and followed him back to the seat.

# CHAPTER THIRTY-FIVE

## LIGHT READING

*E*ddie lowered himself in between a large cluster of trees and bushes. He'd noticed the spot a few days ago and had made a mental note of it. Tall, flowering shrubs surrounded the trunks, providing an excellent cover. The perfect location for his needs. His duffle lay beside him. He moved a couple of the branches of the bush in front and positioned his binoculars, zooming in on the yellow light glowing from the bedroom of the darkened third floor balcony of the house.

He didn't need to check his watch to know it was around five in the morning. The Azaan from a local mosque floated through the air, and a few seconds later, another call to prayer from a distant mosque echoed the words of the first. Soon the sun would rise and the day would start. If his plan worked, it would be a day most of the people in the home would not live to see the end of.

Farah and the baby were safe, out of harm's way. And as much as he wanted to kill Razaa for putting everyone in this hell, his sister made a powerful argument for why he should live. It helped that his story about David's death and how he ended up with Shariff went along with Eddie's theories. Now, if the kid didn't follow through on his promises, he'd be dead before the afternoon.

Eddie dropped his binoculars and unzipped his bag. Time to prep for the morning festivities. A few minutes later, the metal magazine of his .30 caliber rifle locked into place. He angled the weapon and stared into the telescopic lens. A few hundred yards away, on the bottom floor corner, stood a set of sliding glass doors—the target. He positioned the rifle according to what he remembered about the layout of the room hidden behind thick curtains. It would be a clear shot.

To his left, a light on the third level terrace turned on. Eddie lowered the weapon, grabbed his binoculars, and focused on the spot. The door opened. His body tensed as soon as Shariff and two guards entered the balcony. *What the fuck were they doing in her room?* A second later, Alisha joined them.

Two thirds of the men with her had openly discussed the prospect of raping her before they killed her. The final one third was the asswipe who brought her into the house and hadn't been able to keep his fucking hands off her since.

The guards slid trays of food on the plastic table and nodded at whatever Shariff said. While Eddie kept his focus on them, he dug into his bag, feeling for the cell phone with earbuds wound around it.

Alisha wore a light colored top that fit her curves. Considering the company that surrounded her, it fit a little too well for his comfort. Although she seemed calm and collected, Eddie would have bet money on the fact that her knuckles were white. He unwound the wires from the phone and plugged one of the buds into his ear as he turned on the device.

The guards left the balcony and walked out the bedroom. Shariff followed them to the door, shutting and locking them out. Alisha leaned against the railing, and by the time he returned to the balcony, Eddie had the audio up and working. Soon the horny asshole's voice filled his ear. "Not everyone related to me is an arsehole."

Eddie rolled his eyes. *Bull-fucking-shit.* Shariff put an arm around her waist, and when he pressed his groin against her ass, Eddie found himself considering the prospect of grabbing his handgun, sneaking in through her closet, and shooting both of the little dick's heads off.

"It is lovely, isn't it? It takes me back to better times," he said, while staring down her shirt.

"Patience," Eddie muttered under his breath while he listened to their conversation. "Need to be fucking patient."

He focused the weapon on Shariff. His index finger rested firmly against the trigger. One little application of pressure on the metal and a bullet would go straight through the asshole's head. An asshole who stood way to close to Alisha for his taste. A muscle in his jaw twitched as he tried to rein in his urge to finish him off.

*Stick with the plan*, he told himself. Killing Shariff now would make the others run. Escape was not the outcome he intended for any of them. She'd gone through hell. Had her life ripped apart one too many times and today he'd make it all end.

He observed them as his mind drifted to five years ago. In an unfurnished room, he faced a computer monitor watching the same woman, but back then, she was tormented by a different brother. And seated across from Eddie had been her husband.

David's shook with rage as Sayeed tormented his wife. Eddie had considered the man's inability to keep his emotions in check a handicap and regretted bringing him along on the mission. Probably because the woman they had watched meant nothing to him. Just a picture. A name. A means to get the man he'd dreamed of killing for years.

This time it was different and watching Shariff touch Alisha triggered a kind of anger, a possessiveness he'd never felt before. The kind that made it hard for him to think straight and hard to not kill whoever hurt her. The kind David had felt five years ago.

His brows rose as soon as the realization hit. *The kind David felt?* Where the fuck did that come from? He shook it off and lowered his weapon. This was not the time to get emotional, not if he wanted to get her out alive. And he would. For her. For David. His face heated. He'd finish this.

The satellite phone in his jean pocket vibrated. He pulled out the ear bud and pressed the cell to his ear. "Yeah?"

"The kids are all fast asleep," Leanna said. She'd come in the day before, and as much as he hated asking for her help, he was glad he had. He trusted her and knew she'd keep his sister and niece safe.

He dug into the duffle a second time and grabbed a small gaming controller and the rest of the pieces to the remote control rifle system. "Did the kids give you any problems?"

Leanna went along with the coded story. "Nope, perfect little angels."

Eddie screwed the weapon onto the base of the stand as he listened.

"What are you up to?" she asked.

He connected the camera to the top of the rifle. "Nothing much. I'm still in bed."

"Did I wake you?"

"Nope. I was up." The wiring fit smooth into the battery pack. "Doing some light reading."

"Good book?"

"It's a dark read." He turned on the receiver and pressed the arrows on the remote control. Eddie smiled as the gun moved accordingly. "But I like it."

"Is it the book you told me about the other day? I've heard the heroine's easy to fall in love with."

He stared at the balcony and the two tiny figures on it. "Yeah, I'm noticing the same."

The gates to the entrance opened behind him. He looked over his shoulder as the bright lights of a car flashed across the lawn. "Well, I should get back to the book. It's getting really good."

"Okay. Let me know how it ends."

Eddie didn't bother responding. He hit disconnect and slipped the phone back in his pocket.

# CHAPTER THIRTY-SIX

## PREPARING FOR COMPANY

*A*lly sat in the chair Shariff slid out for her and watched him set the cups for the tea. With Alyah and the child safely off the property, the path she couldn't see before had emerged. Hope fluttered its wings deep within her stomach. Farah had the ring. Eddie would find his sister and the baby and get them to a safe place, even if it killed him in the process. Reviewing the mental checklist of lives relieved the heavy weight she carried. Now the only thing she needed to do was to keep herself alive. She eyed the man pouring her chai. That required convincing him she cared.

She stared at the plate of food in front of her and picked up an orange colored sweet and showed it to him. "Ledus were your brother's favorite."

The steam of the fresh tea swirled up when Shariff poured her a cup. "Must run in the family. It's mine and my father's, too."

She returned it to the plate. "He smashed one on my face. It was the moment he told me he killed Umber." She looked over Shariff. "One of the boys he'd adopted."

Shariff paused mid-pour before topping off his cup with the sweet cream drink.

"I've detested them ever since," she said.

He sat beside her and squeezed her knee.

She reached for her tea and took a sip. A warm mix of sweet

cream, cardamom, and a hint of ginger exploded in her mouth. "Was your big brother like your father?"

His smile faltered as he looked out in the distance. "Unfortunately, yes, which is why I would sneak away and wander the grounds whenever either was around. They were both arseholes."

"And when I meet the asshole today, what am I supposed to do?"

He nodded and grabbed a snack from the plate. "You're a bit of a miracle to him. Up until a few months ago, the world believed you died in the explosion. And now here you are, a survivor of the unsurvivable."

Their chairs were positioned so close to each other that when he leaned back, his knee hit hers. "He wants to know if his precious son survived as well."

Ally grabbed a banana from the pile. "And you want me to...?"

He smiled and pressed his hand to his chest. "Rip his heart out piece by piece."

She peeled down the protective layer of the fruit. "I do that by telling him I murdered his son."

Shariff grabbed a slice of apple from the plate and bit into it. "Yes."

He left out the part where his father would then proceed to kill her. She took a bite of the sweet, white meat and forced it down her throat. "You've gone to a lot of trouble to rip his heart out. Risked your life, your freedom to please him. A man who sent you away at six years of age and never looked back until you were valuable enough for him to care about."

Shariff reached over, grabbed the orange ledu, and popped the entire thing in his mouth. "And it will all be worth it," he mumbled through his food.

"From the way you describe her, your mother wasn't like him. Which means you don't need to be like him either." Ally took another bite of her breakfast and pretended not to notice the way he tensed.

He laughed and grabbed his teacup. "And that served her well, didn't it?"

"It gave her you." She turned and watched him finish off the drink. "Do you really think your brother's and father's lives turned out better? Love is a powerful force, Shariff. It's what makes this life worth living and dying for. Look at Sayeed. There wasn't a soul on this planet who loved him."

"Not true. There *is* a soul who loved him. Still loves him." He waved at the driveway. "Speak of the devil."

The motors of the gate buzzed as it opened a second time. She tensed until she saw the servants walking down the path to the house.

He reached for her free hand in her lap and weaved his cold fingers through her clammy ones. "Getting nervous, are we?"

"I'm supposed to confess to murdering Sayeed, and we both know your father will then kill me. I think I'm allowed to be nervous."

She watched the people downstairs while he laughed. The woman in floral yellow met the group of servants and gave them their morning orders, rushing them to start their work because Shariff's father would arrive very soon. "You still haven't told me what else you want me to do."

"Nothing more. You've already done the rest," he said. Ally stiffened when Shariff squeezed her knee. "Have you met Parsa?"

She raised a questioning brow at him. The name sounded familiar, but she couldn't quite place it.

He pointed his cup at the woman in yellow below. "She has been with my family since I was a baby."

"I've seen her around but no."

"She mentioned you paid Bhaabi a visit yesterday, and how the poor woman's been nervous ever since."

Ally felt his eyes probing her, scanning for a reaction. She kept her features as relaxed as possible.

His grip on her palm tightened. "The odd part was after your chat with Bhaabi, she asked Parsa to schedule a car and driver. Any reason why she would do such a thing?"

Her body chilled. Ally shrugged and took another bite of her banana.

"Alyah doesn't speak English." His brows lowered. "Do you by any chance speak Urdu?"

"Not a word." She tossed the peel on the table. "I think my presence makes her jumpy." She smiled. "After all, I was dead to her until a few days ago."

The corner of his mouth twitched. "Of course." He rose from his seat and poured her and himself another serving of chai. "The problem was finding someone who would come so early."

Ally stared at her drink, her fingers digging into her skin.

"Fortunately, I called a friend of mine to drive them." He picked up his cup and looked over at her. "Do you remember the man who met you in the German airport?"

Her heart pulsed inside her ears as his words sunk in.

His phone rang. Shariff pulled it out and glanced at the screen as he talked to her. "Well, he happened to be in town and was kind enough to drive her, which means you're off the hook. Your third task of getting rid of Alyah Bhaabi is being completed as we speak." He rose to his feet and flashed her the still ringing device. "Excuse me, I have to take this."

*Getting rid of Alyah Bhaabi?* Numb, Ally stayed in her seat long after he'd left the balcony. The sound of the gates started up again. She rose to her feet and walked to the barrier. The same car, which drove away with Alyah and Aadam pulled into the drive and parked. Bashar climbed out of the driver's seat. She grabbed the railing for support at the sight of him. He looked up at her and smiled before opening the back passenger door.

The world began to spin around her and her knees weakened. She leaned against the barrier for support. Parsa rushed to the vehicle. She reached in and lifted Aadam out of the car. The boy wrapped his little arms around her neck and his legs around her waist. His tiny voice filled the courtyard as he talked about his trip.

Ally scanned the vehicle for additional passengers, her pulse rising each time she found nothing.

"Chacha! I ate ice cream for breakfast!" Aadam squealed.

Shariff wandered onto the driveway and took the happy child into his own arms.

While the child described his early morning treat, the car drove away.

"Sara Mommy," the child waved.

Unable to respond, Ally helplessly watched Shariff carry the child inside as two other cars pulled up. Doors opened and their occupants exited. The first man to climb out caught her attention and made it impossible for her to look away.

Razaa.

# CHAPTER THIRTY-SEVEN

## ALYAH AND AADAM

$\mathcal{T}$he morning sun chased away the darkness long ago. Now, from her third floor window, Ally could see everything, including Razaa. He stood in the courtyard wedged between the car and its open door, scanning the space, most likely searching for Shariff. The dark aviator glasses he wore made his emotions impossible to read. But she knew when he noticed her, because he stared in her direction for a while before looking away.

Her heart sank. His presence meant either he didn't believe her story or he didn't care. She leaned forward, searching the car. What did his arrival mean about Farah and the baby? And what happened to Eddie? More questions she wasn't sure she wanted to know the answers to.

An older man in a black suit climbed out of the second sedan. He was bald, for the most part, except for the gray hair, which circled around his ears and the lower part of his head. A well-trimmed white goatee covered his mouth and chin. The high collar of his charcoal-colored dress shirt poked out over his suit jacket. She'd bet money his shoes were shiny black leather. Thinner than Sayeed, he looked much like an older version of the man who tortured her for two years and still terrorized her dreams.

His driver walked to his side and put a hand on the old man's arm, guiding him along the gravel path. The black handle of a gun sat above the waistband of the driver's jeans.

Rizwan's serious face morphed into one of joy when Wassim walked out with Aadam in his arms. The old man put his hands on the child's cheeks and kissed his face. "I am your *daada*," he said between kisses. "Do you know how happy I am to finally meet you?"

The shy child shook his head but did not respond.

"Do you know my trunk is filled with gifts I brought for you?"

A second later, Aadam was on his feet, holding his grandfather's hand. The little boy grinned from ear to ear while the driver pulled out package after package from the back of the car. He stood on his tiptoes assessing his stash, unaware that if his uncle had his way, he would never have a chance to play with any of the toys.

The patio door behind her squeaked. Ally turned to find Shariff leaning against the threshold, arms crossed. "You should keep your door locked. You never know what kind of maniacs could sneak in."

She didn't respond.

"I was coming here to tell you that your father-in-law has arrived, but I see you already know."

She rested her back against the railing and copied his pose. "Why aren't you down there greeting him?"

He watched her intently before finally answering. "I'll go when I'm ready."

With a quick prayer for courage, she forced out her question. "And Alyah?"

The corner of his mouth lifted slightly. "My father doesn't care if she shows up or not. All he cares about is his grandson. And meeting you, of course."

"Her husband and son are going to ask about her."

He flashed her a tired smile. "Wassim already has. He seems to think you scared her off."

The sad reality was she had tried to do just that. "The man who dropped off Aadam today, the one who was waiting for me in Germany, you know he helped Sayeed kidnap me?"

He nodded. "I do."

"He's going to kill her, isn't he?" she asked as the faint breeze sent wisps of her hair flying against her face and lips.

"My father would have done it anyway." Shariff approached

her and tucked the loose strands behind her ear. "Soon Wassim will join his wife. He has plans to raise Aadam on his own." He searched her eyes. "I fully intended to kill the child too. But as you see, I didn't. I'm not sure if it was your constant yapping or if the little shit was growing on me." He brushed the tear that ran down her cheek. "I knew you'd be happy."

Hate rose up her throat. Ally swallowed down the bitter taste and tried to hide the emotion from her voice. "Alyah's death will never make me happy," she whispered. "He will grow up without his parents, like you and I did. Don't let that happen."

"I have no control over his outcome." He stared out into the horizon. "And it's too late."

She thought about the man who kidnapped her all those years ago and the hate in his eyes. "Did Bashar kill my husband and Amir?"

Shariff's brows rose but he didn't answer.

Ally grabbed his arm and forced him to look at her. "I'm going to be dead in a few hours. I'd like to leave this earth knowing what happened to them."

An emotion flashed across his face. "Not yours, but he is the reason your friend is a widow."

She nodded. "Razaa killed my husband?"

"In a roundabout way, yes." Shariff rested his elbows on the railing and looked over the grounds. "But I don't want you to die hating him too much. Poor kid showed up at my door six months ago, looking pitiful. He claimed to be one of Sayeed's adopted sons and begged for my help in finding his brothers. So, I introduced him to one of my dearest friends, Bashar.

"As you know, Bashar is not a fan of yours. The man was quite content with the idea of you dead. Once he heard Razaa's story, it didn't take him long to realize it wasn't the case." Shariff nudged her arm with his elbow. "You looked very lovely in your sister's wedding, by the way."

Fear tightened its grip around her chest at the thought of them staring at pictures of her family. She'd put so many people in danger by returning home.

"He took Razaa to the States and convinced him the only way he'd get his brothers back was by shooting your husband dead."

Ally clenched the iron railing, bracing herself for the rest.

"Unfortunately, he walked in front of the car and stood there. He confessed to me later that he couldn't do it and regretted ever agreeing to the plan in the first place. The poor kid's had nightmares about it ever since."

A sad smile tugged at her lips. She had been right.

"Don't worry, though. After today, I'll keep my promise and help him right the wrong and find his brothers."

She thought about the young man two floors below her. "Is that why he's here? Because you promised him you'd find his brothers?"

"No. He's here to bear witness to your murder."

Ally shook her head. What Razaa was about to do would not right his wrongs but add to his growing list of sins. His pain blinded him, and by the time he would realize what he'd done, it would be too late. "And what happens to Farah and her baby?"

Shariff looked her over for a long while before responding. "I promised him that they would be let go once this was all finished."

Ally met his gaze. "And he believes you?"

"He and I have a lot in common. I intend to keep my promises to him."

She prayed they would never find the boys. The thought of them under Shariff, or his father's control, sent another wave of fear shooting through her.

He moved closer, placing his hands on either side of her. "Do you have any concern for your own life?"

Ally's stomach twisted. From the way he stared at her mouth, she knew what he was about to do. She gripped the iron bars behind her and willed herself to remain still. When his lips pressed against her mouth, her fists tightened.

He pulled away, only to return a second time. His desire pushed against her stomach. The bitter taste of acid rose within. She swallowed down the nausea and turned her face.

He kissed her cheek. "You were right. One taste of you will never be enough. And now I will never know just how sweet you must taste."

"Shariff!" A male voice called from somewhere in the house.

"Ahh, the beautiful sound of my name falling from my father's lips." He kissed her cheek one more time before stepping away from her. "Why don't you stay up here for a little bit? Let's get the happy reunion part down before we tackle the rest."

~

Ally stayed on the balcony long after Shariff left. Aside from the two cars, the courtyard below sat empty, like her brain. She had no plan for escape. There was nothing more she could do for anyone. The realization didn't sadden her; it made her numb. So numb, that all she could do was stare out at the blue horizon and see nothing.

A fantasy floated through her head, one she didn't bother pushing away. It was an alternate reality, a *what could have been* version of her story. In this tale, David still lived. He waited outside beyond the trees and fences. An army of men he'd somehow convinced to help stood beside him. She smiled at the idea of him going toe-to-toe with them, most of whom could very well break his neck and not break a sweat in the process. For her, he would have done it and more. The beautiful part of the story was he'd succeed. He always did, and somehow, someway, they'd be together again.

Emotion streamed her face, flowing down her neck, and on to her shirt. "Where are you?" she asked, knowing he'd never answer. A soft breeze caressed her cheeks. She lifted her face, letting it cool the pain burning her skin.

The distant sound of Aadam's voice floated to her ears. She looked at the far end of the yard to see him disappear into the forest of trees. He wasn't alone. Walking beside him, holding his hand, was Parsa.

# CHAPTER THIRTY-EIGHT

## GUEST OF HONOR

*A*lly stood ready before Shariff ever knocked. She'd heard the footsteps approach and knew they were coming for her.

The knock on her door was soft. She removed the padlock and dropped it and the key on the table next to her bed. It wouldn't be needed anymore. She rolled her shoulders back and opened the door, ready for whatever awaited.

Raaza stood in the hallway. He didn't say a word, just stared at her. From the balcony, she hadn't been able to see his features as clear as she could now. A fresh gash ran across his cheek, and his lip was cut and swollen red. Different shades of purple and green colored his right eye, the lid so swollen, he could barely open it. "Razaa?" She brushed her hand along the side of his face. "What happened to you?"

"You happened, dear Bhaabi." The anger in Shariff's voice made her jump. He stood in the hall, a few feet away, his arms crossed. His lips formed a thin line.

Goosebumps rose along her skin as he approached. When she took a step back, his lips curled. "No, Bhaabi, don't run. You're the main attraction today."

He grabbed her wrist and pulled her close. Pain shot through her fingers and up her shoulder. When she tried to pull away, he squeezed harder.

"Shariff, please." She winced.

"Please what? Let you go?" He eased his grip, but his fingers stayed wrapped around her. Shariff moved close and pressed his mouth to her ear. "You've been busy," he hissed.

Ally remained still, staring at Razaa. His face was hard to read, but it was clear he wasn't going to help.

"Who did you find to help you?"

She didn't respond.

"Did you spread your legs for him? Is that how you paid him for his services?" He twisted her arm behind her back and shoved her body against the wall in front of her. "Who the fuck is he?" he growled.

Her cheek scraped against the cold surface as her heart pounded erratically. "I don't know what you're talking about." She kept her voice low, hoping it would calm him.

"Did you hear what she said? She doesn't know which man she sent after you." He yanked her away from the wall, dragging her to Razaa. "Whichever one it was, he does excellent work." He cupped her chin, forcing her to be face to face with the young man in front of her.

"Let her go," Razaa said, his unblinking gaze fixed on her.

It was when their eyes locked that the pieces fell into place. Eddie had found Farah and the baby. She scanned his face for confirmation. Although he showed no emotion, she knew.

"No, I will not. And you want to know why?" His fingers dug into her cheeks. "Only yesterday, she professed her love for you." Ally gasped when he twisted her arm tighter. "Look at his face, Bhaabi. Is this how you show your love?"

Sweat beaded her skin. She was breathless and it had nothing to do with Shariff. "Are they okay?"

Razaa nodded.

Shariff laughed and pulled her away from him. "You're very good. Better than I even realized. Here I was feeling sorry for you, and all the while you were lying to me."

A smile tugged at her lips. Eddie had gotten them out. Yes, Razaa was injured but he was alive, too. "They're safe," she whispered.

Shariff twisted her face to his, digging his fingers into her skin. "But you're fucking not."

He turned her around and shoved her toward the steps. "My father is waiting to talk to you."

Shariff stayed glued to her back the entire time. She scanned the two floors below. Although empty, the muffled voices of men could be heard from somewhere on the bottom.

At the last step, Ally stopped and scanned the space. Shariff put a hand on her back and shoved her forward. "There are no heroes waiting for you down here, Bhaabi. And I sure as hell have no intention of saving you."

The voices grew louder as they walked down the back hallway. She surveyed the kitchen when they passed. It was empty. Another shove to her back kept her moving.

At the end of the hall, Wassim's men stood outside the door, conversing with one another. She gazed at their faces, hoping to find Eddie, knowing she wouldn't. Shariff was right. There would be no heroes for her this time. She ignored the disappointment gnawing at her. His goal had been to save his sister and niece. He'd achieved that. She had even told him not to come back for her. Everything was going according to plan.

The three guards stopped talking and watched her. One flashed her a victorious grin as she passed through the door he held open. Through it all, Shariff's hand remained glued to her back, pushing her along.

The sitting room was large and ornately furnished. A set of sliding doors stretched across the middle of the farthest wall. Thick golden drapes hung over its glass, darkening the space. From the ceiling above them, a crystal chandelier hung, casting the room in a yellow hue.

In front of the draped glass doors, sat a red sofa trimmed with gold and dark wood. Shariff pointed to it as he closed the door they'd entered. "Go sit down."

Ally nodded and looked around as she took her seat. Shariff leaned against the entrance, his arms crossed, his body rigid with anger. Razaa walked toward her. She watched him, hungry to meet his eyes, to tell him she was sorry for everything that had happened to him, but he avoided her gaze. He walked past her and stood in the corner behind the sofa.

She surveyed the space and the other occupants. Rizwan sat across from her in an oversized armchair. His guard stood to at his side. Behind him, against the farthest wall, was a creamy white couch on which Wassim lounged, glaring at her.

Five sets of eyes were fixed on her. There was nothing more she could do for anyone, much less herself. Ally leaned back on the couch and rested her hands in her lap, bracing herself.

# CHAPTER THIRTY-NINE

## QUESTIONS

*A* thick silence fell across the room, almost as thick as the heat pouring down on Ally from the crystal bulbs in the chandelier. Rizwan looked over his shoulder at no one in particular. "Where is the English translator I sent?"

Wassim shifted in his seat uncomfortably. "He did not come today."

"Your wife and handsome translator both disappear on the same day," Shariff smirked. "What an interesting coincidence."

Wassim's face turned multiple shades of red. "What are you trying to say, Shariff?"

Rizwan raised up his hand, silencing them both. "So you do not speak our language?" he asked her in Urdu.

A thin line of sweat formed along Ally's lip. She stared at him blankly. He nodded and cleared his throat. "Do you know who I am?" He spoke his words slow and in English.

She nodded.

He leaned back in his chair and crossed his legs. "You are my *bahu*, my daughter-in-law."

She wiped away the moisture on her lip with the back of her hand. "Yes."

"Your husband was my son." Although he smiled, his gaze on her was anything but kind. He planted a hand to his chest. "He was my soul. My heart. My everything."

Shariff's scowl deepened.

"When I heard he died, it broke my heart."

Nauseating heat blanketed her, making her head throb.

"Until a few months ago, we all thought you were dead too. And now I see with my own eyes, you are not."

Her neck turned slick with perspiration. She fought the urge to wipe it away and focused her attention on the man in front of her.

"I can't help but hope that you being alive means he lives as well."

Her veins turned to ice at his words. She cleared her throat. "He was killed at the compound."

"Can I open the window?" So fixated on the interrogation, Razaa's question made Ally jump.

Rizwan waved his consent and continued. "I have heard a version of the story. Maybe you can tell me if this is accurate."

The morning sun spread across the room the instant the drapes behind her pulled apart.

"Razaa," he said. "You were there when my son died. No?"

When the door slid open, a much-needed breeze wound through the room, cooling them off. "Yes, sir."

He nodded at the man behind Ally. "Wassim tells me you heard her confess to killing him."

Ally's body stilled as she braced herself.

Since the conversation was in English, Wassim sat rigid watching the interaction. At the mention of his name, he rose to his feet. "She is a liar. Don't believe anything she says."

Rizwan rolled his eyes and put a hand up, silencing him.

"Father, if I may," Shariff said.

"No, you may not," he snapped back in Urdu. "Wassim told me how busy you have been with your bhaabi." He looked over his shoulder at his now scowling son. "How thoughtful of you to get to know your brother's wife so well."

"It would be in Wassim's best interest to do some work instead of gossiping," Shariff snapped back.

Rizwan shook his head and eyed Ally. "He sees things you are not able to see. Like how she manipulates you."

Wassim nodded his agreement. "Yes, I do. I know her better than anyone else here. She is a liar and a killer. I stake my life on it."

Rizwan rubbed the temples of his head. "Wassim."

"She killed Sayeed Babba. She killed my guard, and now my wife is missing."

"Wassim," the old man snapped. "If you do not sit down and shut up, I will do it for you."

Wassim talked over his order and continued, "She has had sex with your son. Ask any of the guards. They will *all* tell you."

"I accepted long ago that I have no control over my son's actions, but I do have control over yours." Rizwan tapped his hand on the man standing beside him. "Either kill him or make him leave."

Wordlessly, the guard pulled his gun out and pointed it at Wassim. Shariff opened the door and smirked at him. Wassim's body shook with rage as he stared at Rizwan and stormed out of the room.

Shariff slammed the door shut after him and laughed.

The old man rose to his feet and stared at his son. "You are not allowed to speak. Do you understand me?"

Ally scanned the space while father and son participated in a staring match. The only way out was the open doors behind her. Doors Razaa currently stood guard by. It wasn't until Shariff sat on the white couch Wassim occupied minutes ago, that the older man nodded and focused his attention on Ally. He walked toward her until his feet were directly in front of hers. "Look at me."

She stared up at the man and at the taller shadow that stood behind him.

Rizwan waved his hand at the guard. The gun the man held to his side rose until it pointed at Ally. "The boy behind you tells me you confessed to killing my son. I would like to believe he is lying and to believe my son lives. So tell me, did you kill Sayeed?"

Ally's mouth went dry. If she said no, then he would accuse Razaa of lying and shoot him dead a minute later. "It's true. I killed your son." Her voice was a whisper, but everyone in the room heard it.

The old man's brows rose. His face turned red as he stayed rigid, staring at her. "He is dead? You are sure?"

Terror rocked through her. Not because of Rizwan's anger but because he looked exactly like Sayeed. The way his eyes seemed to shrink in size, and how his brows lowered to create almost one straight line across his forehead. Ally nodded.

He put his palm out. "You killed my Sayeed?"

Unable to speak, she nodded a second time.

The guard behind him handed Rizwan his gun.

She leaned back on the sofa and waited. A gust of wind sped over her head. A second later, a red hole appeared on Rizwan's forehead. His eyes widened, and he reached forward as he fell back onto his guard behind him. The pair landed on the floor. The only sound she heard was her own breathing as she waited for them to move. Blood trickled from them, creating a puddle on the ground.

In stunned silence, she watched the red pool of liquid widen. Someone grabbed her wrist and pulled her to the floor. When she tried to yank her arm away, Razaa sandwiched her hand between his two palms. "Please, Sara Mommy. Trust me," he mouthed. Before he was done, the room erupted in screams.

Shariff was on his feet, his hand on his head. His body shook as he called for the men to come.

While she and Razaa crouched in the corner where the sliding glass and wall met, he ran to the hallway door. The same gust of air sliced through the room a second time. Shariff fell forward. His body slammed against the door in front of him. A line of red followed him down the door as he slid and crumpled to the floor.

Razaa tugged at her to follow him to the open glass door. "We have to go now."

# CHAPTER FORTY

## THE ESCAPE

Ally climbed to her feet and let Razaa guide her out of the sitting room. Once on pebbled ground, he broke into a run, dragging her with him. From over her shoulder, she watched things play out in the room they exited. Two guards shoved the door open, pushing Shariff's body aside and stood at the entrance of the room staring at the carnage. One of them looked out the patio and locked eyes with her. The world became silent as realization flooded his face. This wasn't over. They'd come after her.

It was only then she saw Eddie. He stood hiding with his back to a tree they'd run past. In dark pants and a dark shirt, he gripped his gun with both hands and pointed it at the ground. His focus was fixed on the house. A second later, he sprinted toward the room they'd fled.

Ally turned her attention to the path Razaa took her. Despite the gunshots and the angry voices of men erupting behind them, relief blanketed her. He ran a few paces in front of her, his hand gripping hers. A smile spread across her face as a wave of adrenaline shot through her. Farah and Amirah were safe, Eddie had come back, and Razaa was by her side. For the first time since she boarded the plane, she knew everything would be okay.

They passed the walking trail to the gardens. The sight of the path made her trip on her shoes. Ally pulled her hand away from Razaa and slowed down. Somewhere in the garden was a little boy.

A little boy who had just lost all his family.

Out of breath and his face bright red, he grabbed her hand and tugged harder toward the drive. "Hurry, Sara Mommy. We have to get out of here."

She backed away. "I have to find Aadam."

Razaa's excitement turned to fear. He moved in front of her, his palms pressed out in an attempt to stop her. "My job is to get you in the car and save your life."

She sidestepped him and continued toward the garden. "Leaving you and the boys is something I've never forgiven myself for."

He shook his head as he walked beside her. "It wasn't your fault. Farah *Baji* told me everything. You had no choice."

"But this time I do." Ally looked into his eyes. "If I get in the car with you, it will be because I decided not to help him."

His face fell. "Then I am coming with you."

An idea took root in her mind. "No. Bring the car to the front gate. He's alone with an older woman. I'll get him and meet you there."

He looked over at the vehicle and the trail behind him, as if considering his options.

Ally stopped walking and crossed her arms. "I will not leave him behind."

He nodded and pulled out something from his pocket. Razaa grabbed her hand and slipped it on her finger. "Keep this so I can find you in case I lose you again."

She stared at the silver ring she'd given Farah and smiled. Ally pulled him into a hug and kissed his cheek. "I won't let you lose me again."

"Two minutes," he said, and then sped to the car.

Ally's heart raced as she moved down the twisted road. She didn't know what she was going to say but needed to come up with something soon. She looked on either side as she ran, but there was no sign of them. The trail curved and she followed. When she remembered where it led, she picked up her pace. *They were at the well.*

~

As soon as Alisha and Razaa were out of the building, Eddie ran in.

The two men by the gate were already dealt with. There were seven inside he needed to account for. Three who were now dead and another two who currently stood in the center of the room, their guns cocked in his direction. Their eyes widened when they saw him. The confusion on their faces and their hesitation to shoot was the best gift they could give him. While they tried to decide if he was there to help or hurt, he put a bullet through their heads. He had no choice. They would have figured out he wasn't on their side, and they'd have come after him.

Eddie poked his weapon out the door into the hallway before he stuck his head out. He surveyed the room before entering. Five now lay dead behind him. Two were left: Wassim and a guard.

Senses on high alert, he kept his back to the wall and slid down the empty passage, clearing each room before he moved to the next. Somewhere a clock ticked, a dog barked. But those weren't the sounds he listened for. And then he heard it. Something creaked directly above. At least one of the two targets was on the second floor. That left another unaccounted for.

He entered the living room and cleared the space, his gaze following his gun. At the base of the stairs, he surveyed the floors above him for potential dangers before climbing the steps. It creaked again. His guess was Wassim was grabbing some essentials from his bedroom before he ran.

Eddie crept up the steps to the second floor. Wassim's bedroom was the last door down the hall on the right. When he got halfway down the hall, Wassim came running out, bag and gun in hand.

The target froze at the sight of him and his gun. A wave of emotions washed over his face from relief to confusion and then to fear. "Hassan, she is a liar. Whatever she told you is not true."

Eddie didn't respond. This was the part he hated.

Tears welled in the man's eyes, and he shook his head. "I have a family. Please, don't kill me."

*Fuck.*

An explosion from outside rocked the house before Eddie could respond. Pictures on the wall crashed to the floor as the home shook. Eddie stared through the large windows on the front wall of the building as a second bomb detonated. Tall red flames and plumes of black smoke rose to the sky. By the time he looked back, Wassim was gone.

He stared at the bedroom into which the man had probably run and then out the living room window where the blaze from the car bombs continued. Terror consumed him as the black cloud colored the sky. Alisha was supposed to be in that car.

# CHAPTER FORTY-ONE

## AADAM

few feet from her destination, Ally stopped short. Bashar sat on a stack of bricks, chewing on a straw. She scanned the space for Aadam, and the chill of horror raised goosebumps on her when she finally laid eyes on him.

Barefoot, the child stood atop the ledge of the well. A wooden beam sat on either side of it with a third log secured to the tops of the two. Aadam looped his arm around the post beside him while he swayed on the thin lip of the well. He bent over, looking into the waters below, and talked into the darkness.

She sucked in a breath. Not wanting to startle the child, she walked quietly toward him, in the hopes of pulling him off before he realized what she'd done.

"It looks like we have company, little one," the man announced.

Aadam looked over his shoulder at her and waved. "Sara Mommy, I'm on the well," he said in Urdu.

A shudder ripped through her when his little foot missed the ledge. Aadam held tight to the pole and regained his balance as she got to his side.

Ally wrapped her arms around his waist, pressing his back to her chest. "You are. Tell me why you are up here?"

"Look at that. She understands Urdu." Bashar laughed. "You had us all fooled this whole time."

Ally ignored him and kept her focus on the child.

Aadam pointed inside the cavity. "Ammi is swimming."

Her stomach twisted as the meaning of his words sunk in.

"He wanted to see his mother. How could I deny him?"

Ally looked down to where Aadam pointed, praying she misunderstood. Acid rose up her chest, and she swallowed it down while she stared at Alyah's feet protruding above the dark waters below.

"Hi, Ammi!" He waved at his dead mother.

She should have never told Alyah to leave. Hot tears burned her eyes. Ally hugged the child and stared at Parsa, who lay a few feet away. The woman's face was blue. A deep red line encircled her neck.

She cleared her throat and kept the smile on her face. "Aadam, do you remember the little chipmunk we saw yesterday? The one whose home was under the tree back there?"

"Aha." He stared in the direction she described.

She picked him up and lowered him to the ground. "When I was coming here, I saw his wife and babies running around."

The little guy's eyes widened.

She squatted to his level. "Why don't you go find them? But you have to sit quietly by the tree and wait a long time. Because he's scared. Can you be patient?"

Aadam nodded. A second later, the little boy ran down the trail in search of the furry creature.

Ally stayed on her knees tracking him. "Why did you kill her?" A smile was still glued to her face in case he looked back.

"Which her?"

She rose to her feet and clasped her hands behind her back. "Both."

He shrugged and tossed the straw to the ground next to his gun. "Why not?"

Ally twisted the ring on her finger. "Why are you even here?"

He laughed and stretched out his legs. "Shariff asked me to keep an eye on the boy until things calmed down."

"Letting a three-year-old climb on the well's ledge is how you kept an eye on him?" she asked as she inched closer to him.

"He didn't climb. I put him there." The man grinned.

"Shariff's the one who told me to finish him."

She slid the two gems of the ring together until they snapped. "Well, he changed his mind. He sent a car for us."

His smile widened. He pulled out his phone and pressed the keys. "I wouldn't count on the car if I were you."

Ally felt the edge of the blade and imagined slicing his grin in half. Before she could ask why, an explosion rocked the area. A second later, another one blasted through. The ground and the trees around her shook. She looked in the direction of the sounds. Black smoke mingled with red flames streaked the sky. Her body shook at the sight. It was in the same direction as the gate.

*Razaa.*

"I bet that was the car he sent. Good thing you weren't in it."

Terror shuddered through her as the smoke floated higher and higher in the sky.

She turned to run toward it but stopped when the man laughed.

"It's too late, unless you plan on super gluing all his pieces together. Even then, there's no guarantee you'll find his parts."

Ally's fists clenched at the way his brows rose. The white flash of his teeth when he grinned tipped her over the edge. Tears and hate flowed through her. She lunged at him.

The force of her weight made him fall backward with Ally on top of him.

While he dug his nails into her face, she stabbed the ring's blade into his eye. His screams were her reward. She sank it as deep as she could and pulled it out. When she tried for a second time, he grabbed her wrist, and twisted it until something snapped. Immobilizing pain shot through her, blinding her. He shoved Ally to the ground.

The shoulder above her injured wrist slammed into a bricked side of the well, sending further currents of fire through her limb. She slid toward the watering pail as her body shuddered in pain.

He rose to his feet, a hand covering his bloodied eye.

Her fingers wrapped around the rim of the steel bucket as she waited. When he lunged at her, she slammed the pail at his head. Bashar grunted in pain and fell to the ground. Ally climbed to her feet and ran for the gun. She only made it a few steps before he grabbed hold of her ankle. She toppled to the earth face first.

"You think you can hurt me?" His grasp on her legs tightened as she tried to kick his hands away. Bashar pulled her closer and planted his knee on her back. He bore down all of his weight on the one knee, forcing the breath out of her.

Pressed against the earth and immobilized, Ally rested her cheek on the ground and cried. She cried not only because of the pain shooting through her body, but also because of Razaa.

"Do you know what it feels like to clean up your brother's blood?" he asked as he reached for the gun, which lay a few feet from her. "It's not something I can ever forget."

He shifted his knee farther up her back. "Sometimes I can even smell the scent of it. Feel his brains on my hands." When he grabbed a handful of her hair and pulled, she cried out. He stuffed the long barrel of his weapon into her mouth, silencing her cries. "Do you know how that feels?"

The cylinder stabbed at her throat, making her gag.

"Do you?" he sneered.

She stayed frozen, her fingernails dug into the earth.

"I do. And today. I'm going to feel it again. But this time it will be your brains in my hand."

# CHAPTER FORTY-TWO

## PRAYERS

*No!* The two-letter word screamed on repeat in his head as Eddie ran down the stairs and out the door. He raced toward the burning cars while he pleaded with God. He was not a religious man, but at this point, he'd pray to whatever was presented to him if it would save her life.

By the time he got to the site, fire consumed the vehicle and thick black smoke surged to the sky. The beeping of car alarms were the only sounds he could hear. His fists clenched and unclenched as he watched. His mind fixated on only one thing. She couldn't die.

He covered his mouth and nose with his hand as he ran into the fire. The heat scorched his skin before he ever reached the vehicle. His lungs filled with the black smoke making him cough. When the fumes began to overtake him, he had no other choice but to fall back.

Eddie fell to his knees and tried to catch his breath as he watched it burn. Pieces of metal and other debris lay strewn across the grounds. There was no way anyone could have survived the blast—not even her. The smoke burned his eyes and tears streamed his darkened face. He'd failed her. Again.

"Hassan!" Eddie pulled his attention from the burning car to see Aadam running to him, the dog by his side.

He kept a hand on his gun and scanned the area for others but found no one. After wiping the soot off his face, he stayed on his knees as the child ran into his arms. "Why are you here, little man?"

The kid pointed toward the garden and talked in child words he couldn't comprehend.

Eddie shook his head. "Who is with you?"

Aadam grinned. "Sara Mommy."

~

Eddie ran through the gardens toward the well, only stopping when he was a few feet away. He crouched behind the trees, and everything went silent while he took in the scene. The maid from the house lay dead, red strangulation marks evident around her neck. Also on the ground, next to the well, was Alisha. Pinned on her stomach, Bashar had his knee pressed into her spine. Blood streamed from his closed right eye.

But none of those were the reasons Eddie's veins turned to ice. The man's gun was positioned inside her mouth as he talked to her. Eddie moved in for a cleaner shot, willing the asshole to remove his hand from the weapon. Something moved to the right of them.

A bloodied Razaa held a brick over his head and ran at the target. Eddie's pulse sped. The kid had no clue about the gun in her mouth or that the man's finger was on the trigger. One wrong move and she'd be dead. And there was nothing Eddie could do to stop the scene from playing out.

Razaa slammed the slab over Bashar's head. He shoved the man off Alisha and pulled her away. By the time Bashar rose to his knees, Eddie put a bullet through his head.

He turned to find Razaa hugging an upset Alisha, telling her what had happened. The kid had never been in the car. He'd gotten his ass kicked by the one guard Eddie hadn't been able to find. The man took his car then died a second later in the explosion, which left one body unaccounted for.

Eddie scanned the perimeter. Wassim was somewhere out there. He turned to tell them they needed to leave when Alisha pressed her good palm on the kid's bloody nose.

"Are you sure you're okay?"

Eddie shook his head. Her broken hand hung in a highly

unnatural angle, there were claw marks all over her face, and a gun had just been shoved up her mouth. Yet, she was asking Razaa if he was okay.

It was only then he realized his body shook. Eddie leaned against a tree and wiped the sweat off his forehead, unable to take his gaze off her. She was alive. Up until a few minutes ago, he thought she was gone, and the reality of how close she'd been to death was sinking in. He rested his head on the trunk and thanked the heavens above for letting her live.

# CHAPTER FORTY-THREE

## NEGOTIATIONS

*A*lly sat on the edge of the bed, staring at the sofa shoved against the dingy wall across from her. A few mysterious spots stained its cushions, and there was a rip across one of the pillows. Although it wasn't as nice a hotel as the one Shariff brought her to days before, it served its purpose. Lines creased her forehead when her brows rose. Days? Was that all? It felt like years. She considered all the events of the past fifty odd hours. So much pain. So much loss.

*Had it been worth it?*

The same question floated in her mind a dozen times in the past few hours. And each time she answered yes. She looked down at the sleeping child. Aadam's knees were curled up into his stomach; his head lay in her lap, his thumb safely in his mouth. He had cried for Alyah, a mother who would never again hear his calls. It wasn't until exhaustion overcame him that his tears ebbed, and even then he clung to Ally.

Asleep at the foot of the bed beside her was Razaa. Once Aadam fell asleep, he'd taken over and spent a good portion of the past hour begging for her forgiveness. Hugs and tears later, fatigue overcame him, but even then he refused to leave her side. Her broken wrist and the makeshift splint Eddie created for it rested on the young man's shoulder as he slept. It throbbed, and the ache seemed to be getting worse, but it was the least of her concerns. Too many other problems plagued her. The most pressing of all, what happens to these two?

The man who had the answers was currently on the phone. She looked over at the closed bathroom door. Although she couldn't see him, she could envision Eddie on the other side pacing the floor. Other than a "Yes, sir," and "I understand, sir," he wasn't saying much, but she had a hunch things weren't going well.

When the door finally opened, he walked out, rubbing the back of his neck. He dropped his phone on the table where his other cells rested but didn't look at her.

"Everything okay?" she asked.

"Nope." He lined the phones in a row. "When I get back, I have a meeting with my chief, his boss, and the director."

"Are you going to be fired?"

He let out a breath and nodded. "I kept secrets and left the reservation. In the process, I put another agent at risk. None of which they are impressed with." He walked over to the other side of the bed, behind her, and sat down.

"What are you going to do?"

"Not sure." Eddie leaned his back against the headboard and stretched his legs across the mattress. "Farah and the baby are going to need some help settling in to their new lives. You know, new country and all. So I'll probably stay with them until they kick me out."

Ally played with one of Aadam's curls. "And what happens to these two?"

There was a pause before he answered. She wound the child's lock around her finger, giving Eddie time to break the news.

"Razaa is seventeen. He's an adult, so he's on his own."

Ally felt the young man he mentioned stiffen at the statement. Clearly, he wasn't asleep. She patted him as Eddie spoke.

"As far as the kid, since his biological parents, Sayeed and Alyah are both dead, they'll have to look for relatives who can take him. Wassim legally has no rights over him, and even if he did, he seems to have vanished."

Ally looked over at Eddie. "*They* who? And what happens if *they* can't find his relatives?"

He nodded. "*They* are the Child Protection Bureau. An officer will be called as soon as you're out of the country, and *they'll* find him a good home. The Bureau specializes in helping children. They have a list of vetted families..."

While he praised the benefits of the bureau, Ally shook her head. Instead of it silencing him, her disapproval seemed to make him talk faster.

"Razaa stays with me, and I'm not leaving until Aadam is with his family," she said in the middle of his speech.

Eddie didn't respond for a while, and when he did, his tone was tired as if he knew what was about to happen. "And if they can't find relatives willing to take him?"

Ally rolled her shoulders back and sucked in a lungful of air. "Then he'll stay with me too."

"That. Is. Not an option," he hissed.

He was saying everything she knew he would. She smiled and was sure she was saying everything he thought she would, except for this one part. Ally returned to playing with Aadam's hair. "Either you make it an option, or this little guy and I will disappear."

Silence fell across the room a second time. "You're serious?"

She shrugged. "You know I am."

Razaa cleared his throat. "And I will go with them since I am an adult."

Ally grinned at the sound of Eddie's teeth grinding.

"Alisha, look at me."

His dark brows were raised so high that they seemed to float in the middle of his forehead. The bloodshot eyes and the day old stubble covering his jaw were the only evidence of the hell he'd gone through the past few days. "I have no control over this."

Ally reached over and patted his knee. "You said the same thing years ago in Germany, and it turned out you were in total control."

He slid his legs up and rested his elbows on his knees. "Total control?" He laughed. "If I had been in total control, Alisha Dimarchi would have died back then. You'd have had a new name, a new life like the rest of them. But your husband fought for you. Said you being stripped from everyone you loved would be something you'd never allow. That you'd find a way back to Philly." He pointed at an invisible person in the room. "They, not me, decided to let you return to your home. Why bother going to the trouble of hiding you, if you weren't going to stay hidden?"

She smiled as she thought of David. He'd never told her he'd done that, but it didn't surprise her.

"And, for the record, I don't regret splitting you all up. A group of seventeen people living together in one house is a lot harder to hide than seventeen people scattered over the world. Do you know how many countries they'd have to search?"

Ally stared across the room at the peeling paint while he rambled. He was trying to divert her attention from the issue at hand, but this time, she wouldn't let him succeed. The future of two boys rested firmly on her shoulders. She'd already considered the options and knew there was only one. "This child has lost everything he knows," she said, cutting him off a second time. "I won't abandon him. He deserves a chance at a healthy life. If there is no relative to care for him, I'll do whatever the Agency says, no arguments. As long as Aadam and Raaza stay with me."

"Even if it means walking away from your family and the life you have?"

Aadam nuzzled the back of his head closer to her stomach. She stared down at the child. There was no doubt. No fear. She nodded. "Yes."

# CHAPTER FORTY-FOUR

## PROMISES KEPT

*A*lly stood in the mausoleum and peered through the stained glass window. A few yards away stood four adults. People she knew well. She'd known them her whole life. Well, all but the first four years of her life. People she would always consider hers.

The family faced the gravesite they came to visit. Bhai kept his arm around Mummy while Reya hugged on Pappa, her head resting on his shoulder. Between her parents was the empty spot that was once hers. Everyone had their role, and if Ally stood with them, she'd have been right there in the middle, with an arm wrapped around her parents' waists unifying the family into one complete line.

A bright yellow Mylar balloon with a picture of a rainbow was tied to the tombstone they stared at. She couldn't hear their words, but she knew they were singing. She knew not because she was an excellent lip reader but because it was David's birthday. Her chest tightened. He had hated the whole ordeal but would politely smile until it was over. Which was why Reya always brought him a cake, the gaudiest balloons, and forced them all to sing.

Ally pressed her palm on the glass and watched them, memorizing every detail. A tear slipped down her cheek. Exhaustion and pain was etched across their faces and in the way they carried themselves. And all of it was because of her. Almost three decades ago, they took in an orphaned girl as their own and gave her their hearts. Little did they realize the same girl would one day rip those beautiful hearts to pieces. When they walked past, she moved away from the window and leaned against the wall, trying to hear their words. "They are all together now," Mummy said. "Her birth parents and her David. They will take care of my baby."

Ally's lip quivered but she didn't cry—she smiled. It hadn't occurred to her how comforting the idea of her reuniting with her biological parents and David would be to them. The thought eased her guilt.

She watched them wander away and waited long after they'd gone before she left the mausoleum. When she neared David's grave, she slowed down and focused on the man whose body lay beneath it. In a way, Mummy was right. David was with her and would always be. The tomb she stared at only held his bones, nothing more. He owned her heart and her soul and was a constant presence in her dreams. And he would stay there until the day when they would finally meet again.

"Happy birthday, baby," she whispered.

Funny thing about time. Some people believed it healed all wounds, but Ally knew that wasn't the case. Time only made the wounded get used to their pain. And if they were lucky, they'd find other joys along the way. Joys that could numb the ache, if only for a little while.

A smile stretched across her face as she walked to the parking lot and the dark sedan waiting for her. Seated inside were her two joys. They were her world now. A world she would protect at all costs.

She opened the back door and slid in beside Aadam's booster seat, quickly closing the door beside her. Fast asleep, the bottom of his chin pressed against his chest, raising and lowering between his snores. Puppy, the white dog from the compound, sat guard on the other side of him. The furry creature's nose rested in the little boy's lap while the child's hand lay on the dog's neck. Puppy looked up at her when Ally lifted Aadam's head from its awkward position, leaning his cheek against the side of his headrest. Deeming the situation safe, the dog thumped its tail against the seat and closed its eyes.

"Are you going to tell me where we're going?" Ally asked the woman who was driving as she backed out of the parking spot.

"Razaa why don't you do the honors?" Leanna quipped from

the driver's seat.

The young man in question turned around and grinned back at Ally. His beard had long been shaved clean, making him look more like the seventeen-year-old he was. Other than the pale scar running along his cheek, all physical remnants of his injuries from a few weeks ago were gone. "You got your wish, Mom. We are going to Washington."

Her throat tightened as it did every time he called her Mom.

"Do you even know how to work an apple orchard?" Leanna asked.

Ally smiled at the question. "Not a clue but someone once told me it's the perfect place to retire."

"Well, I've done some research..." Leanna said as she drove to the airport.

While the two in front discussed the business of apple farming, Ally's mind wandered to a night in a hotel room an eternity ago. Razaa was wrong. It wasn't her wish they'd granted.

*"Promise me two things," David whispered.*

*"What?"*

*Soft fingers brushed up and down her spine. "One: buy me a ranch somewhere nice like Seattle, where we can retire early and do something boring like grow fruit or make cheese. And two: After we live a beautifully long life, I die before you. Seeing as how I already had to go through it once, it's only fair the next time around it be your turn."*

She looked over her shoulder in the direction of the cemetery they'd left behind. The corners of her mouth lifted as she imagined a happy David making a check mark in the air with his finger.

# EPILOGUE

*E*ddie stood on his hotel balcony, staring out into the darkened city's skyline. Tiny specks of light glistened like stars from the hundreds of buildings stretching across the horizon. Beside him was Farah, and in the master bedroom of the suite, Amirah slept, oblivious to the nightmare she'd survived.

His sister let out a sigh and rested her head on his shoulder. He wrapped an arm around her, giving her a reassuring squeeze. It was the best he could offer at the moment. Because as long as Wassim lived, he couldn't tell her she was safe. A failure Eddie had no choice but to own. He had the target in his sight and let him go.

Guilt weighed heavily on him. Two good men were dead and their wives were now widows. He went over the situation in his mind a thousand times. Each time, he'd come up with the same conclusion: He could have prevented it.

But now all he could do was keep them hidden until he finished his mission. With a new identity and a new home, Alisha and her two boys were as safe as they could be. Tomorrow, he would take what remained of his family and help them start their new life.

As much as he worried about both women, it wouldn't be Farah that Wassim would come after. And if the man ever discovered who raised his son, he would show no mercy. Eddie gripped the metal railing until it cut into his palms. This story was far from over.

# ARE YOU PART OF KISH'S COLLECTIVE YET?

To stay in touch with Kishan Paul, be in the know about upcoming releases, have exclusive access to ARC's, giveaways, and sneak peaks on the stories she is working on, be a part of a fun interactive group of book lovers.

https://www.facebook.com/groups/KishsCollective/

# Kishan Paul
### *Love stories that transcend all barriers*

# KEEP IN TOUCH!

If you have not already, subscribe to Kish's Connection. Sign up to be a part of Kishan Paul's exclusive mailing list. You will be in the know about exclusive chapters, release dates, and giveaways.

https://app.mailerlite.com/webforms/landing/q0d2q0

# ALSO BY KISHAN PAUL

**The Second Wife Series**
*The Second Wife*: Book 1
*The Widows Keeper*: Book 2

*Blind Love*

*Taking the Plunge*
*Stolen Hearts*

# ABOUT THE AUTHOR

From daring escapes by tough women to chivalrous men swooping in to save the day, the creativity switch to Kishan Paul's brain is always in the 'on' position. If daydreaming stories were a college course, Kish would graduate with honors.

Mother of two beautiful children, she has been married to her best friend for over 20 years. With the help of supportive family and friends, she balances her family, a thriving counseling practice, and writing without sinking into insanity.

## To keep in touch with Kish:

http://kishanpaul.net
https://www.facebook.com/KishanPaulAuthor
https://twitter.com/@kishan_paul
https://www.facebook.com/groups/KishsCollective/
http://www.pinterest.com/kishanpaul

Printed in Great Britain
by Amazon